A Wake

To order additional copies, please contact us.
BookSurge, LLC
www.booksurge.com
1-866-308-6235
orders@booksurge.com

A
Wake

A NOVEL

Andrea Yungblut

2003

A Wake

To My Husband And Soulmate, Mark, For Finding Me. For Unending Encouragement, For Passion, For Love. For Everything.

To My Three Daughters: Emily, For Her Energy, Drive, Sensitivity And Wit, Erin, For Her Insight, Determination And True Love Of Reading, And Madeline, For Her Tenacity, Spirit And Marvelous, Endless Imagination.

To My Parents, Who Raised Me To Appreciate The Written Word As Infinitely Valuable, For Their Love And Support.

To Grandma Esther, "Omi," Watching Over Us No Doubt. For Her Love Of Storytelling, Her Plays And Her Poetry.

Lyke-wake — watch kept at night over a dead body (the Reader's Digest Great Encyclopedic Dictionary, 1964).

-I-

Tolstoy once said pure and complete sorrow is as impossible as pure and complete joy, but he was dead wrong. And it is because Tolstoy was dead wrong that I am standing here at a strange man's house quietly robbing him of his mail.

The door opens. Slams shut again. He is out. Bare feet, smoothly filed toenails. Reaches for the mailbox but neglects to notice the woman with the canvass bag just a few steps away. I could be someone important after all. A relative, the Prime Minister, the Apostle John in robe and sandals. And yet he doesn't even look my way. My heart begins to tighten in my chest. At any point some vital artery could burst and I could collapse at his feet. I can see him now, face pale, rushing inside to call an ambulance and reporting to the dispatcher that some strange woman is expiring inconveniently in his hydrangeas.

But this doesn't happen. My heart races on and does not grind to a halt. He does glance up once but looks back down at his mail again, completely indifferent. I get the impression I have awakened him from an unusually deep and profound sleep and it will take more than a dangerous criminal on his doorstep to drag him from wherever he's been.

He is wearing long pants in taupe, neatly pressed, and a shirt that hints of tangerine. The shirt is buttoned up high as though he's planning on wearing a tie. I picture him standing at his mirror, arms raised and hands at his throat, about to knot the thing around his neck when he is drawn away by a noise at the door, an unusual scraping of his mailbox lid.

He is quite tall, taller than I remember, eyes gray as rain. He isn't in any way attractive. Very ordinary actually. In general a person could walk right past him on the street without so much as taking a second look. Not like Frank. Frank was so noticeable. Women were always quite ready to fling themselves naked at Frank.

I finally manage to move my limbs and take a few steps, glancing back only once to see if he's now watching. But no, still standing in the same place sorting through the mail, shuffling it rapidly in his hands like a deck of cards.

In less than four seconds, he has completely forgotten my existence. Tomorrow he won't think about me once, not even when he opens the door to get his mail. Never reflect on the reason why a strange woman was standing by his hydrangeas the previous day, canvass bag in hand. I have been completely wiped from his mind and erased from his memory for an eternity. Some day I will run into him in a hardware store over a can of CLR and I will say hello and he will say hello back, hesitating a little, uncertain. And those gray, almost colourless eyes will say, *I don't have a clue who the hell you are.*

***

It is a typical spring morning here in the town of Hope; cloudy, a sharp wind that bites the face and hands. But the grass is greening up in a few places and there are little red sprouts starting on the maple branches if you care to look close enough.

Hope is a very ordinary small town in this part of Ontario. A farming community, although the land is marginal at best. One traffic light, a downtown with all the usual stores, roughly a quarter with *for rent* signs in windows. There is, however, a new mall on the north end with a grocery store, drugstore, department store, a number of other run-of-the-mill clothing stores, and of course the bookstore where I work, *A Book A Day*. A bookstore in the town of Hope; just imagine. And that's about it. A town empty of anything meaningful, full of nonentities who come and go, move in and move out, the embodiment of the word insignificant. And still they call it Hope.

A propitious town, or at least people around here seem to think so. They've taken it into their heads to build some new houses this year behind the mall. The town has great potential for growth, they say, seeing as it's so close to the big city of Milan. A bedroom community. People are expected to move here in droves and commute, and they will want new homes. Big new vinyl-clad houses with garages stuck out front, set close together on long narrow lots. One place peering into the windows of the next with hardly space for a stroller or trashcan between. Houses built where someone else's backyard should rightfully be. And the rest of the town is no better. Older homes scattered haphazardly on big, irregular pieces, some curving aimlessly to follow the dirty Hope River. Broken down porches leaning on rotted wooden pillars, shaded by dying trees. Sheds, old garages and other buildings tacked on or placed randomly here and there, without thought to order or form. *Higgledy-piggledy*, Maggie would say. *Slapdash*.

There's a street in the old section called Mill Street, which boasts a long row of houses identical in every way. Yellow brick, two stories, a small porch facing the street, stained glass windows around the door, a half-round window above. Each has a small tower on the southwest corner and a widow's walk upstairs. In a gesture to inconsistency, perhaps a stab at breaking the pattern, a few homeowners on Mill painted their front doors brilliant and unusual colors this past year; mauve, lemon-yellow, tangerine. One even erected an enormous wrought-iron sign at the end of his driveway, *Sixty-Seven Mill Street*, in five-foot-high letters. But that's Hope. Either new and ugly, worn-out and ugly, or simply in bad taste. There you have it.

Yes, I know I shouldn't be so critical. I suppose there are a few things in town worth keeping. Down by the Hope River stands an enormous oak so big in the trunk three people couldn't reach around it and touch fingertips. Maggie says there were once lots of oaks down there and even some elms, planted more than a century ago by the good folk of Hope. But the rest of the trees are gone now; rotted, diseased, worn down by time and old age, cut down to make way for newer things. I visit that old relic quite often, touch its bark, try to imagine the people who planted it here as a small, thin sapling. Or perhaps it was a child who gave it life. A little girl in a long dress and bonnet holding an acorn in her hands, an acorn with a tiny green shoot already jostling for life. She leans over and makes a small hole in the ground, carefully drops the acorn in and covers it, scraping at the earth with tiny white fists.

***

The air is warmer today than it's been for weeks, but not so warm you wouldn't be chilly without a jacket. And there's a cold wind that comes and goes at the bridge where the worst winds always gather. At the traffic light, the only one in town I might add, a group waits to cross. Motionless, no one looking at anyone else or saying anything. The teenagers in the bunch are not dressed for the weather and are cold, though they don't like to show it. Hands in pockets, apathetic, looking dully into the distance or down towards shoes and dirt. One man has both hands clasped around a Styrofoam coffee cup. He blows down into the steaming liquid with quick, ineffectual puffs, looks around over top, first to his left and then right. Other people he doesn't even know are just inches away, elbows pressing against his back. But the man doesn't care. He is thinking about his miserable job at the gas station in Milan, about his wife at home who doesn't see the runs in her nylons or that her pants have become too tight across the backside. Who writes the grocery lists, the potatoes and the hamburger helper and the Lysol, on the backs of the hydro bills and crumples them into her purse.

I walk past them all as fast as I can without raising suspicion. Heaven only knows what they would think if they saw a woman running past full tilt, mailbag in hand. *Thief!* they would yell, *larcenist of letters!*

The street sweeper is out today, scraping the sand, salt and other leftover winter crud off the cracked and aging roads. He follows me most of the way home, which is rather harrowing, all the while producing an enormous racket and raising an intense cloud of dust down Ash, along Front, past the library and all over me.

Next to the library is the old jailhouse. Empty of course, just home temporarily to a few insubordinate teenagers. Apparently on weekends a whole bunch climb in the basement windows and squat in the old cells drinking beer and smoking God only knows what. Ecstasy, they say, or something called Sextasy, a new and lethal mix rumoured to include Viagara. They've dragged some mattresses in there too and some broken down chairs. Fire hazard I'm sure, and yet people around here do squat about it, though everyone knows.

My house on Crawford Street is nothing special. No *curbside appeal*, as the realtors would say. It's the kind of house like dozens, hundreds of others around it. Small, single story, orange-red brick, windows with peeling paint. Number twenty-seven. The yard is cramped and square, roughly fenced with a spindly cedar hedge, yellow and sickly where it faces the street.

When you step in, though, it's really quite beautiful. First off, a small table in the front entrance on which I've arranged an assortment of dolls, just so. Antiques with beautiful painted faces and real hair, dresses of costly fabric, all hand-sewn and perfect. Arranged in a certain order, not tallest to smallest or oldest to youngest, but a certain order nonetheless. The doll with the red velveteen coat and matching hat is always at the back behind the doll with the long black hair and the dress in periwinkle. Real silk.

On the floor stands my wooden bird collection, also in precise order. A friend cut out the shapes for me (thirty-nine in total), and I spent many long winter weekends painting them, all the while carefully consulting my *Audubon Society Field Guide to North American Birds*. A little cheerful family all clustered together and awaiting my arrival each day. No one else seems to care for these things but me. When people come in the front door they cough out the usual compliments, banal generalities, and step over them gingerly. But I know what they are really thinking. *Crass, childish, idiotic.*

It isn't until I've dumped the bag onto my kitchen floor that I permit myself to take a good look. He certainly gets a lot of mail each week, more mail in a week than I get in a year. No wonder he didn't notice I swiped a few today. I rummage around for a while quickly scanning the front of each letter. And then I find it, the one I've been looking for.

Naturally the envelope is sealed. I cradle it in my hands, aware of its weight pressing down on my fingers, its smooth-cool flatness. There are words scrawled in a backward slanted handwriting on the front. Scribbled, extraordinarily sloppy, as though the writer were in some huge hurry. I imagine this person stuffing the letter into the envelope in an enormous rush to get out the door, coat half on, gloves in one hand, snatching a pen quickly and, hardly looking, scratching the address on the front before dashing out the door and dropping it carelessly in the nearest mailbox.

The name Richard Mason peers up at me, blatant and accusing, informing me this letter is not mine. I feel I'm contemplating a murder or some other heinous crime. Any moment someone will walk in and catch me here kneeling, pondering a vile unlawful act, and they will know it right away and call the police. Clenching the letter between my teeth, I reach for the kettle.

Thank heavens he didn't open that door a moment sooner. Thank the high heavens and the saints above. There must be someone watching out for me after all. Some saint. Some bored little angel.

It is typewritten and short. Just one long and tedious paragraph. Hardly a letter at all. I'm not really sure what I'd envisioned, but certainly something with a little more substance. It doesn't matter. I know something at least. I know where the letter came from and I know a name. My instincts were right. There is a woman.

I fold the letter back together quickly; stuff it in the envelope. Will return it later along with the rest.

There's a warm sort of tingling caressing the back of my neck. I am in command today, pleased with myself and the whole world. Move quickly to the full-length mirror in the front entrance. Hair of indefinable colour and style, greenish eyes too large for a thin, lined face. Yes, lined certainly. The years are chipping away now, gravity dragging down hard, tugging at my cheeks and mouth and deepening those black circles beneath the eyes. There is not much else to see here. Nothing noteworthy. Once I was considered to be quite attractive. Now: tall, skinny, depleted. And although I've worn them together countless times, the shirt and skirt do not match each other in any way.

Oh those wretched choices in life and oh how little leeway for anything but perfection.

Maggie says, although she'd never say it to my face, that I've never really grown up. I know. I stumble in restaurants, forget my purse under chairs, run out of clothing stores when approached by salespeople, even the most benign ones. Others make it all look so effortless, so unforced. *Easy as pie*, Maggie says. *Nothing to it*. But she doesn't know. She doesn't know what life is like for someone like me. It's different for her. Everything goes as planned. But for me, I just can't keep it together.

"Can I help you find something?" that immaculately dressed woman in Sutton's Ladies' Wear asked yesterday. But in her voice I detected something disdainful as she looked me over and made her assessment. *Unpolished, gauche, ill bred, penniless.*

So I twisted away, excruciatingly embarrassed. What could she be thinking? What does she know about me? And I started to sweat, really sweat, through brassiere, shirt and sweater.

Maybe it's because I don't know how to shop for things, how to dress properly. I just don't have the knack anymore. And when people come right up and talk to me in a store like that, I feel they're attacking me personally, maybe accusing me of taking something and hiding it in my purse. I always make this big show of holding any item I want to buy way up in front of me, in full view, arms held stiffly away from my body so that they know for certain I'm not trying to rip them off.

Often I imagine myself walking out of a store without paying, by accident of course, and the salesperson storming out after me, grabbing at my arms, and everyone else turning to stare. I can see the policeman arrive, handcuffs in hand. I can see it all so clearly in such minute detail I know for sure it's going to happen one of these days. Like in Dostoyevsky's *The Idiot*, when Prince Myshkin becomes obsessed by this unshaken conviction that he will most certainly break a costly Chinese vase at a friend's party. I understand. I know. It happens.

There is a knock at the back door.

Several long seconds pass. An axe-murderer at the moment of discovery. Squatting down I lunge at the scattered mail, scooping it awkwardly in both arms. Open the pantry door and thrust it all in next to the broom and dust mop, snatch at a letter I've missed and pitch it in too. Crumple another into my pocket. Surely she won't open the pantry door. Surely to high heavens and for goodness sakes, not.

Collapsing at the table I drink deeply, slopping a little on the floor. No matter. Caesar likes cold coffee too. And the floor is dark brown tiles which look clean although they aren't. I feel a clammy sweat begin under my arms and across the bridge of my nose. Lift the hair from the back of my neck and shake it a little.

Come in Maggie.

But I shouldn't bother. Maggie is already through the door and has removed her shoes, tossing them neatly onto the rubber tray at the top of the stairs. She smoothes back a shining cap of short brown hair. Unnecessary. A cyclone could not blow the style from Maggie's locks.

"I tried earlier. You must've been out."

She hardly glances my way, dumps out the coffee maker and begins to fill it with new water, deposits a dog-eared crossword book on the counter.

I try not to glance at the pantry door but do anyway. Closed but not shut tight, damn it to eternal hell.

Maggie is certainly elegant today. I'm not saying this because I just looked at my own reflection in a mirror either. Even in old jeans and a sweatshirt, Maggie looks like she just stepped out of the pages of a catalogue. Ask anyone. Sick in bed with pneumonia and not having showered three days and having just thrown up in a pail, Maggie still looks unflustered, poised, un-ruffled in every way. It's genetic. Her mother's the same way; I've seen her. If someone were to yell out *fire*, Maggie's mom would pour herself a glass of mineral water and check her lipstick be-fore calling the fire department.

"So," she says, "finally you're home. Where've you been? You never seem to be home even when I call real late, and now you're hardly here in the mornings either. Thought you were working evenings this week anyway."

She holds a measuring spoon and jabs it in my direction. "You look like hell Clarice. Great big black bags under your eyes. I told you before, you don't get enough sleep. You look like you've been through the wringer washer."

Pick up my coffee, take another really large swallow which hurts a little going down. Glance at her over the rim of my cup. Sometimes Maggie can be a pain. She has no interests in life aside from her theatre friends and being a mother to me. No concern about anything going on around her either; knows nothing about world affairs. You ask her about war or famine and she'll just shrug her shoulders, roll her eyes.

Who cares. So what. Not my business.

And yet in many ways she has been my saviour these past few years. She knows I need her. Doesn't hesitate to help when she can. I know I would have fallen apart long ago without Mag-gie and she knows it too.

She is looking at me. Forehead creased, eyebrows raised and tilted a little. Reaches over to grab her crosswords from the counter. I know what she's thinking when she looks at me like this. How could any woman let herself go as much as that?

"What does Sally have you doing at that store, read all the

books before you put them out on the shelves? Really, Clarice. All you do is work these days. Get a life."

Maggie pronounces the word really as though comprised of three syllables: Ree-ah-lly. She's the only person I know who pronounces words like this, makes two-syllable words into three, completely at random. She pages through her crosswords and folds the book open flat, studies it a moment, eyebrows angled.

"Is Xylem a word? I need a word that starts with x and it can't be x-ray. Has to end in m."

I don't answer, but if Maggie is ticked off by my lack of interest in her crosswords or in the rest of her life for that matter, she doesn't show it. I don't mean to be so indifferent. I do care for her as a friend, of course, but I just can't get myself involved in her life right now. It all seems to distant, so far away and unreal. The coffee maker begins making a gurgling sound and she turns to it, humming one of her many nameless, tuneless little songs, a small smile on her lips.

"Did I put in four scoops or five? Cutting back on foods with white sugar these days, especially the stuff with fructose in it. Supposed to be converted directly to fat and your body can't use it for energy at all. It's a real scam. They put it in everything these days too. I've been reading all about it." She begins to hum again, this time a recognizable nursery rhyme.

Irritating, infuriating. How does Maggie manage to have her hair done like that every morning with those kids to look after? Man, I'm on a real tirade this morning. Normally I don't care a pin what anybody looks like but today I can't seem to settle down and calm myself.

"I said I think you should give Caesar a different name. He's such a sweetheart. Call him *Cookie* or *Sweetie* or something nice like that. Caesar was such a horrible man." Maggie reaches down to smooth the cat's fur around his neck and scratch at his ears, which he hates. Caesar begins flicking his ears and crouches lower. Laps coffee from the floor tiles, tail thrashing ominously.

"He's been Caesar for ages. I'm not going to go and change his name now for heaven's sake." I bend down to scoop up a clump of fur Caesar has disposed of, dropping it neatly into the bottom of a potted fern and wiping my hands on my pants.

Maggie leans over her crosswords. She is settling in. Evidently I will not rid myself of her for a long while yet. I watch for two minutes, draining the last of my cold coffee. Prod at Caesar's tail with my foot. Pick up a pad of paper from beside the telephone and begin to write, glancing over now and again to make sure she isn't looking.

Richard's mail arrives at nine-fifteen mornings (except today). I mark on the chart *nine twenty-eight* under the left-hand column, which gives the time by the twenty-four hour clock. Pulling out a notebook with lined graph paper from the telephone table drawer, I draw in a bold black line.

"What's that?" Maggie gets up from her chair and leans over my shoulder.

"Just some stuff for the store." I bend over the notebook quickly, shield it with my hand, but Maggie the Terrier can't be shaken, moves closer.

Shut the notebook and grab my purse, reaching inside for a lipstick. It is buried beneath six packages of Kleenex, a comb with two missing teeth, a small album of photos with two elastic bands wrapped around it, an empty pack of Tic-Tacs, a Kinder-surprise toy, a necklace with a broken clasp, and a piano key on an Amway key chain.

"You're lucky, Clarice. You've got so much freedom. A chance to do things right," Maggie says, suddenly very solemn.

I study my reflection in the tiny mirror. I do look better like this: a touch of colour on my lips to bring out the green in my eyes. If only I were confident enough to add a splash of pink to my cheeks and a reckless daub of frosty mauve to the eyelids.

Lucky. What on earth does lucky mean anyway?

Snap the purse shut and glance up at the clock above the stove.

"Sorry Maggie. Got to go. Let Caesar out and lock the door behind you when you're done."

I pick up my notebook; steal a look at the pantry door. She wouldn't dare. Wouldn't dare if her life depended on it.

The chess game is set up on the little table by the window in my bedroom. I am always white. I pick up the white bishop and move him four squares diagonally. The black castle is suddenly in grave danger.

Running to the front entrance, I push open the door and step out. I realize just as I am closing the door very firmly behind me, that Maggie is saying something. I hear muffled words but I didn't quite catch them, and I step away quickly, purse swinging.

-2-

The man in the bookstore stares. He is looking directly at me, eyes open wide; I am quite certain of it. Keep my head down and pull at my skirt, which is riding up again. Three coffee blotches near my navel. Walk quickly to the back and launch my purse onto a chair already crammed with stacks of books without covers. Selecting one at random, I reach for the bathroom door and open.

Brief flash of white belly and hairy male genitalia before a blur of red boxers obscures the scene.

"What the hell, Clarice? Don't you ever knock?"

"Sorry. Just needed to-"

"Like hell," the voice says hoarsely. "Like hell."

Reese emerges, fumbling with his belt and pulling vigorously at tight, tight black jeans.

"You knew I was in there. You just wanted a look at the goods."

Cripes, leave it to Reese to say something like that. A word like *goods* to make it all seem indecent and vulgar. And he knows full well how embarrassed I can get. He knows I can't just turn around and forget.

"I didn't look. And don't worry, I didn't really actually see anything either."

Step past him into the bathroom and lock the door behind me. I am sweating again. Reach down to turn on the tap, splash cold water on face and neck; dab at everything with bits of wet paper towel.

Reese in bright, shiny red boxers.

Tuck stray hairs behind my ears. Flush toilet. Turn the tap on and off three times. Stand and wait.

Sally is in her office when I slip by moving as noiselessly as possible in my ridiculous heels and stained skirt. But she ambushes me anyway.

"That you Clarice? Here, take a look." She pulls me by the arm into the office, motioning towards an open magazine on her desk.

The truth is, smalltalk with Sally is infinitely irritating. She has a way of bringing up subjects that would make even the most brazen squirm; a way of worming out information you wouldn't divulge on your deathbed.

Today Sal is especially imposing: a tailored suit in plum, thick dark hair pulled back into an enormous bun. To my horror Sally has confided in me a lifelong battle with extraneous body hair, rolling up her sleeves to demonstrate the necessity for daily arm shaving to avoid, as she puts it, *resembling a lower primate.*

This embarrasses me, the idea of disclosing a private and highly sensitive matter to someone you hardly know, to an employee who should admire and respect you. Now every time I look at her I am repulsed, automatically examining the area above her lips for telltale signs of five-o'clock-shadow. I am nauseated if she so much as touches me, as though her growths were some kind of fungus, a highly contagious mould.

"You got to see this. Heard he was doing the full monty this month so I just had to take a quick look before I put it out. Quality control, you know. Comes with the job."

"Not bad," I say, peering reluctantly over her shoulder at the very naked man. "Definite improvement over what I saw earlier this morning."

Sally gives me a look of mild astonishment, raises a pair of thick coal-black eyebrows, but says nothing. Feel my face get hot again. Scalding. What on earth has ever possessed me to say this? I know what she is thinking: *who did she wake up with this morning, and still waters certainly do run deep, don't they?*

"What's up with Reese? He ran past without saying a word." Lights a cigarette, an absorbed look on her face, flips rapidly, carelessly, through the rest of the magazine, rips an article out, folds it and thrusts it into her purse. "Usually he'll chat for hours after he's been on the john. Morning ritual."

Red boxers, hairy testicles. Reese will hate me for all eternity and beyond.

"Saw some guy out there in the store when I came in. Reese is likely out there helping him. Maybe the guy is actually buying something."

I have gone too far. Sally tosses the magazine onto the desk, leans back in the chair and frowns at me, taking a long deep pull on her cigarette. One of these days she will fire me for a comment like that. I am about to back away, slip out of the office and make my escape, but she is not done with me yet.

"So, Clarice, did you call him? Tell me."

A direct command.

I look back at her and say nothing. But surely I cannot refuse a direct command. Trouble is, Sally is an expert interrogator. Everyone knows this. She grills people as a matter of policy, as part of her daily routine. I have to admit she makes me very, very nervous. And as a rule I try not to stand too close or look her directly in the face.

"I know about these things," Sally says, picking up the magazine again and paging through more slowly. She lifts one hand and rubs under her nose, brushes her chin lightly. There are little wrinkles all around her mouth from sucking on cigarettes. "You got to be real aggressive as a woman these days. Men expect it. If I hadn't walked right up to John and asked him to that Blue Rodeo concert, I swear he'd have walked out of my life for good."

Taps her cigarette on an overflowing ashtray and leans back, examines me minutely, studying my clothes, my hair, my face with great interest.

How to escape.

"He's a really nice guy. Honest. Just walk up to him the next time you see him and ask him how he's doing, where he works now, how his parents are. Anything. Just get the conversation rolling. Easy as pie."

She must think me crazy not to have called the guy by now. Crazy in general. Every time I walk in the store I catch her watching me, eyeing me up when I walk by the office, or staring at me when I'm with a customer. I catch her and Reese or one of the girls talking quietly, furtively, whenever I'm around. Then they all suddenly clam up tight as wires when I come close enough to overhear. This is the truth; I swear on a stack of Bibles.

"Ask him out. Guys like that." She flicks her cigarette again over the ashtray, spraying bits of ash on table and floor. "They like a girl to take control. John always says he wouldn't have gone out with me a second time if I hadn't been so pushy. Stuck to him like glue till he couldn't shake me loose." Smiles and glances at a framed photograph on her desk.

John. Big, dark-haired, long bony nose that looks like it's been broken a few times. Thin scar running from eyebrow to the corner of his left eye. I picture Sally clinging to his arm, refusing to let go while he struggles to pull away and then finally, reluctantly, giving in, following her thereafter like a devoted retriever.

I move out into the store feeling deflated, as though she has stolen something from me. Suddenly everything I've been planning seems ridiculous, idiotic, insane. Maybe I should forget everything else I've been planning and call the guy Sally wanted to set me up with after all. He sounded kind of nice and he was certainly cute. Brown-haired with eyes that looked back at you sympathetically. The kind of guy who'd come over and make dinner, fix your car.

Reese has finally pushed back the folding glass doors that divide our store from the rest of the mall. The balding guy is gone, replaced by a younger rather attractive man in a suit. I can tell he is reading one of the sex books by the way he kind of holds the book with both hands, sort of shielding the cover, and when I walk past him he closes it briskly and puts it back in the gardening section. Once I'm safely past though he reaches for it again, begins flipping through slowly.

"So how was your date last night?" I say.

Reese is busy stocking the stationary section. Leaning back against the counter I rub at the coffee splotches with a damp thumb, careful not to catch his eye. He says nothing.

He hasn't forgiven me for the bathroom incident then. The full monty. Not that I got much of a view. It was very blurred of course, and then there were the bright red boxers to distract.

"Well if you want to know, it was awful. Date from hell," he says, examining a box of staples minutely, as though counting each staple individually.

"Too bad. Hardly makes going out with you sound enticing." I say this lightly, trying to make a joke, but it falls flat. He doesn't even smile. I lean over quickly to pick up a stack of bookmarks; begin filing them onto the rotating stand in front of the cash register.

"Really liked her at first. Took her to dinner at this nice place too. Unbelievably expensive, but it was damned good."

"Did she like it?"

"You kidding?" He snorts, begins opening a carton of red and blue pens and dumping them on the floor. I crouch down and help him sort. "I mean she didn't hide the fact she was totally bored with me. Bitched the whole time about how overcooked the pork steak was, how she'd much rather have balsamic vinegar in the salad dressing. And then all she talks about is her damned, idiotic dog. An Afghan for God's sake. The dumbest breed alive. The canine version of a Barbie doll." He stops sorting and looks over at me. "You know there's something real funny about a girl who's so hung up about an animal." He gives me a look, full of meaning, raises his eyebrows. "She'd nothing else to say. Nothing. Her dog and her damned horse riding lessons. All I got to hear about was dressage and equitation and heart worm pills."

He leans towards me. "I tried to steer the conversation towards more intimate stuff. You know, about previous boyfriends, whether she likes it when a guy uses his tongue and so on. Just joking of course. Didn't take the hint though. Kind of laughed it off and went back to talking about dogs." Licks a finger, begins sorting through bookmarks.

I nod and try not to look horrified. I wish I could say something interesting, shocking even. Perhaps suggest Reese show this girl his red boxers or even drop them right down for her like he did for me today. I can just see his reaction, how he would look up at me, astounded. His eyes on my face, appalled, but assessing me in a new and calculating way.

"I asked her all kinds of things. I even," Reese leans closer, a wet hand brushing against mine. "I even asked her about what kind of lingerie she likes and if she sleeps with any clothes on."

There are suddenly a lot of customers in the store. Good excuse to walk away quickly. I am beginning to feel a little nauseated anyway. Reese is the kind of person who leaps quite naturally from one self-inflicted crisis to another as often as most people take a shower. It isn't easy, on my end, to appear endlessly sympathetic.

Reese says nothing more to me the rest of the day, just walks around sniffling and sneezing. He has allergies to just about everything and his nose is continuously dripping, but of course he would never think to stop and blow his nose. This bothers me a lot. Ordinarily I run after him with a Kleenex box, but today he just waves me away with that goofy look of his, as though I'm the one with the problem. He has suggested in the past that he carries his own hankies at all times, but quite frankly I believe them to be brand new.

At closing time I head out at a dead run. I know Reese is on my heels and I'm in no mood to carry on another dreary con-versation in the parking lot. Once I am out though I walk more slowly, aware of blisters like loonies on the backs of both heels.

If I drive fast enough I'll get there just before Richard gets home. Most weeknights he comes home late from work, then a quick shower and change before leaving again. He's pretty well never home in the evenings, at least not until very, very late. Strange, isn't it.

His truck is already in the drive when I slide my car in behind the green van a few houses down. Switch off the lights but leave the engine running. Eleven minutes, twelve. Hope no one looks out and sees me slumped over the steering wheel like a corpse.

Fourteen, fifteen. Almost ready to pull out when suddenly the front door opens and he emerges, dressed to the nines, hair still wet.

Queasy, unpleasant sensation. It spreads, moving rapidly

up and across, down my arms to the tips of my fingers. Cold, clammy, disagreeable.

Are you nuts? Are you really, truly and completely nuts?

Clutching the steering wheel with both hands, I bite down hard on my bottom lip. He gets into his truck and backs out onto the street.

Just a few months ago I saw Richard for the first time in many years. Hard to believe I hadn't met up with him in a town the size of Hope before that, but I didn't. Didn't even know he lived here. Naturally I assumed all along it was Milan. When I came across him here a few months ago, he was walking down the street carrying a newspaper in his hands. I stopped my car immediately and watched him go by. I'm not really sure what I was thinking but I kept studying him in the rearview and then, when he was almost out of sight, turned my car around. I had no plan at that point, but I started following him all the way to his house. It was a ridiculous thing to do of course, but there it is.

And from then on I had to do it. It suddenly became the only thing I could hang on to, to keep me together, to keep me from falling to pieces. A habit of sorts, to drive by there and discover what kind of a wonderful, idyllic life he led. Slowly, gradually, little by little, the plan began to emerge. A way, finally to put things to rest. A way to get even.

What if he has noticed my car here again? What if he knows it doesn't belong to a neighbour? He knows all his neighbours. Someone has complained to him already. The police have set up surveillance.

Take a deep breath, switch on the lights, pull out into the street and step down hard on the accelerator.

-3-

His truck turns off the highway a half-hour later and heads down an obscure side road. Follow for a bit, then stop and wait. Another pick-up passes. Heads crane in my direction. *Who is this idiot at the side of the road?* They are discussing me, weighing options, taking notes, jotting down a detailed description for the police.

If I were a normal person I'd turn around right now and head home and put it all behind me. But I am not a normal person. I am a lunatic, truly.

His truck turns down a lane way with big white pines on either side. It is a calm, clear evening. Reach into my purse for a Tick-Tac, pick up the piano key and squeeze down tight. The sun is beginning to sink into the fields to the west, light fading quickly. It's rained not so long ago here, and there's a scent of it still in the air. Cold earth, pine needles, dead worms. The sound of my car door closing is so loud I bite down on my cheek. Has he heard? I begin to follow him on foot.

I could be at home right now in bed reading a book, holding a glass of red wine, or sipping coffee with Maggie. But no. I am possessed. You see if I give up now, I forfeit my only chance to keep myself together. For the longest time I was stumbling around completely unable to go on. And no one knew. Everyone around me sort of assumed I was okay, that I was taking it well, that I was *managing*. I overheard people talking about me, saying how strong I was, how they admired my ability to go on, how they would never be able to face it themselves. But they are all wrong. They have no idea. They don't know how it feels. The hopelessness. It's worn me down. This past year has been infinitely worse. I've now awoken to the pain. It lacerates with every step I take; every word, every face I see. The pain is now alive and lives inside me.

The end of the lane way comes abruptly. An old stone farmhouse looms ahead in a small clearing. Cold, gray, with massive front doors and chimneys on both gable ends. A muted light shines dully from a main floor window. Surely no one will be looking out at this very moment. I could be lost. There's no crime in getting out of one's car and walking to the back door of someone's house. I could be selling something: vacuum cleaners, religion, collecting for some charity. Lots of nice, ordinary, harmless people do things like that. Or maybe even those census takers. I feel in my pockets. No pencil; not one single scrap of paper.

They say when you commit a murder you make at least twenty-five mistakes, and you're lucky if you can think of five afterwards.

Staying close by the trees I make my way around back of the house. The windows are low enough to reach if I can get closer, but naturally there are obstructions. Claw at the bushes and try to push my way between. How is it on television they always make scenes like this look so simple? The pursuer arrives at the house at a crucial moment; a vine or downspout makes climbing to the second story a possibility; a window is left conveniently open. Or the stalker overhears a pivotal conversation. In Shakespeare someone is always overhearing someone else. *Eavesdropping.* I read once that eavesdropping originally meant to stand where the eaves drip. Guess you'd only be willing to stand under dripping eaves listening in on some conversation if the situation were particularly desperate. So, onwards.

Reach the windowsill eventually, breaking branches and cursing repeatedly. Newman once said *ten thousand difficulties do not make one doubt* and that's what counts here. I have no doubt that I must do this. There are difficulties by the bushel, but not one single, solitary doubt. Pulling myself up as high as I can so that my chin is resting on the cement edge of the sill, I wedge my feet into the space between two stones in the wall. From this vantage I can see with some difficulty through sheer curtains. The only light comes from a hallway.

I'd envisioned a kitchen or a living room even, but instead it appears to be a bedroom, sparsely furnished with a bed, an old-fashioned dresser with round mirror, and a rather ordinary wooden desk and chair. On the dresser someone has assembled an assortment of ceramic cherubs. The desk has nothing on it but a fat brass angel, hands outstretched, palms upward. Not one single garment lying on bed or floor. Everything neat as mother's linen napkins: crisply ironed, flawlessly folded and precisely placed.

Suddenly there is movement and the bedroom door opens wide. A light is switched on. In his hands Richard carries papers of some kind, which he drops onto the bed. He appears to be talking to someone out of my view. His lips are moving and there is a muffled sound of words, which I don't quite catch although I lean in closer.

I will not get caught. I know I will not get caught. Bad things just can't happen to me again. This time someone is watching out for me.

Richard sits down and begins writing. I strain to see the doorway better but there is no one else to be seen anywhere. For a few minutes, maybe it's only seconds, who knows, I lean against the window and just watch without thinking at all. Lulled into a kind of stupor and content to just stand there and watch. But then all of a sudden it hits me and I can't stand looking at him anymore so completely content in his own little world: self-satisfied, complacent, living his wonderful, happy little life as though nothing bad had ever happened. As though he'd never done a single thing wrong. And here I am: broken-down, pulled apart, a lunatic. And who wouldn't be, having lost their only child? A tiny sweet child. The most beautiful little girl. While he stood back and let her die, could've saved her and didn't. I wish I could see her now. That little face, that trusting little face the way it was the last time. But I can't. I can't let myself see it or even allow myself to think of about her. It is indescribable this pain. Unbearable. My little girl. My lost little girl. She is gone now; gone from me forever. Buried in that old cemetery at the edge of town. Buried and forgotten by everyone. A tiny little corpse in a tiny wooden box. How I cried when I touched the white lacy dress she loved so much, when they closed the lid. How I cried when they lowered it into the cold, soaking ground. And it was raining so hard that day. Raining and raining and so terribly cold. I couldn't look. I had to turn away. It was unbearable. It was as though they were tearing the heart from my chest, slicing it from me. It's true. A person can really feel that way. *Tearing, slicing.* And I couldn't breathe. I wished I could die. I truly, truly wished I could die. I did die. There is no hell on earth like that of burying a child. Believe me. Trust me. There is no pain more agonizing than looking into the face of your dead child. There is no pain like watching them close the lid, of knowing for certain, and that is the worst part, knowing it is a *certainty,* that you will never, ever see that little face, or kiss that little cheek, or hold that little hand again.

Forgotten. There are probably only a few people in town who even remember what she looks like. In fact, there are probably lots of people in town who don't even know she once existed. Imagine. There are people who don't know me at all, have no idea what I've lost. People who run into me on the street and in the store every day. They think I'm just an ordinary person, just like Maggie. Can't they see it? Can't they see it on my face? In my eyes? It is torture, agony. To walk down the street in daylight and have these people look at me. To wonder whether they know. To wonder what they are thinking. Speculating. How did it all happen? And whose fault? Are they judging me still? To see the pity in their eyes. It is hell. It is hell on earth. I know hell. I have experienced it firsthand. I am still experiencing it and the months and years flicker by. It is not going away, this pain.

When she was only two I took her down to the park by the river. She had this little purse that Maggie had given her for Easter. A little yellow plastic purse with a white daisy flower on the front. She collected acorns from under the big old oak and stuffed them into that purse, pushing them in there one after the other until it was quite literally overflowing with acorns. *Look Mommy, another one! Another one!* I stood back, my shoes at the very edge of the water, and watched. Just stood there and watched her tiny little feet dancing around, flitting from one spot to the other. The small, dark head bending down, tiny perfect fingers reaching for the acorns. It was like there was a shimmering haze around her; a glowing light. It was a beautiful day: sunny and hot and perfectly still and quiet. Complete happiness. As close to heaven as a human being could ever come. I felt it. I touched it. Heaven. Just for a moment. So you see I am right and Tolstoy was wrong. Dead wrong. It has all been stolen from me, and now I am left here completely alone. Lost: a wretch, a broken soul who must steal mail and follow a strange man and peer in windows likes a criminal or an idiot.

He turns a little, looks towards the typewriter again. Did he glance toward the window first, just an instant?

Pull back my chin from the windowsill and let myself fall, come what may.

Has he seen me? Is he even at this moment rushing to the window or to the telephone to call the police? Surely with a town fairly close they will be here in minutes. Lights will come on, flashing. Sirens will blare agonizingly loud and shrill. I can see the policeman's faces: indifferent, feel the steel cuffs snap shut on my wrists, ice cold. *You have the right to remain silent.*

Something claws at my face. Slip down into the bushes, landing with much noise. Nylons snag on a branch and tear as I stumble away. Is he watching from the window? Does he recognize me now? Does he remember?

Run, cursing, inelegant back to the pines, galloping down, down the long lane way to the road and at last, eyes streaming, nylons in unattractive shreds, to the safety of my car. And away.

-4-

But there are no sirens. No police cars on this God-for-saken road. Drive to the corner and pull over. Darkness does strange and terrible things to the human soul. It is only in dark-ness and at a certain time of night that I hear a voice, a cry, a stumbling on the stairs.

I doze off, waking with a start as light floods my car's in-terior. For one awful moment I think it is a policeman after all and that I am truly done for. But the light moves slowly through and then turns away. Richard's black Ford truck, presumably. Fingers numb, I fumble for keys. Hit one-twenty before reaching the highway and pass a half-dozen vehicles, but the black truck vanishes into the darkness and I am left alone with nothing.

***

Most of the streetlights on Church Street are broken and yet no one in the town of Hope ever seems to notice or care. Of course there is no way I could lodge a complaint myself. Everyone would wonder and ask all kinds of questions, and that would just not do at all, would it.

I walk along slowly, placing one foot carefully in front of the other. A rustling of some night creature. A pinecone falls from a tree overhead, accompanied by the barely audible thud of a door closing somewhere in the distance. A hum of music, just faint. Almost impossible to differentiate the individual notes but there, still, if you listen hard enough.

I have walked here so often I don't even stumble when I

come to the place where there are large roots snaking across. I created this little path into the cemetery myself a long time ago by breaking off branches and tramping down the underbrush. Of course I could take the paved road in like other people. After all, it isn't likely I'll meet up with anyone here in the middle of the night. There have been times, though, when I hurried through after dark, crunching noisily on dry leaves with heavy feet, and then came suddenly upon teenagers sprawled in the grass. They were more startled than I. Leapt to their feet snatching at their scattered clothing. Cheeky, insolent little bastards to come here to this place and besmear it with their pantings and groanings and beer cans. I should know who they are but I don't. Don't listen when people tell me family names. Children's names especially slip through and out of my mind untouched, unprocessed now. I retain so little these days, it is a wonder Sally hasn't spoken up more often to reprimand me at work. I know I deserve it.

But there are no teenagers sprawled on the grass or lusting beneath the trees tonight. All is quiet and still and deserted. This cemetery is very old. It was here long before there was a town, when there were just a few farms scratched out of the bush along the river. And now the names on some of the gravestones are all but obliterated. I bet no one ever comes and visits those graves anymore. How long does it take before one becomes just a pile of dusty bones beneath a smooth and nameless stone? Seventy-five years? One hundred, two? Before no one is left alive who has any memories of you at all? As though you never were. Never existed on this earth: never thought and felt and suffered and hoped.

Stop this, Clarice. Pull yourself together. Remember the expression on his face when he came out of his house to get the mail. As though by rattling his mailbox you awakened him from some profoundly deep sleep. Concentrate. Think. Push the rest aside.

It may be dark, but slowly, slowly my eyes adjust, and the headstones begin to emerge as though glowing with their own inner light. Some headstones at the front of the cemetery, the newer ones, flaunt gaudy carved angels and names in bold and ornate letters. Others are smaller and quite plain, self-effacing, perhaps knowing they aren't quite up to snuff. Leaning, ready to topple and sink beneath the grass. Strangling, ruthless, relentless deadly grass, as perennial as the sky itself.

You would think this might be a frightening place for a woman in the middle of a dark night, but you are quite wrong: it is not. I roam around for hours, touching the now familiar gravestones as I pass by, trailing about here and there and feeling quite calm and at peace. There is one grave at the very back that looks to be more ancient than any of the others, with just a simple small stone, name erased completely. I sit next to it and try to picture the person laid to rest here so long ago. Make up stories about all of them: about their lives, the things they did. The minutes pass. And the hours.

As a rule I steer clear of the section with the newer stones, or at least I don't go there very often. I stay close by though. I like to spend my time here amongst the very old, old graves instead. The ancestors. Visit with each and every one individually, moving methodically from one to the next and the next. *Maud Grace Ann Capelin, Esther Elizabeth Mercer, David Paul Cantin. You are not forgotten.* It is lucky no one can see me here drifting about like a real phantom, skipping without purpose in the middle of the night from stone to cold stone, fingers trailing.

She is here. My little girl. She sleeps here every night and every day, year after year after year.

A long time ago I used to sit next to her bed almost every

night and watch while she slept, examine the perfect features, tuck the little fists in under the blankets and smooth back the soft, soft hair. Children are little angels when they sleep. Transformed: all fears, anxieties, transgressions and hopes erased from their faces. They become newborn again, a clean slate, at one with God and no longer a part of this cold earth.

I come here nights to think things over and to make my plans. To tell her that Mommy has not ever, ever, not even for the briefest moment, in any way, forgotten.

When I come here in daylight it is all very different. There are flowers and flying birds and all kinds of noises from the town, and I don't go over to her side of the cemetery at all. There are people. People moving around and watching me. People who can see and judge. They're wondering what happened. *What did you do?* I can feel myself unraveling, coming unstitched. It is much better here at night. So quiet. Also, I can't sleep at home. Or at least very rarely and only a few hours at a time these days. I need to come here. To try to pull myself together again. Sometimes I fall asleep in the grass, and when I wake up morning has already come.

***

Just past the police station in the town of Hope is a place called Expresso Coffee, open 24 hours. Small, run-down, Expresso is exactly like any other coffee joint in a small town. Seventeen little tables, each with four metal chairs, paint peeling. Black marks on the walls where the chairs have scraped. Floor with a black-and-white pattern like a chess game. Feet pass over it and I watch them, imagining they belong to giant chess players moving from space to space.

"What'll you have?" says the woman behind the counter. Tonight she wears green polyester pants and a long T-shirt tight over enormous, swinging cleavage. Hair dyed auburn, but an inch or so of gray at the part that divides her head neatly in half. She looks like a badger. Like the little girl badger in the Francis books who sings to herself: *I know how a jam jar feels: full of jam!* I recite this little Francis song to myself every time I see the Expresso Coffee woman, the badger girl. *I know how a jam jar feels!* Tonight I catch myself murmuring it out loud; glance around quickly to see whether anyone else has noticed but no one looks at me at all.

Next to my customary table sits an enormous gentleman in a brush cut wearing a saggy gray tracksuit. The elastic band of his blue underwear shows at the back. Orders coffee only, triple cream, triple sugar. Wears sneakers, even in winter, untied and no stocks. I can't help staring at the inch or two of fat hairy leg that protrudes from the bottom of his pants. It is mesmerizing, this inch of portly human flesh: white and bloodless as a chunk of dead and dissolving fish. How awful if must be to have flesh like that; skin that looks as though it already belonged to a corpse.

There is another regular, a man who comes in with a newspaper and notebook tucked under his arm. When he orders his medium with cream, the Expresso Coffee woman is transformed, indifference sliding from her features like raw eggs from a pan. Smiling, breasts swinging happily, she spends several long minutes filling his cup and talking rapidly. I can tell with one look he's not really listening. Not someone like him. What could they possibly have to say to one another? They talk for a long time though before she finally hands him his coffee. I see her watch him then after he sits down. But he never once glances up, just writes and writes in his notebook, picking up the coffee cup and drinking without looking. He is rather attractive and mysterious so I make up stories about him. A newspaper reporter on an important story; homicide investigator on a case.

You grow used to a place after a while. Even a dump like this. Sometimes familiarity is a wonderful, comforting thing. The tables here are not always very clean, but it is very agreeable all the same: chessboard floor, aging coffee, donuts molding imperceptibly behind the glass. Even the pale unhealthy faces around me, the spongy bellies hanging out from under T-shirts.

Eventually everyone else leaves, one by one, sometimes en masse, and I am left alone to brood over my cup in the small hours of morning.

When sunrise finally comes I stand up slowly and avoid the intense need to stretch. The early morning risers, the authentic joggers and type A's, have arrived for their morning cup of inspiration. Someone will notice if I stretch. Strange haggard woman with torn nylons and uncombed hair spends whole night in coffee joint. These, you see, are the real, true inhabitants of Hope: normal ordinary people whose lives are proceeding as planned without major crises or disaster or anything terrible at all.

All night I've wondered *why, why, why,* but it is not until I stumble back out to my car that it finally dawns on my clouded, tired brain. Abruptly, like a jet of scalding water.

Of course. *Idiot.* The reason why he drives all the way out to that farmhouse every night. I already know who lives there. I've read the letter. It is all so very clear. The letter, with that curious, sloppy handwriting on the envelope. Richard goes out all that way every night to that old farmhouse just to see *Her.*

-5-

My queen, it seems, is in serious trouble again. Move her back two spaces so she is safe, at least temporarily. The two pawns are acting as guards and this puts the castle in a good position.

Grabbing my canvass bag full of flyers, I head out the door. Today I will walk to Richard's house and to hell with sore feet. But as it turns out, the walk takes longer than I'd bargained. Even with three layers of Band-Aids my feet smart mightily with every step. Also, my all night vigil is beginning to catch up with me and no amount of cold coffee or Tylenol is going to save me from the consequences.

The town of Hope is situated on a hill; not the summit of a hill, but partway down. The section of town where I live is closest to the river, so it's almost all uphill walking to the downtown. Main Street, I'm noticing today, is really quite steep.

At least twenty vehicles in front of the restaurant that quite recently was renamed *In Paradise*. Sounds promising and very fancy, but is not. Before that it was called *The Village Restaurant*, and before that, *Hope Country Kitchen*. But the menu has remained the same, more or less. Mediocre clubhouse sandwiches, limp burgers and fries at noon, liver and onions or roast beef for dinner. Lately *In Paradise* has caused a stir by offering trendy chilled cappuccinos and smoothies for the morning crowd. Smoothies in the town of Hope. Just imagine. I don't believe anyone actually orders them, but they are on the menu all the same and it sounds quite impressive.

I take a quick look in the front window as I walk by. The regulars have arrived. Heinrich Kefner, the operatic composer with a lisp, seated in his usual spot by the pie display, hunched over his black tea. Trudy Martin, who plays the organ at the United Church and owns a glockenspiel. And, inevitably, Gladys Bierman, whose daughter Lisa has long legs and a tremendous, curved nose like a curlew.

The river is down a bit and we need rain. There was rain forecast last night but it never came. Down by the dock there are men at work with shovels. The dock is a bit of a joke actually. The river is so low here that only a small rowboat or a canoe could actually get through without encountering stumps and dissolving refuse. Still, the townspeople are fiercely proud of the place: a flag by the river's edge, picnic tables and raised flowerbeds. Even a small sandy beach of imported sand for toddlers, although the water is dirty as sin and surely a hotbed of infection. I know my mother would never have let us dip a toe in that muck and we wouldn't have argued it either, but people here don't seem to care one way or the other. Likely they don't notice.

There are two parks in town. One down by the river not far from where I live, known as *River Park*, and this one, *Greenwood*, which is substantially bigger and really just a large area of open fields and gravel pathways that loop through a big section of scrappy softwood bush. A favourite spot for joggers.

Jogging was something I used to do, before. The feel of the ground slipping away under my feet, muscles strong and hard, lungs full of clean air. Strength, power. A sensation of incredible aliveness. I don't run anymore though. How would it look? What would people think? But I still come to the park and walk. I must be very vigilant now, though. I must make certain I don't start checking every park bench, every swing set. Usually I catch myself, just in time. Still, I've caught myself moving briskly towards some child, drawn instinctively as a moth to a flame, only averting disaster at the last possible moment. And I've seen the looks on people's faces. I know what they are thinking. No, there is no way I can simply come out here in broad daylight now and start jogging.

***

Arrive to find Richard's driveway empty. But evidently he's been home at some point this morning and left again; the mailbox doesn't have a scrap inside, which is just simply unheard of.

Launching the bag over my shoulder, I glance behind me. A tall hedge surrounds the back yard. There are spring flowers blooming everywhere. Pink, purple and white hyacinths, Emperor tulips by the dozens. Luminous, radiant. A brass bird hovers on the edge of a birdbath, wings outstretched while a stone figure kneels and gazes tirelessly into the face of an old brass sundial.

Step down the cement stairs that lead to a basement door. Locked. But the patio door is not and the screen door is even open a few inches. This surprises me. Somehow I'd envisioned him as very cautious, Ultra-cautious. The kind of person who turns on an alarm system if he's going out for a five-minute walk, installs bars on all backyard windows.

Touch the door handle again. Gloves? Too late and I'm only going to take a very, very quick look. After all, what do I have to lose and so why not.

The house is eerily silent. Move into the kitchen and look around, running my fingers along the smooth cobalt-blue counter. Spotless tabletop, not a morsel. And there are no dishes in the sink either. Not a crumb. Doesn't he ever eat? There are three cans of diced tomatoes, black olives, mandarin orange segments, four different kinds of olive oil in the cupboard. The fridge contains a small carton of coffee cream, parsley, endive, a jar of artichoke hearts, and a red and yellow pepper. No ketchup, no relish, no salad dressing. The freezer compartment is empty aside from one solitary bag of frozen strawberries.

Mail nowhere to be seen. Living room? The gray plush is perfect; entirely without footprints. You can even see the lines left by the vacuum cleaner. But there is no mail here, not even a flyer or a newspaper. Just one large stack of magazines, all of them the *Urban Gardener.* Flipping through I find the page which lists the contents and the staff writers and editors' names. *Richard Mason, editor.*

There is a white shirt draped over a chair in his room. Bed neatly made with a blue plaid comforter. At the foot end, a basket of laundry, clean and already folded. Touch the clothes lightly with the tip of one index finger. Lift the shirt from the chair and hold it up against me. Who has ironed this? Even I can recognize this shirt is neatly, carefully, even expertly, ironed.

Just a quick look. And here I am. Next thing I'll be trying on his cologne, rifling through his underwear drawer.

Fold the shirt again and replace it carefully, but somehow it looks wrong and I try draping it over the chair a second time. Inside the closet are at least a dozen pairs of pants in an orderly row, and several dozen shirts. Underneath, a row of dress shoes, all colours, styles, nicely polished.

On the night table there is a book. Pad past the bed trailing my fingertips lightly over the blanket, and pick it up gently. It is Fyodor Dostoyevsky's *The Idiot.* Dostoyevsky is an amazing writer. He writes about people who are always caught in a situation with several possible choices before them, each of them seeming somehow right and yet at the same time somehow wrong. This seems to me to be very true to life. It is how things really happen. Never a clear road, a single path. We must constantly choose and make decisions and there are endless possibilities and endless obstacles. Hardship makes us grim and ruthless and bitter and muddies those choices even further. My father used to read Dostoyevsky and Aleksandr Solzhenitsyn. Even though he was an ordinary clerk in a hardware store, he read incessantly and read to me every night when I was a child. Took me by the hand once and led me all the way down to the back field to show me a tiny flower seed smaller than a grain of sand.

There are no pictures on the night table or dresser. I wander around the room slowly watching my image in the mirror as I pass by once, twice. This is where he undresses, here, and this is where he sits, and this is the side of the bed where he sleeps, where he reaches over to slip the book back onto the night table and switches off the light.

A sound.

Rush across the hallway and stumble into an adjacent bedroom. Crawl on hands and knees in back of an armchair which thumps noisily against a wall.

Any second now he will come in and switch on the light, pull up the blind. He will grab my arm, march me to the phone and call the police. I can feel how tightly he will grip my arm. See the anger, the disbelief in his eyes.

For ten whole minutes I wait until one calf cramps and I must stand even if there is hell to pay. I'll pretend to be a moron. Not say a word, not even look at him; simply run out the door and out of his life. This time forever.

I move cautiously down the hallway. Silence, although it seems, if I strain hard enough I might hear a bit of music suspended in the air, a scrap of notes, just barely audible. A piano? A serenade perhaps? But then it fades as my foot reaches the bottom stair and something warm and alive brushes against it.

A gray shape streaks past and into the brightly-lit kitchen. And with this only a fleeting impression of two small cat ears and a long tail scuttling out the half-open screen door. I step out slowly, wincing, into the brilliant dusty sunlight, which pours over me like shower of scalding water. But the creature is gone.

-6-

I arrive back home, Braga's *Angels' Serenade* whirling incongruously, insipidly, through my worn out brain. Hoist myself into bed.

Four hours later I emerge from a convoluted dream where I am in a large forest listening to a strange crying child. I stumble towards this pitiful sound, this unknown being, aware I must rescue it or help it in some way. But the trees are endless and I stumble on and on without ever reaching it, hands clasped over my ears to drown the forlorn, miserable, wretched cries.

As I surface slowly and open my eyes to what is real, I become aware of vigorous knocking.

Come in Maggie.

I understand even as I'm croaking out these words that both doors are still locked and there is no way on earth she could possibly hear me. Get up unsteadily, stumble to the kitchen and open the back door.

Stagger back, sit down still half-awake and stretch out my blistered feet.

"Hi there. Thought you were maybe out again. I was getting worried," Maggie says. She's wearing a black and white blouse and coordinating skirt, as perfect together as a matching cup and saucer.

"Sleeping." I say, pushing my hair back from my face. "Headache. Catching a cold, I guess."

"You don't sleep when you're supposed to, dearest, that's the trouble. I'll make you a coffee, and eat this." Shoves a bowl of Special K in front of me, begins mixing orange juice. "I know it's past lunch, but you should have breakfast first. Most important meal of the day. And drink some water. That's your trouble. Ninety per cent of the time you're dehydrated. You feel like a bag of dirt and it's no wonder."

Bag of dirt. Yes, bag of dirt. Describes me well. This is what I am. A sack full of muck.

There is a long awkward pause and I sit fidgeting. Maggie pours water from the kettle into the sink, begins rummaging in cupboards for a bigger glass for my juice. When she looks for something she always holds her hands up and wiggles her fingers a certain way until she finds it. She does the same thing when she's figuring out crosswords; holds the pencil in one hand and in the other does that wiggling thing with her fingers.

"You know it's been years since I've planted Gladiolas. Maybe I'll do that today. Plant Gladiolas," I wave a hand in her direction. "Do you remember the size of the Glads I used to have? Those great big purple ones? Earl next door would come over and actually measure them to see if his were bigger."

Maggie reaches for a glass and pours it half-full. Begins taking tiny little sips, lips barely touching the rim. Looks me over, eyebrows tilted.

"Talk to me Clarice. I want to help. You used to tell me everything."

I think at that moment, still in a haze and heavy-eyed from that dream, with my defenses down and really only half-awake, I might have taken her into my confidence. The fact is, she's right. I used to tell her everything. Everything.

Maggie and I met here in Hope when we were both very young. I was newly married and she'd just given up an acting career at the theatre in Milan to stay home with her babies. We both desperately needed someone to talk to, so confiding in a neighbour the same age who lived just down the street was quite natural. It was always so simple to tell Maggie everything. We had coffee together almost every afternoon after I got home from work, and it wasn't long before it became a ritual. Coffee break with Maggie. A time to tell each other everything.

So much has happened since then. She can't understand. The last ten or twelve years have been so very different for her. No one has altered the course of her life. Her life has moved along, slowly, steadily, conveniently, peacefully, minutely.

But like I said, at that moment I might have confided in her again. Told her about Richard and all my plans. If it hadn't been at that very moment, that critical instant—just like in a play when at a pivotal moment a main character arrives unexpectedly—a key turns in the lock and slowly the front door opens.

Removing his hat and stepping away from the door, he flicks on the front entrance light and tosses the hat adroitly, even expertly, towards the table with the dolls. It lands neatly in front of them without touching a hair. An old habit.

-7-

I stand up and lurch towards the fridge. Pulling open the freezer compartment I examine the contents. What's in that plastic margarine dish anyway? Mull over the possibilities. Five seconds, ten, fifteen. There is no movement at the front door.

It is Maggie who finally breaks the impasse.

"Frank? What are you doing here?" she says. She is at the table, eyes open very wide, lips parted. Quite literally *gaping*. For one long, drawn-out moment Maggie looks perfectly ghastly, as though through some strange transformation she's become the person she'll be in sixty years. But it is only for an instant, and maybe I have imagined it. A moment later she closes her mouth and is back; the same beautiful Maggie I've always known.

Force myself to close the freezer door and move towards him. The wall along the stairs needs painting. There are peeled-off spots. Why have I not noticed this before? Frank hasn't moved from the doorway. He stands and watches, arms crossed, feet just inches from one of my wooden birds. I expect he thinks I will yell and scream and wave my arms about and throw something. Throw him out on his ear, lock, stock and barrel. Really, I am beginning to sound like Maggie.

So imagine Frank's surprise when I simply nod and welcome him home as pleasantly and calmly as though he's only been gone one single, solitary night.

"Where are your bags, Frank?" I say, pushing past him and opening the front door. There they are. The same two expensive brown leather suitcases with the familiar red airline tags, only slightly more battered than before. Reach down and pick them up, drag them through the doorway without a word. The bags are exceptionally heavy.

"Look I better be going," Maggie says. "Like I said before, I'm late already." Funny how Frank always seems to put Maggie on edge. He's the only one who has the power to do this, to make Maggie lose that polished way of talking as though she were rehearsing lines from a play.

"It's all right," I say dropping the bags, which make a thump like an exclamation point. "I'll call you later. Don't for heaven's sake be late on my account."

"See you Frank," Maggie says. "Quite a surprise you showing up like this after all this time. Could almost give a person a heart attack."

Then, as she turns away from him and passes by me she hisses something I don't quite catch. Lips pressed together hard and brow furrowed with an expression very much like my mother: firm, unyielding, inwardly fuming. After Maggie is gone I mix a gin and ginger, adding one ice cube and carefully stirring. Frank has already made himself comfortable on the couch in the living room. The bags have now disappeared.

"Well I see you're back." I set the glass down with a crack on the coffee table.

"You've let your hair grow longer. It looks a lot better that way. You look great, Clarice. Terrific."

An outright lie and he surely knows it.

"It doesn't suit me to have you here Frank. Not at all."

"Then why did you bring in my bags? You could've slammed the door in my face."

Shrug. Pluck at my sweater, which I suddenly notice is covered in tiny lint balls the exact shade of Caesar's fur.

"We agreed we'd stay friends. We agreed, did we not, that

we'd always be there for one another, when one of us needs help." He hasn't taken his eyes off me. Not once. "I take it that's why you're here. You need something. Need my help. Which is fine, but you can't stay long."

"Not exactly," he says. "Not exactly, although you could say I've got a temporary little cash flow problem." He begins to cough and grabs the gin glass, taking a few big mouthfuls. "But that'll all clear up in no time." *Hack, hack, hack.* Settles his feet on the coffee table, leans back. He looks as though he never left here, as though he was lying on this couch in this room all along, for two years, and I just never noticed before. The hair is a shade thinner perhaps and grayer around the sides, but it suits him. In fact, he looks amazing, as though it hasn't touched him at all. It isn't fair. If life has to throw these things at you there should at least be some kind of warning. A few hours to prepare: take a shower and change one's clothes, maybe think of a few important things to say, write a few crib notes.

"For starters you at least better tell me where you've been these past two years," I say.

"Out west. I told you that's where I was headed. Got a job. Quit. Got another job. Quit that too."

"I thought you'd write or something. Send an address. Call maybe. Anything. Two bloody years."

"Typical woman. You want a divorce, want me to get lost, but irregardless you want me to call all the time, check in so you can keep tabs on my whereabouts. Typical."

Frank has this irritating habit of using words that don't exist. This annoys me to no end, and as a result I can't concentrate on what he's trying to say at all. I've told him so many times before that *irregardless* isn't a word, but he still goes on saying it again and again, and not just to infuriate me. He is just careless. Careless with words, careless with his feelings, careless with life. When I told him I wanted a divorce, he just shrugged his shoulders and looked away. *Fine then. Don't matter one way or the other I guess.* He didn't really stand up for himself or for us. It wasn't until after, *after,* that he decides it was all a mistake.

"Well that's fine then," I say. Suddenly I don't care that he's showed up here on my doorstep after disappearing without a word for more than two years. It all seems kind of trifling, unimportant, like the barometer reading for the day or the horoscope in the paper. I find myself wishing I could simply find a sunny spot in the house, curl up like a cat and go back to sleep. Me, wanting sleep. The same person who normally sleeps three, four hours a night at best.

"I'll mix up another ginger," I say, dragging out the syllables.

I head back into the kitchen. How simple it would be to just walk out right now, just turn my back on him and disappear. Maggie would take me in, for a while at least. I see myself bunked in with the kids, sharing a bedroom with Melissa, the oldest. Helping her out with math problems. But I know that I won't do it. I don't have the guts. I'm not that kind of person. I don't have courage.

Frank and I had a very good marriage once. We loved having lots of people around us. Back then I told myself over and over that I was the luckiest woman on earth, that Frank was the best possible husband. And I believed it. Frank brought me flowers. Frank took me out to dinner. Frank washed the dishes and the kitchen floors and cooked dinner. Frank called me every day from work and told me loved me. Frank worried about me and planned my birthdays for months in advance. Lavish gifts and surprise dinners and nights away in exotic locations.

"I have to go Frank." But there is no answer from the other room. Wait, shifting from one foot to the other. Surely he hasn't gone out to his truck again. Another suitcase? Furniture? Heaven forbid he thinks he's moving in here for good. Better put a flying stop to that idea this very minute.

But I am wrong. He is still on the couch. The newspaper lies spread out on his chest. One arm is folded back behind his head. His eyes are closed, face very white, lips slightly parted. For one small moment I think he has up and died, right here on my living room couch. Heart attack. Stroke. Aneurysm. He's at that age now after all. How will I explain it? But he moves one arm a little. A cigarette dangles from the end of two fingers and falls noiselessly to the floor. I move quickly and retrieve it, dropping it into the glass of gin.

But I haven't been fast enough.

On my polished wood floor there is now a stain. A sooty black smear burned into the dark wood that will never, ever go away.

-8-

Hatred is a strange thing, isn't it? Only humans have been given this capacity, this strange and gruesome ability. Certainly animals aren't capable of it. Instinct tells the predator which other animal should be selected as prey and destroyed, but there is no hatred there; simply a logical chain of survival: eat and be eaten. But we humans hang onto emotions of all kinds, don't we? Feed on them until they grow and grow and consume us entirely. Love and hate, but hatred most of all. Yes, hatred certainly. The fuel and motivation for all human action. Love and hatred and of course sex. As Lord Byron once said, *now hatred is by far the longest pleasure; men love in haste, but they detest at leisure.*

***

Holding the doorknob between thumb and forefinger, I turn it very, very slowly. Even so, it makes a smallish noise.

Ridiculous that I have to sneak around here like this, a thief in my own home. I am entitled to leave my own house in the middle of the night if I want. I am an adult. We are no longer married; I owe Frank no explanations. If he wakes, I will tell him I am going out for a walk. It's that simple. But I'd rather he didn't know just the same. If he's going to live in my house for a few weeks or even months, I'd just as soon he didn't see how little time I spend here at night, how unusual my nocturnal habits. Although we are no longer married and he no longer has any hold over me, not the tiniest scrap of authority, I still feel this ridiculous need to make myself into the person he wants me to be, the first Clarice. Even though I tell myself he means nothing now, that it doesn't matter what he sees, I still do not want him to look at me and think, *what is wrong with her? Why can't she be normal? Why has she turned into this unreasonable idiot?* He can't understand someone like me. He looks at me now and is sometimes speechless. I suppose he doesn't see Clarice at all anymore.

Turning onto Church Street, I head towards the cemetery and step quickly down my little path and then in amongst all the familiar stones. My new family: an enormous pink stone with an angel on top, arms stretched beseechingly to the sky, one finger pointing ominously to heaven. And to the left, a half-round stone featuring disembodied praying hands cut off neatly, if somewhat gruesomely, at the wrists. Someone has placed fresh flowers here just recently. Scarlet and oddly crisp and alive. Incongruous as a bunch of blue plastic flowers scattered about in a snowdrift.

I walk for several hours. Finally, when it is almost time to go, I head for the newer section. But I don't go right up close. The headstone is simple and very plain: name, date of birth and date of passing. *Beloved little angel*, it suggests, *Gone to be with God.*

It is not a custom here but I have planted flowers on the entire grave, not just in a small patch in front of the headstone like all the others. I think it is actually not permitted, but I did it anyway and so far no one has said a word. Not the pastor or the groundskeeper, or the old guy in the faded plaid trousers who usually cuts the grass. Maybe in time they will tell me that I am breaking the rules, but let them. This is one thing I will not allow them to take away from me.

It took me a while to determine which flowers, but then I finally settled on purple aubretia, pink bridal veil astilbe, yellow coreopsis, powder blue mist flower, dark rose sea pinks, deep purple asters, maiden pinks dianthus, wine-red blanket flower, white gypsophila, and deep red flame grass. This way there is something blooming all the time for all three seasons. I wanted to plant dwarf iris too and perennial pansies, because they have cheerful, friendly little faces, but there is simply no more room. As it is, the flowers fall all over one another and spill dramatically onto neighbouring plots, which is maddening but simply can't be helped.

***

Caesar has not been himself lately. Since the reappearance of Frank he stays out of sight in a safe place behind the potted fern, and from there keeps an uneasy watch over his food dish. Frank may have set Maggie on edge and made Caesar completely miserable, but he does not concern me one whit. I am free and easy. I have plans, and the whole long day stretches before me with endless possibilities. In the grand scheme of life, Frank's reappearance means nothing. Less than nothing; the little end of nothing whittled down to a point.

He has moved into the spare room. His clothes are everywhere and the bed is never made. Pillows on the floor, bed sheets in a roll and hanging out from under the comforter and onto the floor on one side.

I don't venture into this room very often actually. I don't think I've been in here six times in the past two years. But today I find myself casually wandering in, in spite of myself. You see the whole room has changed entirely from how it used to be, which can be bewildering for anyone. Like a dream when you step into your house and find everything inexplicably different. All the old furniture is gone, even the light fixture. But where? I know this bed and dresser were ordered new and someone came and painted the walls soon after, sewed curtains and even hung them up for me. Yes, Maggie painted the walls and brought curtains. I remember it now. Maggie at the door, paint can and fabric swatch in hand. She was always coming to the door back then with something in her hands, and not just paint brushes. A gift, a casserole. Pity in a covered dish.

Frank used to have a painting business when I first met him. He'd started it when he went to university and needed a job for tuition. He was taking engineering back then, following in his father's big successful footsteps. But he made quite a lot of money painting and decided he liked being his own boss, and so dropped out of university in second year and expanded his business, hiring on two other full-time workers and buying his own truck. He was quite successful right from the start. But of course he didn't stay with that business forever. Ever careless, he dropped it and moved on.

So that's how we met. Frank was hired to paint father's house. I'd insisted my father do something with the old place. Ever since he retired and mother passed on, he neglected it badly. *Falling to wrack and ruin*, as Maggie would say. The roof leaked, windows crumbled, walls cracked. In a befuddled moment, father once let the bathtub overflow so that water ran through the ceiling into the rooms below, rotting carpets, ruining plaster and ceiling tiles, and even flooding the birdcage. But he did nothing. Sat and smoked cigars on the orange-flowered couch that smelled of cat urine, and looked out the window. Went down to the restaurant morning and afternoon for coffee with a handful of chums from the hardware store. Left water pooling under the kitchen table and dishes from the week before rotting in the sink. So I kept after him, and he finally, reluctantly, agreed to have repairs done and then a painter come in to do the whole works.

Frank showed up early one morning in spattered clothing and a greasy ball cap. When I opened father's door, the sun was just beginning to shine through the big windows that faced east, and Frank looked like some Greek god. Tall and dark-haired, muscles rippling as he carried in the cans and rollers and moved rapidly from room to room. We talked about colour schemes and light. We talked about school and family and plans for the future. Frank liked to talk while he worked, had an easy way about him so that anyone felt at once they knew him well. He had no misgivings about revealing every emotion, every thought, every misdemeanor. Most men aren't anything like that. A lot of women aren't either. But Frank was never afraid to reveal himself to anyone.

Frank has a younger brother, a parental deception that haunts Frank to this day. His brother was born when Frank was almost ten, old enough to have come to expect his parent's complete devotion and certainly their exclusive attention. The household had revolved around his needs and wants for so long that he felt utterly betrayed by the arrival of cribs and jolly jumpers and baby bottles. Gone were the long evenings playing football with dad. His father was to have taught him to play golf that summer and taken him to Toronto for a Blue Jay's game. But none of it happened. Troy happened. Tiny toes, blonde, noisy. And beautiful enough that Frank's dark face seemed suddenly monstrous. He realized with alarm that his own big feet seemed like enormous growths on the end of two long skinny poles. There were even thick, ugly hairs growing on his big toes, wiry and grotesque. Before Troy happened, he hadn't noticed any of these things at all.

A sweet baby, everyone said of Troy, *a little miracle*. You should be proud to be the big brother of such a wonderful little baby boy, they told him. Frank sulked and raged and stayed in his room while the little miracle grew up taller, blonder, strikingly handsome, and then to top it off, a prosperous orthopedic surgeon. In Frank's eyes, Troy manipulated his parents from the moment he arrived; ensured that the conversation revolved around him alone, exaggerated the stories he brought home from school, embellished his scholarly accomplishments at the dinner table, and told unfavourable tales about Frank's friends. Frank learned to be very quiet, although to his parents he seemed all at once sullen and secretive.

He asked me out to dinner during his last day painting father's house. I hadn't been out for dinner with anyone for months, having just finished exams. I was also just starting a new summer job at a local weekly. University had been a very isolating experience. I had trouble finding my way into conversations and shied away from parties of any kind. I dated a few boys, but none of them for more than a few months: a series of casual dinners, some dancing, some light groping on cold vinyl seats in dusty pick-up trucks. Carl, my last boyfriend, had been shy and gentle, with a soft voice and small pale hands. He was studying music: majoring in violin and planning to teach school. Nice enough, but in the end dates with Carl turned out tedious and uninteresting. The concerts he took me to were wonderful, but afterwards Carl insisted on a full criticism of every note, arguing noisily if I made any effort to disagree. Instead of gazing into my eyes over dinner in a quiet restaurant, he took me to crowded drinking holes, drew bar lines on paper napkins, filling them with eighth notes and tempos and crescendos to illustrate his point. When he kissed me, he opened his mouth wide revealing a jumble of large crowded teeth that never looked completely clean. I quickly learned to draw my lips in and keep my mouth shut tight. In the end I made excuses, dodged his calls and visits, feigned a number of brief illnesses, and finally called it all off.

Dinner with Frank, who was so much older and more mature, turned out to be radically different. First, cycling through the neighbourhood where he lived, racing down streets and pedaling furiously down steep hills until our tires touched and we almost crashed. Then dinner and a play at a theatre in Milan followed by a visit to Frank's favourite bookstore. I went home energized and in high spirits for the first time after a date. I was going to marry this man. In fact, he said it first. It was the last thing he said to me before we said goodnight on our very first date. *I am going to marry you, Clarice. I guarantee you someday you are going to be Mrs. Frank Forrest.*

-9-

The weather turned cooler this week, bringing with it an irritating drizzle that won't go away. It's left me with a head cold as well, and I find myself roaming the house, soggy Kleenex in hand and nothing much to do. Sally has given me a few days off of work in lieu of overtime, but I have no energy for projects around the house. No interest in gardening or other hobbies. Everything lies neglected.

Frank disappeared rather early this morning, but I don't think it has anything to do with his new business. He doesn't even make the pretence of working these last few weeks. I believe his business partner tunneled out a month ago and the new company never actually materialized. I don't know any of this as fact because Frank no longer tells me things, but I still know him very well, well enough anyway. I've seen how he drifts around here lately. Apathetic, listless, like an old cat with arthritis and bad teeth. And he's so transparent, always was. Even if he no longer tells me everything he is thinking. After his first painting business collapsed, or rather after he abandoned it during the recession, Frank never really found his niche again. Drifted from job to job and refused to return to university or college, despite bullying and prodding from his parents. It seemed as soon as he started to find success in one job, began working his way up the ladder, he would drop it and move on to the next. Start all over elsewhere. Not out of boredom, I truly believe, but out of sheer carelessness, apathy.

Sitting at my desk in my bedroom, I realize I've never actually written Frank a letter before. It seems strange to hold a pen in hand and write his name. So immutable. And so ironic that after having been apart so long and never having written to him once, I finally decide to write him a letter now that he's actually living in my house.

When we were still married, I used to leave him notes all the time. On the kitchen table in the mornings beside the sugar bowl. Love notes, I guess you could say, although they were usually just friendly little reminders. *Hi hon, feed the cat. Water plants. Don't forget banking tonight. Taxes due tomorrow. Remember, it's your mom's birthday tomorrow — get a card in town today!* But they were always signed, *love Clarice.* And XOXO. Just a habit, that XOXO. Zipped those off without so much as a thought. The words themselves meant nothing really. Not that I didn't love him, but I didn't really truly love him at that very moment, that very second as I so carelessly and mindlessly penned that *love Clarice,* and those X's and O's. I felt lucky, certainly. And contentment, yes. Duty. And a sort of wifely love, I suppose. But nothing that entered deep into my soul and cemented me to him forever. It just wasn't like that. Once the first few months of our marriage passed by, our love for one another became routine. All of it. A habit of sorts.

Frank told me his mother used to leave him love notes before Troy was born, little notes in his lunch pail or schoolbag. *Miss You. Mommy Loves You. Hugs and Kisses. Happy Birthday to Mommy's Little Man.* With home baked brownies wrapped in cellophane. Frank claims that once Troy arrived, his mother was always detached and silent when she made Frank's breakfast, not even pausing to kiss him good morning when he entered the room. She worked steadily at the sink, washing bottles and sterilizing in a big pot on the stove, hair in an unruly ponytail. Sometimes she sang to herself, little nursery rhymes. But according to Frank, the special pancakes and all the little love notes disappeared for good from the moment Troy entered the Forrest household.

I am heartless these days, truly. I leave my letter to Frank propped on his pillow like a phone bill. He will find it approximately ten minutes after his arrival home. I can see him moving from room to room, searching for me, clearly annoyed. He will discard his jacket on the back of a kitchen chair, pour himself a gin and ginger, and head to his room, formerly the spare room. He will turn on the television, curse because the old black-and-white has a terrible picture, screw around with the rabbit ears for a long, long time, pushing them this way and that. Then, cursing again, he will collapse on the bed. And finally notice my letter.

Dearest Frank. Don't take this personally, but get out. Today. You know this can't go on. You must see by now how unsuitable it is for both of us. Have a nice life. Your friend always, Clarice

In my bedroom I have four letters from *Her* hidden away in my night table in a locked box. I must return those today while Richard is still at work. It's just been far too difficult this last while doing all of this with Frank underfoot, causing me much grief and worry and certainly the reason behind my catching such a bad cold at this time of year.

I reach for my bishop and move him diagonally four squares; take the black castle off the board and set him carefully on the dresser. Next to three black pawns and a bishop. No question, I am taking complete control of this game

Slip on a raincoat and rubber shoes, and stuff a handful of Kleenex into both sleeves. Close the door firmly behind me, four letters thrust deep, deep into my pockets.

-10-

Sally is in one of her moods today, hiding out in her office and slamming the door shut if anyone comes by. I know what it is. She and John have been trying to have a baby for the past twelve years and Sally is just about at the end of her rope. She'll be turning forty next month and she told me they're almost, almost, ready to give up. Truly, she just can't do it anymore. She is exhausted; they both are. In fact, she has started taking sleeping pills at night and now she tells me she can't go to sleep at all without them. John's blood pressure has also sky-rocketed lately so she's begun to worry about him as well on top of everything else.

Sally invited me to her house once to meet John and to have dinner with them. John did all the cooking for us, barbecuing big thick steaks and foil-wrapped potatoes drenched in butter. Salad with his own dressing. Even a homemade blueberry pie for dessert. Sal mixed the drinks. She drank only mineral water herself, because, she told me quietly, they were trying to get pregnant. She and John exchanged a look when she said that. *Still trying to get pregnant after all this time, after all these years*, it said. And even back then, which was quite a while ago, she seemed too nervous, too overwrought, to manage anything around the house herself. John did it all. I remember thinking this seemed a bit odd, how she seemed to dissolve into this helpless entity within the four walls of her home while at the bookstore she always appeared so efficient and capable.

After supper Sally took me upstairs and showed me the

baby's room. They'd had it all done up professionally years before when they first started trying for a baby. A beautiful hand-carved wooden crib along with matching dresser and change table. Purple and yellow striped blankets and bumper pads with coordinating curtains. Walls a very pale purple with a giant giraffe painted over the crib. The lamp on the dresser was shaped like a giraffe too. Sally picked up the lamp and showed it to me: it had different settings so you could leave it on all night if you wanted. I looked in her face then and saw the desperation, how much she ached for this not-yet conceived child, and how it was destroying her slowly, utterly, inside. This is possible, believe me.

And I think, looking at me, she could almost, *almost,* grasp a little of my pain too, except she was too overwhelmed by her own emptiness to see but a shadow of what could be mine.

At any rate, today something is definitely really, terribly wrong with Sally. She must have lost another baby. She hasn't come out of her office once all day. Every time I go past she is just sitting at her desk staring at the telephone, rubbing one hand lightly over her forearm, no expression at all on her face. A blankness, hardly awake. I really should go in, but I just can't do it even though I know it is the right thing to do.

Reese is quiet all day too, glum and tight-lipped, sniffing continuously and pulling at his wispy little moustache until my stomach begins to turn and I can't stand being anywhere near him. Any time he walks to the front of the store I turn and head quickly for the back, a pile of paperbacks or some stationary item balanced in my arms. March into the storeroom and close the door behind me. Linger there for as long as I dare, knowing full well he will soon come looking, wrestling with the door handle in a way that only Reese can, as though the door were perpetually locked or in some way tremendously difficult to turn. When the end of the day finally arrives, I offer to close up just to speed them both out the door and have the place to myself. This time no one argues or says anything to me at all.

***

There are several lights on at the old farmhouse. Push branches aside, wedge my foot into the space between two stones and hoist myself up until my face is level with the windowsill. He is in the little bedroom again. She, on the other hand, is nowhere to be seen, although I imagine at any moment she will walk in, wineglasses in hand. Or perhaps she is waiting for him in bed, naked and warm and very, very happy. Ecstatic with life. Just waiting for him to join her. How cozy and private and wonderful it all is here for them. What a life they lead, this pair.

And now I know what I am going to do. Truly. It is just a matter of time.

***

Frank must have found my little note, and this time he is gone for good. Blasted out of here never to return. On the kitchen table stands a large crystal vase filled with a dozen yellow roses, full-blown, some drooping already with petals falling. The crystal vase is half empty, carelessly, thoughtlessly filled. So like Frank. I hurry into the spare room to check. Dresser empty; drawers hang open. Bed stripped of sheets. Pillow missing completely.

Caesar is peering in the kitchen window, mouth open in a silent meow. Knock on the window, open the screen to let him in.

Don't worry, I'm back old fellow. Bet you didn't come in at all when he was here alone, did you? Bet you're glad to see the tail end of him, and how come you hate him so much anyway? He's not that bad at all, really. Look, he even left us roses. Just imagine, beautiful yellow roses.

Fill Caesar's dish, bend down and scoop him up into my lap, but he jumps down right away, claws out, and disappears downstairs. I am to be punished then.

Opening the mailbag on the table, I dump its contents. Another letter from *Her*. Again that sloppy, haphazard handwriting on the envelope: some letters leaning one way, others slanting recklessly, crazily, the other.

. . .maybe I'll take this letter and put a match to it along with all the rest. Maybe I'll never send it at all, just leave them here for you to find after. . .

And that's how it ends. As useless as the others and not much of a starting point for someone like me who has so little imagination and must hurry along with all of this.

***

At Maggie's house I pause for a moment before knocking. How long has it been since I last came here? Check my watch. *Nine-fifteen*. But what if one of the kids is home sick? No matter. I'll face them; time I did. Screwed up weirdo neighbour lady. How they'll stare.

"Clarice?"

There is concern and also relief in her eyes. She is wondering whatever possessed me to come back here after all this time. She is thinking I have done something really dumb, like invited Frank back into my life for good, that he is at this very moment lying naked and snoring in my bed, all hairy and sweaty between my blue flowered sheets. She thinks I need her help again.

"Come in, for heaven's sake Clarice. Don't just stand there." She opens the door further and actually grabs my arm, pulling me in.

The house smells of baking bread and Pine Sol.

"Come on, I've got coffee made. Real big pot too. Didn't get a chance when the kids were here. Poured some and it got stone cold. Everyone was late getting up and then Chad forgot he needed money for some fundraiser at school, so I had to run around all over like a chicken searching for change. And Melissa decides on this god-awful blue dress of course, so I had to find stockings to match, which were all in the laundry of course, and I had to iron the dress because it was wrinkled in a ball at the back of her closet and probably dirty, who knows. A little ball like this big. And so of course there was no change anywhere. Nowhere in this total chaos."

This is a lie of course. Everything looks neat and organized in Maggie's house as always. A gleam of copper pots that hang in an orderly row above the stove, smallest to biggest. A ceramic plaque over the stove announces *Blessed Are Those Who Clean Up.*

I cannot under any circumstances picture Maggie rifling through drawers, checking under sofa cushions and dumping out purses in pursuit of stray quarters. A thrill passes through me. Actual goosebumps. I rub my hands over both arms. It is so normal here. So *normal.*

"Well. Is he gone? I thought I saw his truck pull out Friday, but I didn't see whether he'd packed his suitcases in or anything."

"He's gone. Really gone this time."

Maggie flings her arms around me dramatically, pulls me close and hugs me so hard I hear a little crack from somewhere near my left shoulder blade. She reeks of Obsession and, less obviously, Pine Sol.

"I'm so glad, Clarice. I mean it was nice of you to take him in like that but for heaven's sake girl, really, he couldn't just move in again. It was, well, criminal." She lets go of me finally, shakes her head so that her hair bounces. "Would've been such a terrible, terrible mistake. Really, dearest. Paul says the same. You know what? You look great today, Clarice, terrific. You look so much better, really. Not so pale anymore."

A guilty stab somewhere in the region of my chest. For some reason I always want to back away when she flings her arms around me like this, hugs me and kisses me and showers me with little token complements interspersed with never ending motherly advice. I feel it is not genuine, this outpouring: it is all part of being an actress. This is how she traps people. Traps them into thinking that she is much nicer than she really is. In truth, she is thinking something very different, or doesn't really care a whit. And yet for the most part I still try to be like everyone else around Maggie, one of the crowd who accepts her for what she is, who pushes aside any thoughts of insincerity, who accepts her help and show of generosity. Everyone loves Maggie. Who wouldn't? She knows what to say. She makes the right choices and takes the right roads.

And so this is how it ends. Just like old times. I arrive on Maggie's doorstep staggering with the weight of my catastrophe on my shoulders, the sheer enormity of my ineptitude. And Maggie offers advice. Motherly, kindly, pityingly, with perhaps a covered casserole or a dozen muffins on the side.

***

I have trouble concentrating at work in the afternoon. I am supposed to be restocking best sellers, but I keep taking down new ones and putting back old ones. In the end I give it all up and let Reese take over while I cover the till. It's busy all evening, which is a godsend. At least I am occupied. Twice when I'm counting back change though I have difficulty adding up the dimes and quarters and mess everything up. Customers look at me strangely and glance at one another. *Idiot,* they are saying, *Imbecile.*

When at last there is a lull, Reese, who seems in much better spirits today, abandons the best sellers and wanders over to chat, leaning towards me in his irritatingly intimate manner, edging further and further into my space until I begin to feel sick to my stomache yet again.

"But you weren't doing anything tonight. You told me so yourself. Anyway, I thought you said you were dating again these days."

"No thanks Reese. I'm not in the mood. Really. I'd be really rotten company. Maybe another time. And no I'm not dating. Not at all, actually. I don't know where you got that idea from."

He scowls at me, begins cracking his knuckles. *Crack. Crack. Crack.* Picks at his nails which is quite unnecessary. They are long, yes, but round and smooth. Kind of strange for a guy. So neat and long and shapely, and the hands so moistly white. He reaches up and shoves at his glasses, pushing them back until they touch his eyebrows. Yanks at the forlorn little moustache with thumb and forefinger. I want to tell him that his glasses look foolish like that, all pushed up and smushed against his eyes, and the moustache is simply a mistake. But every time I start to say something he looks me straight in the eye and I must close my mouth again, unable to choke out one single, solitary word. Coward that I am.

"So how's Charlene anyway?" I say finally instead. "Did you go to the dance?"

"We went, but I've decided that's it. We hardly even danced. She kept complaining it was too hot and too smoky and just sat there without saying anything so I took her home right after."

"Sorry Reese. Thought it might work out for you. She

seemed real nice. I mean when she came in the store I thought, now isn't this a nice girl. Pretty too. That shiny blonde hair."

"I just knew she was a loser. I just knew it. I mean with the Afghan dog and everything."

How is it a person like Reese turns into such a walking disaster when he's around women? Roughly forty, tall and thin, with brown eyes that are really quite nice if you can see past those horrible glasses. Yet there's something about him that's definitely off-putting. That wispy moustache is somehow effeminate and that alone is enough to turn a girl off. I can certainly see why he has major troubles in the woman department. He is pleasant to chat with and that smile seems sincere and kindly, but one simply couldn't imagine being held in those doughy white arms.

Maybe that's what men think about me these days. The same sort of thing except from the male point of view. There's just something about me, some little thing that always turns them away. Certainly no man, aside from Reese of course and he doesn't count, has made any kind of a pass at me in ages. Nothing. As though I were completely invisible. A fly speck. A jot of dust.

I resume my post at the till and begin sorting MasterCard and Visa slips. Must tell Sal we're running short.

A young female shopper is now standing in front of the romance section and Reese is closing in. She looks as though she's at least seventeen, but who knows. Twelve-year-olds look so grown-up these days, she's probably hardly past Grade six and Reese likely won't care. I'm just reaching for a book someone has abandoned on top of today's newspapers, when to the right of the big display of hardcovers I see Richard walk past. Just like that. *Richard.*

As usual tears are not far off and easily summoned, child that I am.

"Reese, tell Sal I got really sick and I'm not coming back. Swear you'll tell her." This is not really a complete lie. I do feel sick, wipe at my teary eyes with the back of my hands, and choke back a sob, a real throaty choking sob that is rising in my throat like vomit. Run out of the store. Stop short and scan the hallway trying to see past a group of stout female shoppers, then move away quickly again, tottering in my shoes. One woman shouts something at me as I brush by. Looking back over my shoulder I see she is balancing a bowl of goldfish on one arm, which evidently I almost dislodged on my way past.

I begin to run in earnest. And then, from somewhere far behind me, I hear Reese's voice sailing out over the noise of the mall crowd, wailing and high-pitched as a little girl's.

"You're crazy Clarice. Completely crazy. You're one weird, screwed-up crazy bitch and I ain't telling Sally anything at all."

-II-

I push past a female shopper in a huge swinging floral dress, buttocks two axe-handles wide. Next, an assembly of teens, hands in pockets, crotches at knees, green-tipped fingers clutching little jean handbags. But I lose him again.

It occurs to me as I open the mall doors that maybe I was mistaken, that it wasn't really Richard at all, but I don't really believe it. I am not a lunatic. I am not seeing visions or apparitions or hearing voices in my head. Trust me, I am perfectly in control, and I can think just as clearly and lucidly as the next person.

When I get home I find Caesar has regurgitated on the kitchen floor in three gray, still surprisingly mouse-like piles, and once on the mat at the front door. Akin to frothy felt. The remaining roses from Frank have now lost most of their petals and I pitch them, along with Caesar's presents, into the backyard under the cedar hedge. The phone rings. I have missed another dentist's appointment and the secretary is scarcely civil.

Sorry, sorry, sorry.

Hang up, aware suddenly of an ache in my top left bicuspid, ever so slight, but definitely an ache. I envision a gaping hole, a long exposed nerve already inflamed and worsening by the minute. I must make a note to ask Maggie which dentist she visits in Milan. The telephone begins to ring again, piercingly, but there is no way I can answer it now. The house feels hot and I walk around slowly opening windows wide and counting under my breath.

Seven, eight, nine, ten rings.

Who would let it go that long? How ridiculous not to hang up after the fourth ring. Who on earth takes nine whole rings to get to their telephone? If you don't answer after four, you're either not home at all or you're on the toilet and otherwise indisposed. I pace, trail my fingers along furniture, move to the front entrance and examine my dolls. They are beautiful. Perfect, ageless and changeless. Adjust my little bird collection before heading out the door. Just as I am leaving, the telephone begins to clamour again.

***

A startling, wonderful and very significant discovery. I find Richard's truck parked in front of a bar in town called *Sunny's*, which is not really in the downtown area, but further east, close to the arena and the Legion on a street called Mistake Street. Leave it to the town of Hope to have a street named Mistake. *Sunny's* is not a very agreeable place to be perfectly honest: tired-looking, with a patchy roof, a sagging porch, and a screen door that doesn't shut properly. The truth is I sort of assumed it shut down a number of years ago, and if I hadn't started roaming around tonight in areas where I otherwise never go, I'd never have happened across it at all. Richard at *Sunny's*. Who would have thought?

I hadn't been able to figure out where it was he went every Friday after work, and this was starting to get irritating. I knew he didn't go home and I knew he didn't show up at the farmhouse until very late, but somehow because of my own work schedule at the bookstore, I'd never managed to follow him here. But now I know, and things are finally beginning to move forward properly. Just like a chess game when all at once the pieces on the board begin to fit together in a perfectly executed design and you know your opponent's life is yours.

Still, there is no way I am actually venturing inside Sunny's tonight, believe you me. I need to go home and wait and make my plans first of course, and be very, very certain about everything. It would not do to be hasty or imprudent, would it now?

***

It doesn't take much to retrace the route I have now traveled so many times. I find the lane way easily, and park the car as I did before on the side of the gravel road, hidden by the trees. No vehicles approach.

The farmhouse, when I arrive, appears quite deserted. *She* is not here either then. I weave through the pine trees and approach the house from the back. I am now quite cold and wrap my sweater as tightly as possible around me, pulling my hands into my sleeves. What excuse if someone comes out?

But there is no one. Proceed recklessly to the back of the house, try the brass knocker and wait. Silence. Ring the doorbell, twice, three times. Lift the brass knocker again and pound it down hard. I will think of something if someone comes. I used to be a reporter. I can talk if I have to. I used to be able to talk myself in and out of corners. I could ask anyone anything. Somehow I will find the words. I have not turned into some kind of an imbecile.

Wait. Silence, apart from the gurgling of a few tree swallows which are soaring, plummeting vigorously above and around me.

There is a short flight of concrete stairs that lead to a basement door. Just to the left is a small basement window, open partially from the inside. But there is a screen and when I try to open it, I discover it is painted shut. One corner of the screen has a small tear in it, which I yank at until I can stick my hand in. Then shove my arm down as far as I can until I feel a nail. Persist for a few minutes until it finally gives and I am in.

Through the shadows I see two enormous old freezers and a large concrete cistern in one corner. The air is dank and unpleasant, tinged with something foul akin to rotting potatoes and cat urine. The door at the top of the stairs leads to a hallway. I move down this hallway and walk into the first doorway on the right.

Now I can see why everything appeared so deserted outside. It *is* deserted. Unlike the bedroom I saw before when I looked through the window, everything here in this room gives the give the impression of being somehow forgotten, discarded. The furniture isn't covered in sheets or anything, but there is dust everywhere and the air is very close, as though doors and windows are seldom open.

A heap of dead cluster flies lies on the sill of a window. Black mildew along the edges of the window frames. A grandfather clock stands silent in one corner, weights resting at the very bottom of their chains. Evidently it is the living room, although it is quite gloomy and sparsely furnished.

I walk back out and up one of the two oak staircases on either end of the house. The upstairs looks much more lived in, although there are still piles of dead flies at the windows. At least there is furniture in every bedroom and the beds have blankets and pillows. In one room, the antique bed is so inviting that I must touch it, run my fingers over the warm wood and the beautiful quilt. A lovely, elegant room. I am convinced all at once that this room must surely be *Hers*. The closet is full of clothes. There are dozens of dresses and I pull one out for a closer look. Apparently *She* is slim and tall and her clothes are very expensive and tasteful. I work my way through the whole closet, taking out dress after dress and examining them all, checking labels and running my fingers over the fabric. Lay them out on the bed and take a step back.

And then, on the little night table with the slim, curved legs, I see the photograph of a young woman smiling at me. No, I am wrong. *She* is not smiling at me at all, even though her eyes appear to look straight into mine. She has blonde sleek hair and the blue eyes are certainly a little narrowed, as if wincing a bit, straining to see past someone or something. And that alluring, provocative sort of smile, as though she is quite intimate with the photographer. Richard, of course; I am sure of this. As certain as if he'd just walked in, camera in hand, and told me so himself. The young woman's expression is decidedly self-possessed. She is supremely self-confident, convinced that the person taking the picture is deeply in love with her.

And as for me?

I am merely the intruder, the criminal, the lunatic. I am uninvited, a stranger in her house, unwanted and unwelcome, touching her things, holding her clothes, staring morosely at her photograph.

And Richard? Richard does not even know that I exist.

-12-

The sun is shining and it's warm enough for a tank top and shorts today, but as soon as I get dressed I become conscious of the rough whiteness of my legs; bony knees standing out like faucets, blue veins crisscrossing thighs and calves in all directions. And my arms: thin, pitiable, with wrinkled skin on hands and wrists.

But I persevere, resist the urge to change, force myself to walk past the front entranceway mirror without once looking.

I'm sweating a little by the time I reach Main Street. My heart begins to beat faster and faster and faster until I must slow down and pull my shoulders back, breathe deeply a few times and close my eyes. Sometimes when I am aware of my heart beating like this, I imagine in the next moment, in the next second even, my heart might cease beating entirely and that will be it. A snap; a tiny explosion. And then the end. It is possible after all; it can happen.

As usual at this time of day, a whole row of dirty and mostly rusting pick-ups line the street in front of *In Paradise*. Inside, the restaurant emanates a warm, verdant glow, owing perhaps to the orange ceilings and olive-green walls. Sunlight from the front windows outlines a thick, gently swaying pathway of dust in the air amidst faux green ferns that hang suspended from the ceiling. Evidently no one else notices these details but me.

I sit down at the first empty table making much noise with my chair, but no one looks my way. Order plain coffee with cream from a young teen waitress I've never seen here before.

Brick-red eye shadow, black lipstick, a badly cut shag that looks substantially shorter on one side. Surely she could pass for thirteen. *Maureen,* she mouths, when I ask her name. *Maureen King.* Not that I'll remember by the time I'm finished my coffee. She looks bored and pissed off that I've asked, and takes my order with a dismissive nod. A jaded woman of fifty-five in a child's suit.

I drink the coffee quickly, although it's very hot and thin and not to my liking at all. The black-lipped waitress keeps coming back to ask me if I want something to eat. *You're not eating a thing?* She says several times, with much emphasis. I'm sure the others, that group of oily old men in blackened coveralls in the corner, for example, have not eaten anything either, but I notice she leaves them alone. Only coffee cups and ashtrays litter their table. They are noisy and they don't care who overhears. Complain of the weather, the wars, the rising Canadian dollar, and of course the dandelions. Someone suggests that this year the dandelions are worse because they've mutated and there are literally hundreds of new strains resistant to any form of chemical. The others nod, slurp coffee and look glum.

Three women roughly my age sprawl in the booth next to me, robust bare thighs sticking to the vinyl seats. Oozing cellulite. They are discussing children's baseball and soccer schedules. One woman mentions Botox, and the others immediately stop frowning and concentrate on brow furrows and crow's feet. They don't notice at all when at first I stare and then begin rummaging through my purse, finally dumping everything on the table and sorting through systematically. When I've found what I'm looking for, I get up and leave quickly, just as the waitress with the bad shag approaches for the fourth time.

***

"Are you listening or what's the problem here, lady? It's called *Living with Leanne*. Supposed to be a bestseller, but I sure as heck don't see it with your bestsellers anywhere." The customer looks up at me curiously because she's asked three times already and I still haven't responded.

Trouble is, I can't concentrate at work at all today. I walk through the shelves of books and past all kinds of people and all I see in front of me is that house and that long, curved staircase, that elegant bedroom upstairs. It takes several long minutes before I grasp the fact that it's me this absurd little shopper is addressing, that I'm here at the bookstore, at work, that something is expected of me, I have a job to do and I'd better wake up.

The worst part is after I looked at that photograph in *Her* room, I thought I could almost feel *Her* cold hands on my arm, touching me lightly. And then suddenly I became aware of myself standing there in that room, almost as though I was looking down on myself from above like a dead person. It was an appalling feeling, as though I really were crazy; some mad psychopath lurking about touching other people's things and planning foul murder. Such an odd, creepy feeling, I tell you I quite literally ran from the room and almost toppled down the stairs in my hurry. It was all I could do to make myself stop long enough to patch up the screen, albeit roughly. And I ran and ran and ran all the way back to the car, drove like a mad woman back into town, clutched the steering wheel so hard my hands still have the marks.

"Likely up there somewhere." I motion vaguely with my hand and look back at the shopper who is now paging impatiently through some other book, glancing up every now and then as though I were some kind of moron.

She is not deceived at all, this insipid little shopper in her ridiculous green dress.

"It was on the bestseller's for ages. You must have it here. My daughter said she saw it in every store in Toronto." She rolls her eyes and slams the book down hard. "Don't tell me now after all this looking around wasting my time that you don't have it. I've been waiting quite literally for hours."

"We must be sold out at the moment. Yes, they're all gone, but only temporarily of course. We did have lots. That was weeks ago, of course, but everyone, everyone wanted one. Couldn't keep it stocked. We have trouble getting them from the publishers these days." I pull out a pad of paper and a pen from my pocket. "We've reordered, naturally. They'll be in again in no time. We get shipments daily. But these publishers, you know." Wave my hand in the air.

She is not so easily put off. I begin to walk away, but I'm not rid of her entirely until I head for the storeroom. She follows me right to the back, stopping only when I go through the door. I watch from behind the storage shelves while she stands uncertainly in the doorway for a minute or two, peering in, twisting her head this way and that, at last marching away arms swinging, an angry olive-green blob.

Where is *She*? I suppose on a trip somewhere, a long business trip, or visiting aging, ailing parents somewhere far away. Push the hair from my eyes, tuck it behind my ears. Maggie would be absolutely horrified if I told her about the things I've been doing. Following a strange man, going to his house and breaking in. She'd be appalled, to say the least. And her brother-in-law an RCMP officer to boot. I can't tell her about any of it. For all I know, she'd turn me in. In fact, the more I think about it, I'm certain, absolutely certain. Yes, she'd feel compelled to turn me over to the police in a heartbeat and when you think about it who could blame her.

"So guess what?" Reese says walking past me, an enormous

stack of books in his arms. Reese always carries too many books and he's forever dropping them. Sally gets really mad because he's wrecked a bunch of the expensive hardcover books that way, but he refuses to use the trolley cart we have. Says it makes him look like a waiter or someone who cleans rooms in a hotel. Very fussy about his image these days. Afraid people will look down on him if they think he's just a lowly sales clerk or stock boy in a store. He wants to look *management*. He tells people he is management. And there's no point in offering help, in trying to take a few books out of his arms. He'll only sniff and slap at me and turn away like a too often fussed over child.

I step quickly out of his way and flatten myself against the history books, but I am too late. His left arm brushes my shoulder and a dozen hardcover books slide to the floor with a catastrophic thump.

"Oh shit," Reese says, glancing back over his shoulder to see whether Sally has noticed. But she is still in her office; it's one of her hide-from-the-whole-world days today. An old lady with a black velvet handbag and very short thin hair looks up and frowns at me. She assumes I am the one with the foul language.

I bend down, help Reese collect the books and carry them to the new bestsellers section. Fortunately, none of them look worse for the wear and will not need to be marked down this time.

"Well, what then?" I say.

He seems to have forgotten what he was going to tell me, and is pulling instead at wisps of beard and sniffling again. I reach into my pocket, feel around for a Kleenex.

"You'll never believe this, Clarice. Never in a million years."

"Charlene called and proposed," I say. "You won the lottery. You're moving to Brazil."

"Better than that. Much better. I bought a horse. A real live horse."

He's right. I would never have guessed in a million years. But what an idiotic thing to do. Of all the most idiotic schemes he's come up with, and there have been many, this is by far the most asinine. It even beats the time he took his chainsaw and turned a tree in the front yard of a girl he was dating into the approximate shape of a bear standing on its back legs. The bear was holding what was supposed to be a bottle of wine or a fish or something in its front paws, but unfortunately it turned out rather phallic-looking and the landlord sued for damages. The girlfriend promptly told Reese he was obscene and dumped him on the spot.

"A horse? What the hell, Reese," I say. I can already picture the catastrophic results: broken bones, damages to property, lawsuits. "Why in heaven's name a horse? You don't even know how to ride. You've never even suggested you liked horses. Not once."

"Well it was a real deal. I couldn't turn it down."

"But you don't ride. You don't know anything about horses at all."

"I'm taking lessons at the place where I'll board it. Starts next Saturday. Besides which, it's already a done deal. He's paid and signed for. So now I am the proud owner of a real live horse for the first time in my life, a real beauty. And I do so know a lot about horses. Tons of stuff. A lot more than somebody like you would know. You, Clarice, have never even been on a farm."

He smiles smugly and turns away. I am slapped and dismissed.

***

Maggie called the store today during lunch hour and asked

me to meet her at *Gabriel's* for dinner. *Gabriel's* is a fairly expensive restaurant located at the same mall where I work, but I've never actually eaten there before. I suppose I said yes because I knew if I said no, I could never think of a logical explanation which would make me sound like I was still a normal, rational, ordinary person.

We meet at the store and walk over to the restaurant together. Maggie looks stunning as always in a black pantsuit with enormous hoop earrings and matching choker necklace. Hair parted at the side and swept back expertly.

I tug discreetly at my brassiere which is riding up again and giving me a rash. Also, my shirt seems somehow too short all of a sudden, and is hanging out over top of my skirt. Some day I will be one of those wandering old ladies with her dress on backwards, the buttons all done up wrong, small flat boobs hanging down at the front like two saggy little loops.

"Oh Paul doesn't mind looking after the kids for one night really," Maggie is saying as we sit down. But she is also looking at me with a somewhat bewildered expression. I wonder how long I've been sitting here like this, staring down at the water glass, twisting it in my hands, watching the water trickle down across my fingers and onto my plate.

"He knows I need away time," she says, "which is why the girls and I go out on Fridays sometimes. He doesn't mind usually if it's a Friday, although sometimes he kicks up a real fuss. It's just there's always something going on, soccer practice or hockey or concerts. Rush, rush, rush. But today I decided I just had to get out, get away. You know."

I don't know, but I nod and nod, dry my hands on a napkin and examine my menu without reading.

"Fish good here?"

"Paul and I had the pork here once. Not bad. The pasta's great too. You'd love it."

I sip from my wineglass, look around at the other tables. Everyone is so dressed up.

"That Reese guy at the store sure seems nice enough," Maggie says without looking up at me, voice suddenly very quiet. An attempt at sincerity I suppose. "He said hello to me when I came in and he was very polite and helpful."

Cripes, do I have to get into all that now? Explanations about Reese, his whole history explored, just to prove he's not for me?

"Look, Reese is okay, but he's not my type, Maggie, so lay off okay?"

"I would never, ever suggest such a thing Clarice, dearest. I didn't mean that at all. I just. . ." She tries to look hurt but it's not very convincing. Maggie has a way of not finishing her sentences, leaves them trailing, unraveling at the edges like some old towel. My theory is she herself doesn't know where her sentences are leading, that there are just partial thoughts floating around in that little head of hers. I bet even if I wasn't always interrupting her, she would have trouble completing one idea before meandering to the next.

"I'll have the scallops." This to a harassed-looking waiter who is just going by and not at all equipped to take my order.

"This isn't my table," he begins but then resigns himself, pulls out a notepad. "Scallops and what?"

"Scallops and another half-litre of the Merlot."

As soon as he's walked away I polish off the second glass and promptly pour another. I'm feeling very relaxed and happy and a little drowsy now. Maggie hasn't noticed. She's telling me all about her week, how she's planing to get back into acting again, how she's contacted the theatre in Milan and they've agreed to hire her. She is very animated, cheeks flushed. I begin attacking the scallops, which the waiter has just brought to our table. Maggie has ordered the curry chicken special, but is too keyed up for food at the moment and leans closer.

"So when are you finally going to start dating again Clarice? I really think it's time. It isn't good for you to be alone so much. And I don't see what's wrong with this Reese guy if he's available." She takes a small bite of chicken, chewing thoughtfully for a moment and dabbing at her mouth with a napkin. "You need to go out more. We both need to get out more for that matter."

"You're right, Maggie I need to get out. I was actually thinking maybe even this Friday night. Not with a guy, of course, just out. Maybe to a pub or something, you know, just to mix with people. Get to know a few new people."

"Finally. Heavens, Clarice, I'll even go along with you if you want. I mean Paul won't mind if I tell him it's really important. He's always going out with his buddies and leaving me with the kids. And it'll be a Friday night, which means it doesn't matter if the kids get to bed late or not."

The last thing on earth I want: Maggie tagging along. I can see her now sidling up to Richard and smiling suggestively. *My friend over there is just dying to meet you.* And me, squirming in my chair, mortified, trying not to look, dripping perspiration. He would hardly look at me. Just smile up at Maggie. *You'll have to tell your friend I'm terribly flattered but I'm already engaged, you see. Getting married this summer. . .*

"Wonderful of you to suggest coming along Maggie, but I think I need to go out alone this time," I say. She's about to protest so I add, firmly, "Alone, Maggie, but thank you so much anyway. It really is something I need to do by myself. To give me some confidence. A new start, so to speak."

Now that this little matter has been decided and she's

calmed down enough, Maggie eats her chicken with speed and efficiency, ordering another large glass of water, Spanish coffee and pecan pie á la mode. I manage to divert the conversation, rather adroitly I might add, to literature; the merits of some popular American author I know Maggie adores. I ask about a book. She tells me snippets, warms to the idea, voice rises, ends up revealing the entire plot between mouthfuls of ice cream and pecan pie. I smile and nod and poke at my plate and let my thoughts waft about without really trying to concentrate on anything at all.

He will be with *Her* at Sunny's, of course. I try to imagine them together, the two of them seated next to one another at a table in a corner, and myself seated a few tables away, just watching. She will notice me staring and will look over at me a few times. I will look away hurriedly, pretending I didn't see, but she will lean over and say something to him, and he will look over at me too, frowning a little. He will make some comment to her then and they will both laugh. And then, dismissing me as unimportant, an idiot, they will drink their wine and talk about something else, and he will reach for her hand, and they will soon forget that some crazy woman is staring, *gaping* at them just a few tables away.

Maggie has begun another long, complicated tale about her older sister. "Imagine, twelve years she's fooling around on him right under his nose, right in the house even, in their own bed, and he doesn't see it. In the end, she had to tell him herself."

I nod and nod and spend the rest of the evening stirring my scallops around my plate. And polish off, with little effect, the rest of the half-litre of Merlot.

-13-

I decide to search the basement for gardening tools. As a general rule I avoid the basement completely. There's nothing wrong down there, you just can't really walk around at all, mainly because it's so full of boxes and cartons from my parents' house. Some of the boxes are really old; mother's things that dad kept stored away in his attic. There are even some of her old dresses, heaps of ancient albums. Some day I plan to go through it all. Sort through the letters; figure out what needs keeping. I imagine the clothes must be pretty well ruined by now, down there in the damp for so many years. I never thought to put out mothballs either.

Mother would never have let things sit like that to rot. She was a schoolteacher, started out with a one-room schoolhouse and never stopped thinking that way. Structured, systematic, orderly. Things were always neat as a pin at our place, our days regimented and strictly controlled. My sisters and I were permitted one toy out at a time. The rest were carefully packed away in the toy trunk. Dolls were never left strewn about naked or with tatted hair like they were at friends' houses. Oh no. In our house, even the dolls were bathed regularly and their clothes washed and faithfully ironed. Each doll had brand new hair ribbons, and mother made sure we tied them neatly before placing the dolls back in their special cradle, tucked in with a white, white blanket soft as fresh snow and bleached spotless. Three dolls; one for each of us. Books were put on the bookshelf each time we were finished reading, even if we hadn't completed the book. *On the bookshelf,* mother would say, voice rising in a note of warning. *In the right place, alphabetical please.* Dog-eared corners made her furious, so we soon learned to be careful about bookmarks.

My sister Martha had a hobbyhorse, given to her by my grandfather. Brown satiny fur. Real horsehair mane and tail and a special leather bridle. I loved that hobbyhorse, but Martha didn't let me ride it, ever. Only my youngest sister Jennifer was given the privilege. One day in a fit of jealousy I ripped a satiny ear right off while Martha was outside on the swing. Mother switched my hands so hard I couldn't sleep the whole night.

I give up my search for the gardening tools when I find a box of old things that came from the spare room; her little things. Perhaps Mother was right: I should have listened. It is good to be careful with possessions, to put them away neatly and tidily in tissue paper and in pretty boxes with tight-fitting lids. I cover the box with an old curtain, push it in back of a big stack of Frank's old *Sports Illustrated.*

Run back upstairs quickly, retrieve Richard's file from the telephone table in the kitchen and bring it into the bedroom. On the first page I have written: Richard Mason. Occupation: magazine editor, the *Urban Gardener.* Address: 647 Oakland Street, and a long list of other personal data.

On page two is the chart recording his daily activities. On the next page is a graph, and on page four I have written a full description of his house in town and one of the farmhouse. Enclosed in the file is one of the letters which I have not yet had a chance to return. I take the letter out, then carry the rest of the papers back to the kitchen and after lighting them all with a match, drop them into the sink. They catch fire slowly, pages curling up and blackening one by one.

I've decided, whatever happens on Friday, I'm not doing any of this anymore. I must move on finally.

Water begins to fill the kitchen sink. Ashes float to the

top. Turning off the water, I take the letter to my bedroom and thrust it inside my copy of *The Idiot*. Place my white queen a few spaces closer to the black king and head out the door.

-14-

Florence Bishop, whose house sits so inconveniently between Maggie's and mine, will be complaining again. *Earl, that Forrest woman is wandering around our yard half-naked again.* And then, more sharply, a few decibels louder, *Don't look now, for pity's sake.* Earl, a thin balding man dried up as an old ear of corn, will shrink back from the window with Florence still plucking at the creased and fleshless arm. He will wait until she turns away before stealing a quick look. A half-bare breast? A rounded rump?

Once, soon after Frank and I married and moved here, we were kissing in the back yard, clasped in each other's arms, sheer lust compelling us to disregard the possibility of an audience. And there was an audience. Earl Bishop in his backyard, binoculars in hand, flagrantly spying through sizeable gaps in the cedars.

I didn't notice at first, but Frank caught on right away and put on a real show, pulling off my shirt, unhooking my brassiere with one hand and unzipping my jeans with the other. My pants were around my ankles and Frank's well on their way when Florence arrived on the scene.

The fury of God destroying Sodom and Gomorrah was nothing to the rage of Mrs. Florence Bishop at the moment of discovery. A mighty squeal like that of a piglet snatched from mama's teat.

"You old goat. You stupid old goat," and then seizing the offending binoculars from Earl's perspiring hands, turning her indignant wrath upon me.

And I, looking back at her over my naked shoulder, hastily

zipping jeans, running mortified and sweating to the house, felt I should surely now be transformed into a pillar of salt. Frank alone was enormously pleased with the whole affair, winking knowingly at Earl before sauntering slowly, brazenly back inside, not even bothering to do up the zipper of his pants.

At Maggie's door I hesitate before knocking. Years ago I would have walked in this house three times a day without once so much as stopping to think, let alone actually knocking. Now it is all out of the question.

It takes her at least three minutes to answer the door and I am almost ready to turn and go.

"Clarice. I wasn't expecting company this time of day. Come in." Something is not quite right. The smile is forced. For once she looks tired and put out. Her lipstick has all but worn off. I follow her into the kitchen, feeling my mood deflate with hers.

"Sorry to just show up this early," I say, pulling the housecoat tighter and retying the belt.

"Oh no, don't worry about it. So would you like some coffee? Made muffins this morning too, morning glory, whole wheat, no white sugar. The kids just gobble them up. Chad took four in his lunch today, but Paul didn't like them at all."

"Thanks, but no."

She waits. One minute, two. Finally she moves to the stove, brings muffins, pours two mugs of coffee.

"You're not letting Frank move in again, are you? That's what he seems to think. He came over here trying to worm out some more information yesterday, so watch out. And don't you dare let him move back, because that's exactly what he wants. You have to listen to me, Clarice."

She sets a mug down in front of me, begins stirring sugar into her own. The spoon clinks noisily against the cup and she stirs and stirs, faster and faster. "You're crazy if you even think about it. Crazy."

"I might," I say. *Clink, clink, clink.* I want to grab hold of that cup and dump it out. I want to reach over and slap her hands. Anyway, did she not say she was cutting out all white sugar?

She studies me, eyebrows angled, moves back to the stove. "Didn't sleep much last night. Melissa and Chad both had a touch of the flu, but they seemed just fine this morning so I sent them to school anyway. Figures, huh? Chad told me I was a bad mother. I should let him stay home and sleep all day."

"Sorry Maggie. Look I better go," I rub my feet together under the chair. Why in heaven's name did I come here anyway? I can't tell her. I just can't.

Glance over at the clock. There are hours and hours and hours to fill.

"By the way, Clarice," Maggie says suddenly, whirling around to face me again, "your mother-in-law Margaret called. Can you beat it? Your mother-in-law of all people."

It takes a moment for this to sink in. The idea is about as bizarre as an occurrence in a Kafka novel. If Maggie told me Paul turned into an enormous insect overnight, I would've been more inclined to believe it.

"You can't be serious. Margaret? Why in heaven's name would Margaret call you? I didn't think she even knew you."

"Couldn't believe it either. Took me ages to figure out who she actually was when she called. But she was really, really nice. Invited me to the big fancy party they're having for the *Princess Theatre*, black tie and all. That's why she called. She's on the board of directors now, and since I've been hired back, she's invited me too. Everybody's going. The whole acting company. And a bunch of family and friends, so you're going to be invited too, of course. Least ways that's what she told me."

"I don't believe it. Margaret called you," I say.

"Well you better believe it girl. It's on the twenty-seventh, or the twenty-eighth. I'd have to check the calendar. The last Saturday in the month anyway. I can't wait. It's been ages since I've gone to any kind of a party. Paul never wants to do anything."

She sits down at the table again, bites into a muffin, dumps another spoonful of sugar into her coffee and begins stirring. "And I'm going to get myself a new dress. Great excuse, huh? So we'll have to go out shopping together. For new dresses. Just like we used to."

I want to tell her that I cannot possibly go to this party; there is no way someone like me can show up at this kind of a celebration. But I don't know how to say it. Maggie will look at me from under those angled brows and she will frown, toss her spoon onto the table so hard that it clatters. And then she will continue to nag and press and push until I give in. *You have to go Clarice. They're expecting you. You can't hide out in your house forever you know. You've got to get over this.*

So I say nothing, just nod and listen to Maggie's stories about the theatre, about all the plays in which she'll soon be performing. Lead actress. Model Mom. Devoted Wife.

After twenty-five minutes I let myself out and wave in the direction of the Bishop house. It is sunny and warm and I know where I will go. All I need is a good pair of running shoes.

***

Richard's kitchen as usual is spotless; not a crumb. But there is mail on the counter by the fridge and I sift through it casually, tossing it back as though it were my own hydro bills and bank statements. Today there is nothing from *Her.*

Although I have no business there I am drawn, irresistibly,

up the stairs again to his room. *The Idiot* still lies on the night table, closed, a bookmark thrust inside.

I pick it up gently and it falls open to the part where Nastasya Filipovna flings her fur coat at Prince Myshkin, mistaking him as a sort of servant, ordering him to announce her to the others in the drawing room. *What are you carrying my coat for? Ha, ha, ha! You're not mad, are you?* And then, when he stares back at her speechlessly, she cries, *Oh, you idiot!*

Oh, you idiot. I drop the book quickly, turn and walk down the stairs.

There is a sound.

I was wrong. He is home, after all. Or at least he is home now. A loud, scraping noise, a door slamming, and this time it is decidedly not quiet little cat feet. There are actual footsteps.

Without thinking I reach back behind me and open the closet door, step inside. Has he heard? Hold my breath for as long as I can, not daring to make even that small sound.

But there is nothing for a few moments. I count sixty seconds. One hundred.

A door closes. An image of my shoes sitting where I'd so carelessly tossed them by the screen door. Shift slightly from one foot to the other, stumbling over something and almost falling. Jackets push up against me, smothering, sleeves lifting up: encircling, constricting. There is a smell of leather and sweat, and I realize at last that I am standing on a heap of boots and other footwear. Bending down I pick one up, feeling it all over. A woman's shoe: small, narrow.

There are footsteps. They pass by quite close and then up the stairs. If he is coming, I must face him with dignity and not in a cramped old closet full of reeking shoes. Wait for a moment, hand resting on the doorknob, then I turn the knob very, very slowly.

Move quickly into the kitchen. The shoes are still in the same place where I left them. Fling back the screen door, no longer caring how loud, and run into the backyard still in socks, shoes in hand; turn my head once to look behind me.

Richard's cat is sitting there. Staring, unblinking, as insolent as only cats can be, the fur on his back twitching slightly. He turns his head slowly and begins licking, biting at his fur. But I know he is still watching. This licking is all an act. Cats are really so very much like people.

Any moment now the police will come around that corner and haul me away. Richard is calling them already. *It's her again. She's here. The one who stole my mail, who broke in here last time and touched my things.*

Finally I run. I don't remember how I get away. I just recall almost smashing into two kids with a bike, and then a brief flash of a large man pushing a lawnmower: great wads of hair, a sprinkling of moles, and two naked sagging brown breasts.

-15-

Frank's mother Dorinda, his real mother, has always insisted everyone call her Dinny. And we all do, although I cringe inwardly every time, even after all these years. It's one of those names that never comes easily to the tongue, that always sounds in some way made up, artificial. A name that sneers at the world, if you will.

Dinny is a small, tidy sort of person, very attractive, with shoulder-length, ash-blonde hair that hasn't changed a bit in seventeen years. She's been living with her new man, Michael, for four or five years now, having divorced Frank's father, Douglas, when Frank was only fifteen. The truth is, I haven't seen any of them for a long, long time. When Frank and I split up, they sort of gave up on me, and I guess that too was to be expected. I certainly didn't do anything about trying to stay in touch, so I suppose I am to blame as much as they are.

Frank's father looks like a grown-up Frank. The eyes are identical, and the same big-boned frame and dark, glossy hair. But Douglas is bigger and heavier, with deep lines from nose to chin, and a look about the eyes as though he is uneasy with himself, always a bit ashamed. His new wife Margaret is very bosomy and squat, with protruding eyes set close together and a short nose like a Pekinese. But she is tolerably friendly, talkative and essentially benign.

"Margaret sure is one hell of a talker," Douglas said to me on my wedding day. "Talk the feathers off a crow." I don't really remember Frank's dad saying anything else to me at the wedding, just smiling and nodding while Margaret made a commotion over my dress, and told a very long, twisted story of her own first wedding. Douglas kept his arm tight about her shoulders the whole time, knocking back glass after glass of rye. I would've been mortified had my new husband drank that much in public, but Margaret didn't seem to notice. She just carried on with the story about her seven bridesmaids. Every one had worn the same dress in different shades of the same colour but, alas, the dresses were not finished in time, and Margaret and her mother and sister were forced to stay up the entire night before the wedding to complete the sewing themselves.

"Just imagine," I said, clicking my tongue. "How terrible. Well, well."

I felt sorry for Frank. He was trying so hard to make our wedding day a success, attempting to be the perfect bridegroom, the life of the party, moving energetically from group to group and talking to everyone. He danced with all the women, old and young alike, several times each, which wasn't at all necessary I remember thinking.

But Troy spoiled it for him. Brother Troy with his striking face, the unruly blonde curls and raucous laughter that echoed around the room so that everyone turned to look. The obsequious, toadying comments to the women; false and loud, but no one else seemed to notice. Oh that must be the doctor, they all said, Dorinda's youngest son. The successful one. Isn't he good-looking? Isn't he talented? Isn't he just the nicest young man? I could see Frank wince. All that laughter. I'm sure he thought it was aimed at him. Jokes told by the little brother at the older brother's expense. Stories about their childhood likely; all of Frank's most embarrassing moments revisited. His grievances, his childish jealousies and resentful little skirmishes. But maybe it wasn't true. Maybe Troy, loosened up after a few glasses of scotch, was just telling our wedding guests about his work and his own life; harmless little anecdotes about troublesome patients and lovesick nurses.

But it made me uneasy watching them. Frank pushing his way to the opposite side of the room whenever Troy came near, and Troy so oblivious to his brother's scorn and resentment. Even Douglas, when he wasn't clinging to Margaret, had his thick arm slung about Troy's shoulders or was smacking him across the back. Chip off the old block. The apple never falls far from the tree. It wasn't easy for Frank at all.

Then I noticed that Frank's mother was giving me this look. As though she was very surprised her eldest son had chosen someone like me to be his partner for life. I saw her watching my face, just staring and staring, as though she just couldn't believe that this was what Frank had bound himself to forever and ever, till death do us part.

"You look so pale, Clarice," Dinny said finally, voice raised so the group of ladies by the door could hear quite clearly. "You need some colour on your cheeks. If you'd like I'll lend you my blush. I could put it on for you myself in the ladies room. I'd be happy to. You don't have to be embarrassed. It would be no trouble at all. You're always so pale and sickly looking. You definitely need something to brighten you up a bit, and don't argue. White just isn't your colour, is it dear? Quite washes you out."

But back then I just waved her away, shrugged her off like a blow fly. Dinny was wrong anyway. Everyone else kept complimenting me, saying how beautiful I was, how gorgeous my dress. Brilliant even. And I felt brilliant that day. I had so much confidence. Loads of it. My hair had been put up by a talented hairdresser; an intricate bun with tiny flowers woven in. I wore mother's veil too, which trailed to the floor and made me feel like a goddess.

I was happy, ecstatic. Truly the happiest person there was. Yes, even that is possible sometimes. But only briefly in this life, I'll admit. Just a glimpse.

-16-

Before my little girl was born I never imagined I'd make a good mother. I didn't think I knew how. My own mother had been so brusque and exacting in her parenting and my father soft and pliable and careless, though certainly well-meaning. I wasn't sure I'd ever learn to strike the proper balance, that I even knew what it meant to be a good parent. I had no one close to me but Maggie who could give me any advice. Just don't sweat the small stuff, Maggie kept saying. Don't let a bit of dirt in the house bother you when you have a baby to look after. Have fun. Enjoy yourself.

So I made sure nothing in our home was regimented, nothing was done by the clock. Breakfast was sometimes at 6:00, sometimes at 10:00. Lunchtime was a sloppy affair, with crackers and cheese and apple pieces just about anywhere in the house or yard, at any time of day. Supper was often late. Bedtime came and went without any of us ever looking at the clock. Yes, I was strict about the toys. I made her place them in her toy box and the books on the bookshelf when we were finished reading them. But the dolls were naked, hair tangled and matted. Doll clothes were mixed in with puzzle pieces. Bits of Lego hid under couch cushions. And half-read books loitered about the living room and on the windowsills in the kitchen. There was no rhyme or reason to our household. It was all pleasant chaos.

She ruled this little untidy kingdom with tiny fists grasping acorns in one hand and dolly's hair in the other. Always smiling. Chattering and singing and telling stories. She believed there were little rock people in the garden. That tiny pebbles changed themselves into little people when we weren't looking, and then larked about in the begonias and under the raspberry canes. She was always poking around the garden with a stick, turning over rocks, examining little stones for signs of feet and hands. *Look Mommy. Look at the nose on this one. I saw it run from over there. It tried to hide from me Mommy. It did! It did!* Very convincing. It was easy to believe anything she said in that wise little voice, so grown-up and full of reason.

I lost her one day. She was just old enough that I could let her go outside alone in the backyard, which was surrounded by a cedar hedge thicker than any fence. All morning she would putter about with stick in hand examining stones and playing with them on the back patio, lining them up in a long winding row. She made houses for them out of grass clippings, and little beds out of moss and flower petals.

The morning I lost her she was outside and alone no more than fifteen minutes. I was making sweet potato soup and when I looked out the kitchen window to check, she was gone. I ran out in slippers and searched the backyard, concerned but not yet panicked. Then I began combing the neighbourhood, running up and down the street both ways, housecoat flying, panic rising quickly. It must have been at least forty-five minutes before I heard her voice from a yard eight houses down. The Wilsons. A middle-aged pair with three teenaged children. She had discovered a pond in their backyard with lots of brightly coloured stones and a fountain and goldfish and frogs. She was perched in the middle on a big flat stone, a bright green frog in each hand, golden eyes bulging. She was singing quietly and didn't even look up when I called out her name. When I lifted her out of her watery kingdom I discovered her pockets were filled with stones of every size and shape. Although the pond was perhaps only three feet deep, if she'd fallen in those rocks might have dragged her right down to its mucky bottom where water plants buried their tangled roots.

I went on a journey Mommy, she said happily. *A rock people journey. And I found a whole town of them living here by this lake. They said they would like to come and live with us at my house now. Can I Mommy? Can I take them home to live with us forever?*

-17-

It is finally Friday night.

New jeans, new cream-colored shirt; casual but tidy and smart. Even the brassiere and panties are new, matching if you will and it can't hurt.

Outside it is windy in gusts and beginning to rain, but I am not going to let the weather dampen my mood. I feel, instead, that everything bodes well for my mission tonight.

When I arrived home from work today, I found a little note from Maggie stuck between the front doors.

Hi Clarice, I looked in but there was no sign of you. It's like you've totally fallen off the face of the earth this week. Hope you remembered to get your hair done at that place I told you about. Lots of luck tonight going out on the town. Make sure you call if you want me to come along and call if you need a ride home. I'm sure Paul won't mind. Hugs and kisses, Maggie. P.S. Don't chicken out! And wear a nice skirt and don't drink too much! Love, Maggie.

I must not have been home yet when Maggie the Terrier arrived. Unshakable, immovable, muffin-tin, notepad and pencil always in hand. Thankfully I wasn't home yet. Thank the high heavens for small mercies and good timing at last.

I am just about to leave when the telephone rings.

"Hello?" I say. "Hello, hello?" My voice sounds scratchy and hoarse, as though I am coming down with a bad chest cold. I clear my throat several times and cough into my hand. The absurd thought crosses my mind that it might be Richard himself calling.

"Clarice? It's Margaret. How are you my dear? You sound sickly. Are you ill?"

"Margaret," I clutch at the phone, trying not to drop the receiver and begin coughing again as quietly as possible, "what a surprise. I'm just fine. How are you? Haven't heard from you in so long."

"Yes, I know," she says. There is a brief pause. "We're both very well, Douglas and I. We've been out golfing and just came in the door because it started to rain, and I said to Doug we must try Clarice again. I've tried so many times and haven't been able to reach you, and he said of course it would be a good time to try, that you'd likely be home from work. And almost dinnertime. So I just called. I hope I'm not interrupting. There isn't someone there is there?"

"Oh no," I say. "Oh not at all."

"Well good then. Your friend Maggie likely told you about the party already, the anniversary party for the Princess Theatre. On Saturday the twenty-sixth, seven o'clock at our house. That's of course why I'm calling, to invite you. Did you get the invitation in the mail yet? We had trouble with the printers and they didn't come until last week. Like I said, I'd tried you a million times. Douglas and I have wanted to have a party ever since we built the new house here in Milan. We've lots of room for it, you know. With the big front room and the music room and the kitchen open to the great room, and we've just finished decorating too. Gold tones and whites. So you can imagine we're just dying to have a fancy party. You know, with everyone all dressed up in tails and long gowns, and show the place to everyone. Just for the neighbours of course, and family and friends and the theatre people. To celebrate the anniversary. It seemed like the perfect excuse."

"Oh," I say, "I'm not sure. But thank you. Thank you anyway so much Margaret. It sounds terrific."

"Oh yes. Well good, so you'll come then. You have to, you

know. I already told everyone you were, and so they're expecting you. We all are. We'd all so much like to see you again. It'd be such a disappointment if you couldn't come. And don't forget it's formal: black tie, long gowns, the whole bit. With all the theatre people and actors and so on, they expect that sort of thing you know."

There is a pause while she fumbles for something. A scratching sound on her end. I shift the phone to the other shoulder and sigh.

"I'll add your name to the list then, all right? Goodbye then Clarice. Look forward to seeing you again. It's been far too long. We'll talk at the party. You can tell me everything you've been doing these past few years. Everything. And I'll fill you in on us of course. Douglas and I have been travelling all over. So take care of yourself now. See you at the party; don't forget."

There is a little click as she replaces the receiver and I am cut off.

-18-

I came here years ago with Frank. Sunny's was quite different then: smokier, more crowded and confused. A jostling of elbows punctuated by drunken laughter. Rank puddles under barstools accompanied by the cacophony of those whose inhibitions have long been lost to alcohol. A despondency that hung over the whole room and clung doggedly to walls and ceiling.

Today it is quiet and there are only a few patrons here and there, silently quaffing. The place has definitely changed. Brighter and less squalid, though the screen door still doesn't shut properly and the wood floor is two decades filthier. And yet, the gloominess that used to persist has somehow been cleared away.

For the first time it occurs to me that I may not see Richard here tonight. After all, what are the chances? Why hadn't I thought of this possibility before? I've always had this idea that if I think through all the potential bad things that could happen before I do something, they just won't happen. They simply can't happen because I am prepared, forewarned.

But my fears are all for nothing; he is here of course. Even with his back to me and from way across the room, I can see very plainly it is Richard.

Tug at the front of my shirt discreetly. My new brassiere is already riding up. I feel creased and uncomfortable and sweaty. Sit down positioning myself in such a way that I can still see him quite easily. Open handbag and rifle through; search for a calendar so I can turn pages. Something to look at so I will appear busy, professional, here to unwind after a long day at the office. Not some crazy woman haunting a bar, lying in wait for a strange man.

To my left is a largish man in a black muscle shirt. His mat of black hair is tightly curled and tangled, and he smells of sweat and something that reminds me vaguely of my father's fishing boat. To my right, two stools down, a very thin man is swigging from a line of small glasses containing a ferocious looking, gold-coloured liquor. He looks nowhere else but down, grunting energetically with each swallow.

I play with an empty glass someone has left at the bar, and order a glass of wine. What would the bartender say if I told him the whole story, asked for advice? The look. *Disbelief, incredulity.*

Glance over at Richard. Seated across from him is a man I don't recognize. Animated conversation. I can only see the back of Richard's head at the moment, but this other man is facing me and is moving his hands very rapidly while he speaks. Richard is just listening. From time to time his head moves slightly and he reaches for his drink.

Twist the empty glass in front of me. Fish around in my purse, finger the piano key. Pull out a pack of Tic-Tacs and pop one in. What now, Clarice? Walk over and interrupt? Perhaps it's his boss, the publisher himself offering him a big huge promotion. Chance of a lifetime.

"What can I get you?" says the bartender. He is drying his hands, which look very dirty, on a striped towel with unraveling edges. The top two-thirds of his head is balding and lumpy with prominent bones. Short bristled hairs stand out like hackles from just above his shirt collar.

"Just red wine please." I regret this instantly. Why didn't I think to order a cosmopolitan, a martini, or at least suggested a good wine? I would have seemed so much more interesting, sophisticated. The bartender would perhaps have been impressed.

A martini please. And be sure it's very dry. Just wave the vermouth cap over the glass. Yes, that's it. And I could have waved my hand like this, just casually.

"Your wine," he says, sliding it in front of me, "compliments of the guy down at the end of the bar."

Turn and look down the line of barstools. The Expresso Coffee man of all people. The one who comes in the coffee shop with the newspaper and notebook under his arm, who sits and writes and writes while I make up stories about him. Watched by the big-boobed waitress who resembles the badger in the *Francis* books. I wonder whether he's mistaken me for her. Glance down furtively at my chest, look back over. He smiles right away, and I wave and nod and push at my hair. *Thank you*, I mouth with great exaggeration, pointing down unnecessarily to my glass.

What now, Clarice? If Mr. Expresso comes over here and sits, you're sunk.

Why in heaven's name does he pick tonight to notice me, when I've been going to the same coffee shop for years and he's never so much as lifted an eyebrow? I stare down at my drink; feel myself getting hotter by the second. I am actually beginning to steam. Did I remember to double up on deodorant? Perhaps he'll just go away. Maybe it's just one of those spur-of-the-moment things and doesn't mean anything at all. He probably buys drinks for all the single girls here. Purely a matter of courtesy.

Glance around. Sure enough, I am the only woman sitting all by herself tonight. A few more women are scattered about here and there, but they are all sitting with someone.

Glance over at Richard again. Alone. Drink rapidly, mopping at my mouth. I am suddenly very cold. And just a minute ago I was as hot as sin, thoroughly drenched and could've broiled eggs under my arms.

Here's your chance, Clarice. Your one big huge chance. So don't blow it.

Don't knock over your stool. Don't trip, and don't, whatever you do, drop your purse and scatter embarrassing personal items all across the floor.

What will I say? Why didn't I prepare anything? I had weeks and weeks. Months even. Maggie would've memorized her lines; Maggie would've rehearsed for this moment until she knew every word inside out.

Get up quickly and move across the room, pulling my sweater around me tighter and crossing my arms in front. His shirt looks freshly ironed, crisp and perfect. Glance back. Is that other man really gone for good, or did he just go for a pee and is now coming up behind me?

But there is no one.

Clutch my purse and march around his chair, less than gracefully, but at least I haven't tripped or collided with anything. I have not caused a scene.

"I know this sounds stupid and rather idiotic," I say very rapidly. "I mean it sounds like one of those typical pick-up lines you might hear in a bar, that is what a man might say to some girl in a bar or some woman might say to some man she doesn't know. But I'm sure I know you from somewhere, and I've just been sitting over there the last few minutes trying to remember where it was I saw you before. I mean it wasn't here. I don't normally come to some bar all alone anyway, and I haven't been in this place for years and years either. So it must have been somewhere else..."

That's it. I cannot possibly say anything more. It's like sitting in front of an essay question on an exam. You've said everything you know about the subject in a hundred different ways, and although you know your answer should be five hundred words longer, you cannot possibly think of one single, solitary word more; not if your very life depended on it.

And so I am silent.

He looks up, startled, gray eyes open wide. Looks into mine for so long without saying anything that I feel as though I've just fallen off something very high up and must suck in my breath hard to prepare for the crushing impact. But I can see right away by his frozen face, that uninterested look, that he is wondering how to extricate himself; what words can he say to make this strange woman just go away.

"You're quite right," he says, looking away finally. "I feel the same way exactly. I noticed you the moment you came in and sat down over there at the bar, and I was just saying to my friend Bob before he left, I'm certain I know you from somewhere too. Quite certain. Here, sit down. Have a seat. Please."

Reaching for the chair and shifting it back gives me a chance to begin breathing normally again. I have landed, safely, survived the impact.

"Oh I didn't mean to interrupt," I say, "if your friend comes back...I hate to..."

"Don't worry. Bob's gone. Girlfriend troubles. She hates it when he comes in here for a drink Friday nights. If I were her I'd be glad to be rid of the beggar at least one evening a week. So I guess we should figure out where it was we met, right?" He pushes aside several beer bottles and mops at the table with a napkin. Waves at a passing waitress who comes over quickly.

"What are you drinking tonight? You look like a lady who would enjoy a glass of an excellent red wine, and believe it or not they have some pretty good stuff here."

I nod and he motions to the waitress. "A glass of the Folonari Valpolicella for the lady and the Glenfiddich again for me."

"Gardening," I say. "I mean, where we met. A gardening show, or something. The big *Home and Garden Show* in Milan. Maybe that's where we met."

"That's it," he says. "That's it exactly."

He sounds so certain that for a moment I almost believe this story myself. I can see myself wandering dreamily through crowds of flower enthusiasts, past displays filled with asters and zinnia, and then spotting him standing alone, just waiting for me to come and ask him a question. I can see us starting a conversation, heads bent over a rose, examining the leaves for aphids. It is all so believable. Almost like it really did happen.

I look up at him. He smiles and I am suddenly afraid I will burst into noisy tears. Tears are so easily summoned these days.

"...editor of a magazine called the *Urban Gardener*," he is saying. "Maybe you've read it. And yes, I've been to all those shows around here, all of them, even the big one in Milan in June. The magazine always has a display at that one for sure. There's a good chance we might've met there. But I don't forget a face, as a rule." He smiles again, holds out a hand. "I guess we should formally introduce ourselves, shouldn't we? I'm Richard."

"Of course," I say. "Of course. Clarice. Clarice Forrest."

I grip the seat of my chair and bite down on my lip. Why not say his last name?

"Clarice. An unusual name. But very beautiful. I like it very much."

The wine and scotch arrive and I sip anxiously. What now? What next, Clarice, for gosh sake?

"So what do you do, Clarice?" he says, looking past my shoulder at the couple seated behind us.

"I work at the new bookstore here in town. In the mall. I haven't worked there that long actually. I was a reporter before, but I quit."

"Before?"

"Yes, that is years ago." Heaven help me if I mention Frank at a time like this. I gulp at my wine and swallow hard.

"That's maybe where I've seen you before. I've been in that store a number of times since it opened. You know I always wished I could own a bookstore somewhere. A small one, where I'd get to know all my customers, talk to them about favourite authors and so on. Not easy to make any money in that business these days though I gather."

"I love to read too," I say quickly. "I like the classics. Especially the golden age of Russian literature. Pushkin, Tolstoy, Chekhov, Dostoyevsky."

I am about to mention *The Idiot,* as an example, tell him how impressed I am with Dostoyevsky's insight into the darker places of the human mind. But I realize he isn't listening. He has turned his attention once again to the couple behind me and is only nodding to be polite.

"Do you know Dostoyevsky? Have you read his work? You know Dostoyevsky stood before a firing squad once?" I say this as loud as I possibly can without appearing ridiculous, moving my chair back and leaning forward over the table. "He'd committed some trifling political crime and was about to be shot to death. Just imagine, standing there against a wall in front of a line of rifles, blindfolded, about to be shot to death, and at the very last moment, the eleventh hour, at the moment when he knows he's going to die, just when he is saying his final prayers and preparing for the bullets to tear through him, he receives an official reprieve. Someone reads from some official government document. Sentenced to hard labour in Siberia instead. Just imagine how he felt. The unspeakable terror. Unspeakable. He wrote in *The Idiot* that the death penalty is an outrage on the soul. That the worst pain is the certain knowledge that in an hour, in ten minutes, in half a minute you will no longer be alive, and that it's certain, the main thing is that it is certain. And for the human spirit this knowledge is the most terrible thing of all.

Just imagine the suffering. The human mind cannot conceive of the idea that in an hour, a minute, a few seconds, it will cease to exist. How his outlook on life would've changed from that moment on, irrevocably and forever. Your very soul would be shattered, and you'd see things so much more clearly, with a sharpness, as though every detail around you were suddenly in perfect focus. And you'd possess a knowledge that no one else would have."

Appalled, I finally stop speaking, begin twisting the glass in my hands. I feel cold all over and my fingers begin to tremble so much that I can't control them, fold them in my lap and squeeze down hard. He is looking at me but clearly he hasn't understood a word. He thinks I'm crazy. An idiot. Whatever possessed me to bring up Dostoyevsky and the firing squad? A really cheerful story. Perfect light conversation for a bar on a Friday night amongst a bunch of guys slugging back beer. The sort of thing strangers talk about all the time. I'm not sure what came over me. Utter lunacy again.

"I didn't know any of that," he says slowly. "What an interesting life he had."

But he is not thinking about me or my little lecture on Dostoyevsky at all. Inscrutable, unreadable, those cold gray eyes. He is thinking about something else. Someone else perhaps. A few long minutes pass and neither one of us speaks.

"They were all great, weren't they? Turgenev, Tolstoy, Pushkin, Chekhov," he says finally. Moves his scotch glass so the liquid sloshes around. "What else can I get you to drink, Clarice?"

I notice then to my horror that I've already finished my entire glass of wine while he has hardly taken a sip of the Glenfiddich.

"I'll order more wine. A half-litre this time."

"Oh no, nothing more at all for me please," I say. "It was just I was thirsty before. But not now. Not at all. I'll have water." Fidget in my chair. My brassiere is really riding up now and I wish I could reach down and give it a yank. Also my panties are digging in and I feel damp all over. Maybe if he looks the other way for a moment. "So where do you live in town? Do you have a big garden yourself, or maybe you don't have time with your work at the magazine?"

"Not big exactly. Not much room in my little backyard. But I'm actually thinking about putting my house up for sale, moving to the country where there's some space for things. Maybe starting a greenhouse business. Landscaping, that sort of thing. That was the plan anyway, down the road."

He is silent again, but it is not an uncomfortable silence now. He looks around the room and sips his drink quietly while I twist a beer coaster in my hands and try to look relaxed. At least the trembling in my fingers is beginning to subside on its own. Richard's eyes keep returning to the couple behind me. His eyelids are now half-closed. How much has he had to drink before I arrived? He certainly looks as though he's relaxed now, drowsy and quite possibly only half awake. That pleasant warm and mellow state when one has had just the right amount of alcohol to drink and has forgotten about the world.

If *She* were here at his side, slim and tall and blonde and perfect, he would not look away or get sleepy and bored. He would not look past *Her* and stare at other people. She would smile at him in that alluring, provocative way, just as she did in the photograph, and he would be fascinated. He would take her hands in his and gaze into her eyes, and they would talk for hours about Dostoyevsky and Aleksandr Solzhenitsyn or a hundred other things. And no one, no one else in the whole room could make him look away. I bet if a glass fell, a whole tray of glasses right behind his head, he wouldn't turn to look. If a man beside him suddenly, spontaneously, burst into flames, he wouldn't lift an eyebrow hair.

"You live here in town then? I mean for the time being until you sell. Where in town?" I will not let the subject rest; he must think me mad.

"Not far from here actually. And you? You live here too, in Hope? I've never seen you before. Such a small place and it's amazing how many people you don't know. There's people down the street that have been living there for six years and I've never met them once, not once. I don't even know their names. Now it seems too late to go up and ask. I would feel awkward and a little ashamed. As though I should have made the effort years ago, but was too inconsiderate to bother."

But you have met me before. You have. How could you forget? How could you forget her? How could you have turned your back on her as though she meant nothing at all?

"Yes, I live here in Hope. On the north end. Maybe that's why, total opposite ends of town. Just a small place but it's plenty big enough for one person. One person and one cat," I say.

Now he knows that much. Alone. Glance down at his hand. No ring either. At least not yet.

"How old are you?" he says suddenly sober and unsmiling and looking straight into my eyes.

"That's not something you should ask a woman, just point blank like that," I say very quickly, looking down at my hands. "It's really not the gentlemanly thing to do. Time certainly slips by doesn't it when you get to this age? I can't believe high school was so many years ago. One day just turns into the next and the next. One season after the other. Faster and faster and faster."

He is smiling a little now, amused, the corners of his mouth turned up slightly as though at some small private joke.

Well, she isn't twenty any more, is she? Just look at her face. The younger girls at the store, the part-time students, when they thought I couldn't hear: discussing me. Scratching, dissecting.

"I'm quite certain I'm older than you are, believe me. A lot older. And I'm sorry I asked. You're right. I wasn't being a gentleman at all. Inexcusable. Comes from living alone for so long. You just remind me of someone. Look, I should maybe go now." He glances again at the couple behind me.

How do I detain him? I shouldn't have talked so much. What was it I was saying there a moment ago? Something about time slipping away, faster and faster. How awkward. I can't just let him walk away now. I can't approach him like this in a bar a second time. My only chance is now. If I want to settle the score with him, then I need to act now. Lay out my plans.

I reach into my purse and pull out my wallet, scribble on the back of an old receipt and hand it to him. I should be mortified, ashamed of my brazen, self-indulgent behaviour. But I am not. This time circumstances most definitely allow.

"My number," I say. "Oh yes and address. Maybe we can get together again sometime and really figure out where it was we met. Maybe another drink or something."

"Thank you. I'd love that. I could drop by the bookstore sometime. When do you work next?"

"Tomorrow," I say quickly. Thank goodness it's Saturday and thank the heavens and the saints above Reese asked for the day off to go ride his new horse. There is some angel in heaven looking out for me after all. "But I work next week too, every day but Friday."

"Well good then." He leans over to grasp my hand and holds it lightly for a moment. His hand is very warm. Mine, on the other hand, surely must feel like a clump of frozen match-sticks. "I'm really very glad we met, Clarice. Can't tell you how much good it did me to sit here a while and just talk like this to someone like you. Bob, you know, he's got his troubles, with the girlfriend and so on, so I'm just someone who can listen well. So it was wonderful chatting with someone like you. Refreshing." He hesitates, then reaches into his pocket, out of politeness only, and retrieves a business card. "Here. This is mine. My home number is on there too. Give me a ring some time. If I'm not home, which is very likely, there's the machine. I generally check it every day. And I'll think about how we met before. I know if I think long enough I'll figure it out."

And then he turns and simply walks away.

She would have leaned over first and kissed him full on the lips. And to *Her* he would not have said *it was nice chatting with someone like you*. He would have said, full of meaning, *let's go somewhere where we can be alone*.

This makes me feel angry, yes, and also a little depressed, disheartened apart from everything else in a way that I just can't explain.

I am just some ordinary stranger with whom he shared a drink and exchanged a few common pleasantries after listening to a friend complain. I am someone who filled in a few more moments of time with idle chatter, gave him the excuse to order just one more glass of good scotch.

And, because he was inclined to feel idle tonight, because the chair felt comfortable and the drinks made him a little drowsy and maybe a little lazy too, he stayed on a few minutes longer and listened to this peculiar woman who was clearly just lonely and wanted to talk to someone. He will go home now, feeling warm and relaxed and very tired. He will not remember where he met me before. He will not give our whole conversation or me, for that matter, a moment's thought. By tomorrow he will forget I ever existed. Until perhaps one day, by pure chance, by accident alone, he will wander into the bookstore at the mall and see me.

But trust me, I will not let this happen. I will make him remember.

-19-

There are white squirrels in the town of Hope; I've seen them. At the very least there are two. I saw them earlier this morning in the river park. They were chasing each other around in the grass under the big oak, and they weren't afraid of me at all, fearless enough to let me come within ten feet and then only scamper as high as the first knothole, watch me from there with two pairs of bright, bright eyes.

I've actually seen them here once before. That time they were near this tree as well, so likely they must live here. The first time it was very early in the morning. The sun was just touching the sky to the east and it was still quite dark. I was walking back from the cemetery and there they were, flitting about, rushing up and down that big old tree as though the very existence of the whole world depended on them. At first I thought they were little white ghosts. Furry banshees tumbling about from some time long past. That my nightlong vigils in the graveyard had rendered me suddenly sensitive to apparitions or hallucinations.

But as I got closer I could make out every last detail. Tiny little paws, so much like hands, wise bright little eyes, long twitching tails just a little gray at the ends. A smudge of dirt on a belly, a torn ear-tip. There was no mistaking it; they were real. Every hair. Of course there was no one else around, no one with whom I could share this brilliant though probably useless discovery. To verify the fact that I wasn't seeing things.

And now today again, white squirrels.

I watched them for quite some time. They ran to the very top of the tree and in no time back down again, darted across the grass to the willows by the river, chasing one another as though undergoing some complicated rodent ritual. I tagged along as best I could, attempting to keep up although I was terribly slow and awkward. They weren't afraid at all, seemed hardly aware I was close by. At one point I walked right up to one sitting on the ground, acorn in its paws. It peered up at me cannily, nodding its head and turning the nut over and over, but did not move away. I reached out to grasp the long white tail hairs and only then did it melt into the shade of the trees. Strange, how silent they are, my two little white rodent ghosts.

After the squirrels had gone and I was alone again, I suddenly saw her. Or at least I thought I did. But only for a moment. Fortunately I caught myself in time. Turns out the child was someone else's; a complete stranger and naturally quite different in so many ways. When I got close enough, I could see how very different she was and was surprised I could have been so mistaken. I reached up and covered my eyes with both hands, let my head fall back.

Idiot.

This time I knew almost right away, was able to spare myself the worst pain. I quickly made myself think about something else, about the white squirrels, about Maggie, about Richard at *Sunny's*. And sure enough, when I looked up again, the little girl was gone. Maybe she just walked away. Maybe she was still there but behind the tree on the other side. Impossible to tell. All I know is she was gone and she wasn't mine, and I got through it somehow this time without the expected collapse.

Something I must face from time to time. Something that happens. I can't help myself. Usually I can catch myself, but only just.

I am so tired. I walk down the path out of the river park and back onto Main Street. Just my luck, I meet up with Gladys

Bierman in front of *In Paradise*. Her daughter is with her today. Six feet tall in stocking feet and towering languorously over us both, which is really quite disconcerting. She is wearing hip-hugger bell-bottoms and a very short crop top that reveals her sunken bellybutton and a large section of bare brown midriff. She looks smashing and very youthful. In my sweat pants I feel like a dreary gray blob next to the pair of them. Gladys is wearing a gorgeous peacock-blue suit that likely costs over two hundred and definitely did not come from a store here in town. Guess she needs to be well put together to be a successful interior decorator; youthfulness is so important these days. And I suppose you wouldn't want some ancient and sloppy-looking interior decorator telling you what type of broadloom or throw cushions you need. But still, I can't forgive her. Gladys's unrelenting insouciance is too irritating for words, let me tell you.

"Been meaning to stop in to see you for ages, Clarice," she says, taking my hand and smiling blithely. "So glad we ran into one another finally."

Meaning she's been too ill at ease to stop in; doesn't know what to say to someone like me and likely doesn't care, if she were to be honest.

"Do you know," I say pulling my hand back quickly, "whether anyone has ever seen white squirrels in town?"

Mother and daughter exchange a look full of meaning and no one answers.

"Down in the park. The river park. White ones."

"My goodness, no," says Gladys finally. "Certainly not. What I meant to ask you, Clarice, is whether I could come over some time, you know, to look around your place, give you a few tips maybe, some decorating ideas just for you. Totally free of charge of course. And I could help you out. With the painting and draperies and so on. I've quite the talented crew working for me now. We've been doing a lot of work in some of the newer houses in Milan."

Bending her head down a little so I can view the long curlew nose in profile, Lisa examines her chipped green fingernails. Bored, jaded, cheesed off. Likely her mom talks to people on the street about curtains and fingertip towels all the time.

"Thanks so much Gladys," I say. "Maybe sometime in the winter. I'm so busy at the moment, I haven't really the time. And I'm not sure what I'd like to change in the house. I'll have to think about it. But thank you anyway."

"Well, suit yourself Clarice, dear. Florence Bishop said you could use a hand. You know, decorating and so on. That you were thinking of listing the place."

"Oh no," I say. "Not at all. I wouldn't dream of selling it. Where did Florence get such a curious idea?"

"Oh well, who knows," Gladys says. Glances down at her watch, rubs at her foot with the toe of her other sandal.

"I better go," I say. "Work awaits." Walk away abruptly and cross the street.

Terrible of me to stomp off like that so suddenly, but I can't help myself. Gladys gives me the cold chills and I always start to feel a little sick after standing next to her. That cropped hair, all spiky and streaked and perfectly gelled with make-up just so. Always grabbing hands, touching shoulders. And that daughter of hers. A giant. With that naked midriff and that wretched nose I simply must stare at and stare at.

Look behind me. Lisa is walking the opposite way down Main, long brown legs moving swiftly, arms swinging. A brown-bellied curlew in flight.

***

Maggie arrives not long after I arrive home.

"Raining cats and dogs out there now," she says, shaking her wet hair, radiant as ever.

Just like Maggie. *Raining cats and dogs.* Who actually says things like that anymore? But Maggie is the kind of person who can get away with it. She peels off jacket, rubber shoes and spills into the kitchen.

"Just look at my hair, will you." Slings the jacket neatly over the back of a kitchen chair. "A perfect fright."

Wet or not, she looks flawless to me. Short-sleeved pale yellow shirt, pants a gorgeous shade of moss green, brand new. Like a daffodil about to burst open.

"Thought you'd stop in," I say.

"So tell me everything." She leans toward me pulling at my arm. "How was your night out? I would've called but it was too late last night. Did you meet anyone new? Talk to anyone?"

"Oh there's not much to tell," I say. "Went to that place called *Sunny's.* You know, over by the curling club on the east end. I didn't even know it was still open. Hadn't been there in years. So I had a few drinks, nothing too exciting. It's much nicer inside now than it used to be."

"See anybody interesting?"

"No, not at all. Hardly anybody there. Like I told you, not very exciting. Maybe next time I'll head into the city to some other place. Maybe we can go together."

She doesn't quite believe me. There is more to the story and she knows it.

"Here, I'll pour coffee." I get up to grab the pot to give my hands something to do.

Caesar emerges from the basement and eyes Maggie suspiciously. He threw up on the basement stairs again overnight, and I stepped in it this morning when I went down to get bread from the freezer. Maybe he needs to see a vet. I can't even remember when he last had his rabies shot. Maybe he has worms.

"Forgot to tell you something," she says. "About Frank. He called yesterday when you were at work. He wanted to come by. I don't know what he's after but I imagine he'll show up here again so I just wanted to warn you. You better tell him off this time, Clarice. Really tell him off."

Dear forever latched-on-to-me Frank. I can't feel sorry for him anymore. He has his own life and I have mine. We were happy together once. We would have been the kind of couple that grows old together. With rocking chairs and long walks and a cottage by the lake. Frank golfing and me writing a gardening column for the local paper. We would have gotten used to each other, leaned on each other. Bored, but content and very ordinary. A sufficient measure of happiness.

"Thanks for the warning, but Frank doesn't bother me one bit."

Reach into my pocket for Richard's business card which I shoved in there this morning. But the pocket is empty. Begin a thorough search of both front pockets as discreetly as possible so Maggie won't ask.

Maggie is helping herself to the muffins on the table.

"You know these muffins aren't mine," she says. "They don't taste like mine at all. And I'm positive there's nuts in my recipe. It was mom's recipe and I'm sure it said nuts. Walnuts. A whole cup, walnut pieces. I didn't find any nuts in mine. Not one. Did you find any nuts?"

"They're definitely your muffins, Maggie. You brought them a while ago and I stuck them in the freezer and took them out just this morning. You know I don't bake."

Maggie polishes off a second in silence, while I sift through a stack of old mail.

"So, I forgot to tell you. Margaret did call and invite me to the party," I say.

"That's great, Clarice. I knew she was going to. You're going of course?"

"Didn't give me much choice. Sounds like she and Douglas are definitely expecting me. I suppose Frank will be there too and Dinny and Michael. Margaret would never leave them out for something like this."

"Who cares? You know you have to go, Clarice. They'd be so disappointed. And it'll be fun anyway. We'll go shopping together for dresses. Get our hair and nails done. Look, I got to run," She sets her mug carefully into the sink and wipes at the counter with one long, perfectly-shaped fingernail. "Thanks for the coffee. Told Paul I wouldn't be more than a minute and as it was he rolled his eyes and grunted something at me. But I'll call later. We can make plans."

When she is gone I sit down and take another huge swallow of coffee.

Gone. The only tangible evidence of having spoken to him at all. I could have showed up at his office with that business card in my hands and said, *Richard gave me his card, said I should stop by and see him sometime. . ..*

I drag the garbage can to the middle of the kitchen floor and dump it out completely. Begin sifting through and find a phone bill, unpaid, and my new address book.

I'm still kneeling on the floor in the midst of all the garbage and unfolding the creased and soggy telephone bill when there is a knock at the door.

Frank.

"What in the hell do you want now Frank," I say as I fling open the door.

But it is not Frank.

It is Richard.

-20-

I stand in the doorway quite calmly holding my housecoat closed, hands crossed over my chest, elbows in tight. My stomach feels hot, compressed, unsettled.

He has come to my house and I didn't even have to do anything to make him appear.

"Hello, Clarice. Hope this isn't a bad time to stop by," He looks a little embarrassed, folding his arms self-consciously in front of him as though he doesn't know what to do with them, and looking past me, searchingly, into the front entrance. He is holding a magazine rolled up and is tapping it restlessly against the palm of one hand. "I wanted to stop in at your store yesterday but I had someone I had to go see and it ended up taking the whole day. So I decided I'd come by here instead this morning. Your address was on the card you gave me."

"Yes it was, wasn't it." I hold the door open wider for him. "Please come in. It's not a bad time at all. In fact, it's a great time."

He is dressed in blue jeans and a plain white T-shirt. Like I said before, very ordinary. Most people would never notice or remember him if they met up with him once. Those pale gray eyes, that long narrow nose in that wide face. Lines around the eyes, and much deeper ones on the forehead. Blonde hair, but a dark blonde, gray-brown almost, and inoffensive. Tall, but narrow in the shoulders and really quite thin all over. *Too thin*, people would say. *Could use a little weight-training.* And pale in the face as though he doesn't get outdoors much, despite his claims about gardening. Yes, quite ordinary. An office worker, you might say, a computer technician, a banker. Very run-of-the-mill. Not at all like Frank: flashy and gregarious, handsome in a dark and dramatic and sexual way. *Drop your pants gorgeous*, Maggie said once. Her words, not mine.

"Come into the kitchen. I'll make coffee."

It is not until I'm actually through the doorway with him directly behind me not two steps back, that I realize the garbage—eggshells, cat puke, soggy paper towel and all—is still scattered about the floor. As though some catastrophic event swept through my house, and my house alone, sometime early this morning.

"Wow," he says, "I thought I sometimes left sweeping up too many days in a row, but it seems you have me beat."

A flash. His pristine kitchen, freshly vacuumed carpets, immaculate bedroom.

I am amazed at myself. I cannot believe how calm and controlled I am. For a moment I assume I am not really awake, that this is some bizarre but quite convincing dream from which I am about to awaken with a jolt. So I can afford to be calm. Alice in her Wonderland

"I actually had a bit of an accident this morning as you can see. The cat made a mess. I was just cleaning it all up when you came. Have a seat." Step over the disaster and begin to bustle about with the coffee, grinding beans and measuring, finally turning my attention to the floor. But he is already at it, on hands and knees with a dustpan that he's found all by himself.

"You have a cat?" I say.

"As a matter of fact yes. Quite an old guy actually, so all he seems to do is sleep these days. But he's a great companion. Likes to sit at my desk and watch while I write. Knows exactly what time it is, I swear, and he lets my know when I need to quit and go make dinner. I must say he's never pulled a trick like this with the garbage in all his years though." He raises his eyebrows and looks around him. "Yours must be quite a tiger."

"Just a stray. Showed up at my back door one day. Not that much of a terror usually. But he doesn't like men."

Richard looks surprised. "Really, why not?"

"Oh, I don't know," I say. Don't mention Frank for heaven's sake, Clarice. Not at a time like this. I busy myself with the coffee and the teaspoons, rattling about and making a lot of noise so I don't have to look directly at him. But he seems perfectly at ease now, gazing around the kitchen with interest, taking everything in and bouncing one knee, just slightly, up and down.

"So I finally figured it out. Told you I would," he says, getting up and stretching his arms a little. He is examining my potted fern, looking underneath the leaves and peering into the soil.

"Figured what out?" I drop a spoon and it makes an enormous clatter on the floor. In spite of myself, I jump to one side a bit, actually take an idiotic little hopping step to the left.

"Where we met. I told you I never forget. It's one thing I've always had. A great memory for people's names and faces."

"So where?" I say, slowly reaching down to retrieve the spoon, "I haven't a clue."

I feel like someone who just met up with a person they haven't seen in years, and remember that the last time they saw this other person they had had far too much to drink and said a number of embarrassing and regrettable things, then proceeded to knock a glass of red wine down the other person's shirt. You keep waiting all through the conversation for it to be mentioned, for the dreaded subject to be resurrected. Parties and wine glasses and white shirts. The anxiety is terrible.

"You sometimes deliver flyers or something like that, don't you?" he is saying. Sits back down and reaches for his coffee.

"Yes, certainly I used to." I am surprised at my voice: flat and quite ordinary.

He smiles. "Thought so. Took me a while Friday night after I left, but by the time I got home I'd remembered. Like I said, I never forget a face."

"Actually, I don't deliver flyers anymore at all. It was just a temporary thing, sort of a favour to a friend. I'm far too busy at the store these days."

"And all yesterday I kept thinking I must stop in and see her and tell her that I'd figured it out. I thought it was kind of interesting how you just walked over and introduced yourself like that. Most women would be afraid to do that sort of thing. Shows you have grit."

Stare down into my cup. It looks murky, and there are bits of coffee grounds or something worse floating around in it. *Grit.* Not someone like me, surely. He is quite mistaken.

And then it hits me. What if he should get up from the table, quite unexpectedly, and walk to my bedroom. Just like that. It is possible, after all. It's only just down the hall. He could ask to see the rest of my house. He could ask to use the washroom. I couldn't refuse him that, could I? What if, by chance, he should go in the wrong door and walk into my room instead, walk over to my night table and pick up my copy of *The Idiot.* Not that implausible, really. After all, if he saw it lying there he would naturally pick it up, comment on the fact that he too is reading this same novel at the moment; ask for my opinion. And then, he could open it, just a little, or it would open of its own accord, fall open to the place were I left off reading. And to his feet would drop the letter. The letter from *Her.* I can see him now, how his face would change, how a look of friendly interest would alter suddenly, horribly. Incredulity, anger. The horror-struck expression of one who only now realizes he has been cruelly betrayed.

"The other reason I thought I'd stop by was to give you the latest copy of my magazine. You said you loved gardening so I thought you might be keen to see it, you know, if you've never read it before. We're always trying to reel in new subscribers one way or another. I've signed up quite a number of my friends who don't even have backyards, let alone gardens." He smiles a little.

"Wonderful," I say. "Thank you." But I don't really understand what he is saying at all. Something about gardening. About friends without backyards. It is all very confusing. The only thing I can think about is what to do if he gets up now and asks to go to the bathroom. I must not let him drink too much.

But my crazy little fit is suddenly over. He is not simply going to get up and walk to my bedroom. That sort of thing just does not happen in real life. This is not a horror flick. And if it should, I will be prepared. I will come up with a plan. It is good I've thought of it already so that it won't happen. And I know what to expect now if it should. There are all kinds of things I could do.

"I'd love to read your magazine. Thank you so much. And you will have to stop by the bookstore sometime," I say slowly. "We've all the classics that most stores wouldn't think to carry. Most of the big stores in the cities these days focus almost entirely on the new stuff, the popular authors, the recent best sellers, romances, mysteries and so on. We specialize in the classics; some of the old books that have been around for years and everybody should read."

The Idiot on his night table was likely just on loan from someone, a gift he himself had little interest in but was reading out of courtesy to a friend. Or he isn't reading it at all. At this very moment it lies totally forgotten on the night table, the bookmark still in the same page where it was the day I last saw it. Someday he will notice it there and take it back to work, hand it to a co-worker, saying he is finished with it but had rather a lot of trouble getting through it. That it wasn't his kind of book. Or he will place it, carelessly, along with dozens of others, on his bookshelf, somewhere near the bottom with a stack of other books he has never read.

"Well, I'll definitely come by."

"So tell me more about yourself. I mean I know nothing other than that you have this friend called Bob with girlfriend troubles and you work at the *Urban Gardener*. That's it."

"There isn't a whole lot to tell actually. My family's in the states now, mostly Arizona and California. I've a brother and sister. My sister's a nurse and my brother's in construction, both married. I never saw my grandfather, but everyone said I looked like him. He was a farmer and when I was five, my family moved to his house near Milan. My dad didn't farm the land though. Rented it out. I always wished he'd quit his job at the canning plant and buy some cows. I had this vision of us operating a dairy farm together. Father and son partnership. A lasting legacy I could take over when dad got to be too old. I knew my brother would never be interested. It could all be mine someday. But then I hit my teen years and joined the basketball team and played football and decided living on a farm for the rest of my life was a really, really bad idea. And anyway, Mom and Dad sold the farm soon after and retired to British Columbia. So I went to Western and took journalism and traveled around a bit until I got the spot at the *Urban Gardener*, and then bought a place here in town. Didn't know a dahlia from a holly hock back then when I started, but I soon found out that this is what I was really interested in. Writing for the magazine, gardening. That sort of thing. And this was where I wanted to stay. I feel at home here even though my parents have moved away. All my closest friends still live around here too. I just can't imagine wanting to move to the U.S. or out west like my parents. To some strange place like that. I'm not the adventurous type at all I guess." He pauses for a moment, turns his head away slightly and puts down the coffee cup. I sense he is going to get up any second now, place the cup in the sink and say he needs to go, perhaps lifting one hand up to his mouth to suppress a small yawn. "Well? You? You haven't said much about yourself either. Family?" He smiles and leans forward. I was wrong. He is not going to get up and leave. A least not yet.

"Oh, I don't really have family any more, so to speak, at least not anywhere close by. My dad died a while ago and mother's been gone for years. My sisters moved away to the Ottawa area and we've kind of lost touch, to be honest. It's too bad really. We were quite close once we got to be teenagers. We learned how to band together to outsmart my mom, to make her bend the rules a little so we could go out with our friends. We even covered for each other so Mom never found out some of the things we were doing. We had a lot of good times together. But their lives are so different from mine now. They have families. Big families, and I don't know my nieces and nephews at all really. I went to visit them all a number of years ago and it was a bewildering experience. All those kids. The chaos and noise. Picnics and all kinds of family get-togethers just about every weekend. They all live quite close to one another now. My oldest sister has twin boys and then another two younger boys, and I could never tell any of them apart. They all looked so much the same. Like their Dad, who is only five-foot-nine, but has a chest and shoulders like a horse and the darkest curliest hair you've ever seen and back hair like you wouldn't believe. All the boys look like him. So I kept saying the names all wrong, and after a while I think they sort of resented me being there staying with them. I should've taken a hotel room maybe. Or rented a place. It was too much for me, especially on my own. I didn't know what to do with myself and I didn't know how to help Martha. I haven't been back at all since then. I've written and asked them to come and visit me here of course. But they just don't have the time right now with the kids in school and then soccer and ball in the summers. They keep saying they want to visit, but the truth is there's nothing here for them. The kids would be bored and so would my sisters, believe me. They don't like it here. This town is too small and there's no place to go. Even Milan seems like a farm town to them. So it's just me. On my own." I am surprised I have told him all of this. It just came out, quite naturally and unforced. The truth is I normally don't like to tell people anything about my family for some reason. I usually keep all of that to myself. Fiddle with my spoon and for the first time wonder how I must look: hair uncombed, face unwashed, a dirty housecoat instead of proper clothes and here the morning half gone.

"So why did you give it up? Journalism? You told me before you used to be a reporter."

It takes me a good thirty seconds before I can find the answer. It isn't easy to go back. It isn't a simple thing for me to just go back in my mind and resurrect those days when I was a different person; the other Clarice. The *first Clarice*. "If you're a reporter you report on other people's lives. You follow people who do interesting, worthwhile things. You watch them. You write about them. They're the ones doing the remarkable things, while you're only writing about them. You have to be subservient and admiring and obsequious. I just couldn't anymore. I changed a lot over the years as well. People do change. They have to."

"Surely as a reporter you write about interesting things as well. Events, places, music, plays. Not just remarkable people."

"Well yes, it is interesting in a way, of course. But I always felt I wasn't the right sort of person. It's much better working in a bookstore. Quieter, calming. Do you like your job at the magazine?"

"Yes, I do like it. Very much actually. But sometimes I think I spend too much time at work and not enough time doing other things."

He looks around and I can't shake this feeling that all of a sudden he has remembered *Her*. There is a faint line between his eyes and he begins bouncing his knee up and down again, ever so slightly. His eyes rest on mine only briefly, then flicker away, look past me toward the doorway. Restrained, circumspect.

"I should be going, Clarice. Thanks for the coffee. You probably have things to do. The rain's finally let up and I should get to work in the garden. Can't believe the weeds in there already at this time of year. Sunday is sometimes the only day I have to get things done."

He goes back to the front door and picks up a copy of the *Urban Gardener* that he must have tossed there on his way in. Hands it to me with a small smile.

"There's a good article on page twelve about dahlias."

"Thanks," I say. "I can't tell you how happy I am that you stopped by like this. Sorry I'm not even dressed and sorry about the mess in the kitchen. Normally I'd be dressed a lot earlier on a Sunday, believe me."

"I shouldn't just drop in without warning like that. Maybe I'll give you a call sometime. Or I'll stop by the store."

He says this politely enough, but there's no warmth in it. He doesn't really mean it at all.

Opens the door, steps out and is gone.

-21-

Despite our big sale on hardcover books at the store today, Reese has been exceptionally quiet, ignoring all customers and leaving all the fetching and carrying and questions to me. Normally he's quite a pest, following people, all but asking to carry their shopping bags, and showering them with a steady stream of unsolicited advice. But today he hardly says a word and stalks about like a petulant child, glaring balefully at anyone who approaches. His allergies are really acting up again and I've placed a box of Kleenex on the cash desk and in a few more strategic places around the store. But he's left them all untouched and wanders about the store looking uneasy and avoiding my eyes, nose dripping. His nose is really quite narrow and pointy at the tip and a little droplet often collects there, a round little bead that wobbles and trembles for a long, long time before it falls. I can't help staring, just can't stop myself, which is endlessly irritating, and I find myself casting all the blame on him. Does he not feel anything wet there at all?

When it's time to shut down for the night, Reese begins closing up without being told and I finally, reluctantly and against my better judgement, ask him what is wrong. It turns out it's girlfriend troubles. He's simply very depressed about being alone. The last three girls he asked out turned him down flat, and the one that he was supposed to see this past weekend simply didn't show up at the appointed time and now won't explain why or return his calls. Also, he tried out his new horse on Saturday and ended up face down in a field with two big bruises on his knees and a sprained little finger. Consequently, he's now having second thoughts about the horse after all, even though he informs me this has been the Big Dream since he was a small child. What nonsense. It is very difficult for me to keep my temper. I have the urge all day to take him by the shoulders and give him a good shake.

Even Sally, who is usually too preoccupied by her own troubles, has noticed the change in Reese. "What's with Reese today?" she says as she strides past, tapping two pencils together in her hands. "He hasn't said two words to me all day and normally I can't get him to shut up at all. In fact usually I have to chase him down and tell him to lay off the customers. He's such a pest, it's embarrassing. And today I haven't seen him near anybody even once."

She's one to talk. She's been a bear all day herself, mostly because she hates having sales and she doesn't do well under pressure these days. But she's finally beginning to relax and lighten up now that it's almost closing time. Evidently it is not one of those days where she holes up in her office and hides from the world because there are definite signs she is in the mood for a long chat. There will be no escape for me.

"I don't know," I say. There is a gray fuzz beginning to appear above her upper lip and I have to force myself not to look at it. "He's been strange all day. Avoiding the customers if you can believe it." I don't want to get into it with her, explain all of Reese's girl problems, and now the whole long story about the horse. In fact, I was really hoping for a quick getaway tonight, so Sally in a talkative mood is not a good thing at all.

"Come to the back for a minute, will you? Reese can finish up. I want a word with you." She tucks a book under her arm and walks away, heels clicking. What could she possibly want? Did she hear when I snapped at the fishwife who complained about the price of the new hardcovers?

"Get in here. Sit," Sally says as I approach the doorway.

My underarms feel wet. Truth is, I really am afraid of Sally. She intimidates me. If I were a chicken, I'd be on the very bottom of the pecking order. I'd be the one with some tiny little imperfection that all the other hens pecked and pecked at until I was dead.

She looks me over closely, leans back, taps her pen on the edge of the table. *Tap, tap, tap.* Each tap runs through me like a small electric shock and goose bumps appear instantly on the top of my arms. I rub at the area above my upper lip with one index finger and try to look unconcerned.

"There's this guy I know, friend of John's. Single. Really great guy. I'll set you up some time, Clarice. You'll love him. I wanted to tell you a bit about him so I ..."

The telephone rings. I wave good-bye quickly and back out of the office as she reaches for the receiver. By the way her mouth changes, molds into a long, thin line, I can see this is an important call. She even closes the book and turns her chair away so she's facing the window. A sign for me to go.

Please, please please let it be a baby for her this time. Please let it happen. Show me there is someone up there watching out for us after all. It is not all random; it is not all absurd and pointless.

***

I drive past Richard's house. Believe me, this is really very necessary. I must get on with my plans. It's time he realized what he's done to me; it's time there was some justice here.

No lights on anywhere. What do the neighbours think, him being away every evening like this? Don't they wonder what he does? Doesn't anyone want to know where the man goes every evening? It must seem strange: a grown man well over forty, all alone, no family of his own, and out until very late every evening.

In the backyard I stop and look behind me again. Not a soul, only the stone figure, a strange dwarf-like shadow kneeling in the muted light. I almost expect it to look up this time, nod its head, put a finger knowingly to its lips. But of course it doesn't. This is the kind of nonsense that dances around my head these days. The trouble is I've been awake so long and I know I need sleep very badly, but sleep has become elusive. Real sleep that is. The kind that lasts uninterrupted for hours and hours and hours. Never far off, but there, just out of reach, just past my fingertips. There was a time when I took sleep for granted. When I climbed into my bed without thought or concern, and then fell asleep as effortlessly and instinctively as taking a breath of air. And I slept seven, eight, nine hours at a time without once even waking up. And when I did, I didn't think twice about it. Took it for granted completely. Imagine.

I move around to the back door, nervous, on edge, remembering how it was the last time I was here. At least it is getting dark. Rush to the stairs and go up, two at a time, move quickly to his room, push open the door. Yes, the book is still here. Lift it gently and open. I was wrong about him again. He has read some more of it, after all. Ah yes, the part where Aglaya sends the prince a hedgehog as a present. When the prince, who was sitting alone in deep despair having just returned home ridiculed and banished by Aglaya, sees this present, he looks like one who's just risen from the dead. *Risen from the dead.*

Close the book slowly and place it on the night table. For a long while I just sit and wait, watching as darkness closes in and the minutes turn to hours. Finally I get up and move around the room, touching his things lightly with two fingers. Not one single photograph. Slip around the house anyway from room to room, opening closet doors, dressers, peering inside drawers. But there is nothing. Not one photograph of *Her* anywhere in this house. How strange is that?

***

The enormous man in the brush cut has just come in. He is ordering his coffee, triple cream, triple sugar. Very satisfied to see him again, I wait until he's already walking toward his table before going up to the counter and placing my own order. I feel very content. Completely out of character, I look the donuts over as though deciding which one I should choose. What would she say if I actually bought something to eat today.

"Coffee, large, black." Snap. Snap. It comes out sharp, an order. I hesitate, thinking I should've at least said please afterwards, but wait too long and then it's too late to say anything else.

"Is that all?" says Francis the badger from behind the counter. She reaches down, sorts a few donuts, placing some up higher and moving an assortment of muffins down. Tonight she is wearing black pants and a lime green T-shirt that is too short and exposes numerous tummy rolls. She is chewing gum and blowing little bubbles. I wonder if she knows how unattractive her mouth is when she speaks. A crooked line, with the words forcing themselves out through one corner only. And that pulpous squishy nose over top.

"Oh, no. Just coffee."

She pours and I hand her the exact change and say thank you very loud. Twice. She says nothing at all, snaps her gum, and I turn and walk rapidly to my table.

The man with the newspaper and notebook is not here tonight. Was he offended I took his drink and then didn't say one word to him Friday night at the bar?

When my coffee is cool enough I begin drinking in big

mouthfuls, swallowing hard, but I tip the cup back too hard and some of it spills and drips down both sides of my cheeks and onto the table. Clutch at a handful of napkins, daub at my face. The big man in the saggy, gray tracksuit has noticed and is turning his head, angling his brush cut my way to get a better view. I leave the rest of the coffee and walk out quickly.

When I arrive home, I notice Maggie the Terrier has already come and gone. Let herself in through the back door, which evidently I've failed to lock again, washed my dishes and scrubbed the kitchen floor. Oh yes that's right, I guess I did overlook washing it after the garbage can incident but that doesn't mean I need Maggie to do it for me.

There is a batch of fresh muffins on the counter neatly covered with saran, and a note. For some reason this irritates me. This obsession of Maggie's to do all these favours for me, these ridiculous little acts of charity.

Clarice, I just thought I'd bring these muffins by. I think they're better than those last ones I brought you. Sorry I had to rush out in such a hurry Sunday morning. I noticed later there was a strange truck in your drive. Frank didn't get a new truck did he? I hope he's staying clear of you. Let me know if I can help in that department. Take care, love Maggie. P.S. Florence Bishop told Beatrice Fielhaber that some strange man is moving in with you. They're spreading it around the neighbourhood. Ha Ha.

I'm strangely elated that Maggie saw Richard's truck in my driveway Sunday morning. It proves he really was here. Also, I'm quite satisfied with the rumours old Florence is spreading. It is very pleasing to be talked about for other reasons at long last. Very pleasing indeed.

I walk into the bedroom and examine the chessboard. Move my queen two spaces to the right. Check. Wander back into the kitchen and unwrap the muffins, take a largish bite. Solid as a bullet. I am trying to chew and my mouth is completely full with a hard muffin clump when the telephone rings.

"Hello," I say, trying to swallow the whole bite at once.

"Hello, Clarice," says a voice now familiar. "It's Richard. Richard Mason."

-22-

For a brief moment I want to tell him. Tell him that I've been following him; that I've been in his house just tonight and held his book in my hands. I want to shock him, confront and challenge him until he is shaken. I want this all to be over somehow.

But truth is, I am a coward. I do not have *grit* at all.

"Well hello," I say again, trying stupidly to think of something clever and witty, but nothing else comes out.

"Good, how are you?" He sounds nervous, on edge. There is a catch to his voice and he clears his throat sharply, several times. For some reason this calms me down and I suddenly feel a little better, almost warm towards him again. "I was hoping to get you at home," he says. "Sorry I'm calling so late. I was out tonight. Tried to call you as soon as I got back, but there was no answer. I'm not sure why, but I just sort of assumed that you were the kind of person that stayed up late at nights, like I do."

"I should have an answering machine. I'm always missing people," I say cheerfully. There are still muffin remnants in my throat. I try to swallow them quietly but make a little gagging sound. I imagine his face: the look of surprise, a little sickened. Reach for the fridge door to get water, but the cord will not go that far and I almost yank the entire telephone to the floor and must lunge like a madwoman to grab hold of it.

"I wanted to ask you about Friday night," he says.

"Yes?" I say quickly. "Yes?"

"I just wondered whether you might be free for a drink

like you'd suggested. I mean after today I already know Friday shouldn't be too busy for me. I had some appointments cancel and so on. A couple things got moved forward to next week. So I thought maybe you'd like to go out for a drink. That is if you're free."

"Oh yes. Definitely. I'm free on Friday." I begin to tear at the drawer under the telephone table in search of the calendar. Flip through it frantically looking for Friday, but the whole month seems to have disappeared. If I'm supposed to work late, the hell with it. Reese or someone will just have to cover. I don't care if his horse is entered in the Kentucky Derby or the Belmont Stakes this weekend, he just has to.

"Friday would be great. Perfect. Same place?"

"Same place would be great if that's what you'd like." He sounds relieved, which is a little surprising. After all he gave me no indication on Sunday that he was even the slightest bit interested in going out with me. On the contrary, he seemed put out I'd even suggested it. As if he was just glad to be making a hasty exit from my house and hoped never to have to meet up with me again.

"...Unless you'd like to try some other place?" he is saying. "There's a restaurant in Milan at the north end that's really good. We could have dinner. Much quieter too and they have wonderful wine. I'm not really all that fond of *Sunny's*, unless you're just going out for a beer and you don't feel like driving all the way into the city. There's no food to speak of."

"Oh well, whatever. That sounds fine. You decide." I hope I don't sound too flippant, too dismissive. But I can't let him know how much it matters. I've been fiddling with my desk calendar, trying to find the right page and almost drop the receiver again.

"Hello? Hello? You still there?" he says. These is an edge

now to his voice. Irritation? He believes I am the nervous sort, jumpy and easily alarmed. The type of individual who has trouble looking anyone in the eye. The kind who steps aside quickly when confronted by a group of people on a sidewalk, forever ill at ease and insecure.

"Oh yes. Sorry. I just about dropped the phone." I laugh and shift the receiver to the other ear, pressing it in tight. "That place. The restaurant you were just talking about in Milan. It sounds great. Dinner would be wonderful. I'd love that."

Is there some way I can finally bring up the topic of *Her* when we go out? There must be. Maybe if I mention Frank, clear the air about my own past. Maybe that would be the catalyst to his own confession. But I am afraid of this. Afraid of what he might say. Terrified to bring up something in any way connected to the past. And yet I need to move on with things. Move forward with my plans and keep my mind focused on the task. Every time I do this, I feel so much better inside.

"Okay," he is saying. "I'll pick you up at 6:30 Friday. That okay?"

"Yes, that's fine. See you then. At 6:30. And thank you Richard. Thank you so terribly much."

Thank you so terribly much. He must think me an idiot. A romping, nervous, panicky idiot.

"I'm already looking forward to Friday, Clarice. Talk to you later. Good night."

There is a faint click and he is gone. I run to the mirror in the front hall. This is just an automatic thing for me at times; I'm not really sure why. I mean I'm not the type of person who sits and stares at herself all day in a mirror or obsesses about personal appearance, but at this moment I simply need to.

Nothing has changed. A myriad of horizontal creases across the front of my skirt. A run up the nylons on my left calf. Hollows beneath my eyes and, yes, even more lines around the corners of my mouth than last time. Small, but still there if you look close. Behind me looms my own shadow on the wall; enormous, hulking, limbs long and grotesque and even rather frightening.

Perhaps I am running a temperature. I turn away from the mirror and head to the bathroom, spend fifteen fruitless minutes searching for the thermometer and then uncover an earring I thought I'd had lost. Of course by then I've forgotten what it was I was searching for. My mind is numb. I can't remember why I came in here after that phone call. Slip on my runners and tuck the laces into the shoes. If I hurry, Maggie might still be awake. I can check and see if there are any lights on and then knock on the back door. She won't mind. She never turns in early. She'll be in the kitchen likely, baking or cleaning floors with Pine Sol.

Sure enough at Maggie's house there are lights on in the living room and kitchen. I tap at the door very gently, twice, and wait. A full minute later Maggie opens the door, just a crack. She squints out at me, face anxious and full of shadows.

"Clarice, for heaven's sake girl. You scared the hell out of me. I thought I'd heard something at the door, but then it was so late I thought it must be cats or something. I was just going to check the doors were locked before turning in. Usually Paul does, but tonight…"

"Sorry Maggie," I say, suddenly wishing very much that I hadn't come at all. What has possessed me? What am I going to tell her anyway? That I lied about the bar Friday night? That I met some strange guy there and we've now made a date to go out to dinner? That I am not the person she thinks I am? "I thought you'd still be awake."

"Well yes," she says, looking over her shoulder, "but Paul's gone to bed already ages ago, and the kids are asleep too, I imagine. But come in and have a drink and we'll talk. I take it that's why you're here. You need to talk. Is something wrong? Is it Frank again?"

I'm almost tempted to say I better just go back home, that there is nothing I need to say. But it's too late. I follow her into the kitchen feeling foolish and sit down. She pulls out a chair across from me and sits down heavily, folding her legs underneath her. She is in a dressing gown; hair pulled back for the night in a terrycloth hair band which matches the shade of her nightgown precisely. Her face is not all done up in cream, and if there are wrinkles, they are not in any way noticeable. She looks quite perfect, as though already showered and rested and fresh for a new day.

"So," she says, breathlessly, "what's up? What in the world brings you here at this time of night?"

"It's not that late," I say, trying to sound offhand. Maybe if I adopt a devil-may-care attitude from now on, people will believe it; perhaps I will even start to believe it myself. "I just wanted to talk. Thanks by the way for the muffins and the note and for cleaning up. You didn't have to you know."

"I know. I wanted to. Did Frank show up?"

"Maybe I should just let him move back in, Maggie. Maybe I should give him a chance."

"Surely you're not serious, Clarice," she says. A look settles on her face as though she thinks I am a foolish small child and that I need to be handled like one. But at least I've turned the conversation to new waters. I've changed my mind about telling her. And now at least I don't have to mention Richard and try to explain everything. She thinks I've come here to talk about Frank.

Richard. Panic begins to set in. How will I manage it? A real dinner date. It will be quiet and formal and there will be candles and good food, and he will be expecting me to act like a normal, ordinary woman on a date. Like the first Clarice: young, eager, self-confident, willing to take risks.

"The thought of you and Frank getting back together is absolutely insane. You're crazy you know, Clarice. Totally off your rocker."

I look away, push my chair back a little from the table. Love is a kind of temporary insanity, isn't it? It only lasts a short while though. One wakes up soon enough. As though humans weren't meant to experience that kind of happiness for very long, at least not here on earth in this existence. In time, life kind of drags that sort of insanity out of you in little pieces. Or, worse: it shatters it completely in one short, horrible instant.

I let out a huge breath of air. The kitchen smells of Italian food, something spicy and saucy. I sniff and find myself suddenly enormously hungry. I've had little to eat all day. Dry toast this morning, an apple and a banana at lunch at the store, and then that rock-hard muffin just before Richard called. Nothing else but cold coffee all day.

"You know your cat's been here a lot lately. Showed up again today at lunchtime. Not that I mind, really," Maggie says. "He's such a sweetie. I said *Cookie, Cookie,* and he came right up to me and let me scratch behind his ears. I'll have to put cream out with little bits of bread for him again so he doesn't starve."

"I'm dead tired Maggie. I just can't sleep. And there's something I need to do that I should tell you about."

But she is not listening. Looking around the kitchen as though contemplating the dinner menu for tomorrow night. Perhaps noting a stray cobweb up there in one corner that needs attending to.

"He likes to be called Cookie. It suits him. I think he might have ear mites though. I checked, and it's all black and grubby in there. Don't you take him to the vet at all?"

"He's been to the vet many times. Really, Maggie, you make me sound like a criminal."

"Are you hungry?" she says. "You look so thin these days. Way too thin and so pale. You don't take care of yourself, Clarice. Do you want me to get you something to eat?"

I am about to say *Yes, yes, I'm starving. I'll have some of whatever it was you made for supper. Italian food. Loads of it: big steaming, parmesan-cheese-covered platefuls of it.* But at that moment there is a sharp noise and then a click.

Paul is suddenly standing there blinking in the light. He is naked, aside from a very short, tight, shiny black g-string affair with big pink lips printed all over it. Right over the crotch and written in florescent green letters are the words KISS ME. He squints at us, one hand up to his eyes to shield them from the light, the other fluttering down self-consciously to his crotch.

"That you, Maggie? I swore I could hear something out here. Voices." He looks at me with eyes half-closed, limply, as though I am just a really bad dream that is about to dissolve momentarily.

I stare stupidly at his groin, trying not to look but unable to draw my eyes away. It's just not the kind of thing one would imagine someone sensible like Paul ever wearing. I'd have sooner thought he'd wear a pair of lacy woman's undergarments than this absurd little thing. Does Maggie mind? I expect she does. I can't imagine fastidious, fashionable Maggie giving him something like that. *Liking* something like that. Not even for a joke. She doesn't have that kind of sense of humour at all.

"I haven't slept a wink," Paul says. "Not one minute. Not one second even. There's some damned, stupid cat howling outside the window again."

***

Twenty-five minutes later I find my way down the little path I made at the cemetery. It is another dark, dark night. I walk slowly, as lightly as possible, placing my feet carefully one in front of the other and trying not to make a single sound. My feet find their way easily over the big roots that reach across the path, and I do not stumble even once.

The headstones emerge rapidly from the darkness. Familiar now, like family. The night is absolutely quiet. I wish I could hear something: music or some kind of traffic noise from town even. But all is still. Still as death if you will, and I sit down again, wide awake, alert to even the smallest sound or movement, and wait patiently for morning.

-23-

"So," Richard says, leaning towards me, "what do you think of this place? Nice, isn't it?"

What can I say? It's gorgeous of course, very elegant. Small and intimate, tucked into a corner of Milan I've never even seen before. Not that I come to Milan very often. Likely Maggie has been here with her theatre friends before. I'll have to figure out some way to ask her.

So far I've made no critical mistakes. I've managed to walk from the door to the table without lurching in my shoes and we are now safely seated, like any ordinary couple on a date. Richard appears relaxed and comfortable, much more so than when he was at my house. I wonder whether he has had a drink already at home before coming to pick me up. Something to take the edge off. Why didn't I think of it?

"Wonderful," I say and smile at him. "It's so nice of you to suggest coming here. Much nicer than Sunny's, for sure."

"Wait until you try the food." He picks up a menu, begins skimming through.

I pick mine up as well, but I can't concentrate. Flip through it uneasily and turn to the back. There is a list of desserts as long as my arm. And my goodness, how expensive. It sounds as if he's been here many times. Appears to know the menu well, referred to the waiter who seated us by name, even asked for a specific table here by the window without first looking around the room.

"I think I'll have the swordfish," he says, closing his menu briskly and placing it at the side of his plate.

Just like a man to come up with something that fast. Every man is capable of making split decisions when it comes to food. I, on the other hand, can't make up my mind at all, pore over the stir-fry options again and again. Emu or wild boar? I should be more blasé, offhand. Handle my menu carelessly. Instead I bite on my lip and flip back and forth through the pages without any idea of what I want at all, gripping the plastic cover so hard I leave dents.

Glancing up over the top of my menu, I can't help but stare. Something about his eyes and the way he looks at me and says nothing. I can't explain it. My heart is beating fast in my chest. I can feel it thumping hard, erratic.

What is he thinking? What in heaven's name could he possibly be thinking about? A strand of hair falls from my updo and I push at it impatiently trying to tuck it back in.

"You might try the shrimp," Richard is saying, taking a long drink of beer and looking out the window to his left. "It's really very good. Or the marlin. Marinated in olive oil and fresh herbs. Grilled lightly. Sublime."

"You've been here often before then?" I squirm a little. The chair feels hard and narrow and I try to sit up straighter and tuck my dress down around my knees.

"Oh yes, but it's been a couple of years at least, I would think. Place hasn't changed though. It's a pretty popular place around here."

He rubs his hands lightly over his temples. It almost looks as though he's stifling a yawn. Maybe he's bored with me already. I have let him down. He is expecting someone more witty, someone who talks a lot and has stories to tell. Someone charming and sophisticated like Maggie. I imagine Maggie sitting here fingering a long strand of pearls and smiling up at him, hair smoothly parted and swept back, telling him some amusing story about scuba diving down in the Cayman Islands or about acting the part of Silia Gala in a Luigi Pirandello play. Which one was it now that she was so proud of? I strain for a moment trying to recall the name, but it eludes me. Stupid that I can't remember anything at all these days. Mind is porous as sand.

A waiter arrives bearing water glasses and wine. I gulp at my glass of beer. Richard is already finished his and handles his wineglass with expert hands, holding it up to breathe in the bouquet.

"Rules of the Game," I say, suddenly remembering the name of the Pirandello play. I glance up at Richard, but he hasn't heard me. He is now sipping his wine, cupping the glass in both hands, absorbed in his own thoughts and glancing every now and again out the window to his left.

Rules of the Game. That's it, isn't it?? Just a game, all of it? He thinks we are both abiding by the rules of the game, saying what people are expected to say when they go out on a date for the first time. He doesn't know it yet. For us the rules do not apply and this is certainly not a game.

"You look great tonight, Clarice. "Really nice."

"Thanks," I say. "You look very handsome yourself. Maybe I should have worn something more formal." I glance around me. Everyone is dressed up. That lady at the table next to us has an expensive gold necklace as thick as my little finger. I am wearing a simple black dress. No jewelry aside from small silver earrings. My hair, which I tried to do the same as last Friday night, has not turned out this time at all. There are little bits and pieces falling down already at the back and sides, and here with dinner not even served.

"Oh no," Richard is saying. "You're perfect."

Pat at my hair gently, attempt to tuck more stray pieces behind my ears.

"Did you know I'm divorced," I say, shoving aside my beer and picking up my wineglass. "A few years ago now. It just didn't work out. He and I, his name was Frank, we made a lot of mistakes. We just couldn't make it work together. You never asked, but I thought you should know." I wish at once that I'd said it differently, broached the subject more casually. Maybe I should've waited until after dinner, until we knew one another a little better and felt more at ease.

"I knew it from the moment I saw you last Friday. I said to myself, I bet that girl was married before, or at least engaged or something. I imagined you got married in high school, maybe, when you were really young. Anyhow, I just had this feeling. How could an attractive, smart woman like you not be taken already? I just knew it. I knew if you were single it had to be that you were married before and only recently on your own."

I anticipated he'd be surprised, shocked even. I could've told him at the bar, or at least at my house. I could have said, Richard, *I was married before. I'm divorced. I have a history, baggage. I'm not the person you think I am. You probably don't want to become involved with someone like me, with so much behind them, with so much failure in their past.*

"So, what about you?" I say quickly. "What is a smart, good-looking guy like you doing single? I thought the same about you when we first talked. Surely there must be a hundred women out there chasing after someone like you. Surely this man must be married or at least must have been married before at least once."

He raises his eyebrows, begins cutting his bun and spreading butter carefully on both sides. His hands are white, as though he hasn't been outside very much lately. The fingernails are very short and trim and clean.

"Definitely not. Certainly not a hundred." He turns toward the waiter who has arrived with our salads. "I've changed my mind. Could I maybe have some soup and the marlin instead of the swordfish? That would be perfect. Clarice, will you have some soup as well?"

"Oh no, not for me," I say a little breathlessly. "I'll have lots to eat with this enormous salad and the shrimp. It's probably a huge plateful anyway. I won't be able to manage soup as well."

He is wearing a suit tonight, deep navy, almost black, and an expensive-looking silk tie, and he looks quite attractive, much more noticeable than before.

"So you haven't been married before?" I say, reaching for my water and swallowing a big mouthful that hurts going down. "Or engaged?" Prying, false. I should just let it drop but I need to know. I need to see how he reacts.

"Oh, I've dated some," he says. "But not for a while. It's been so busy for me this past year or two with the magazine. I haven't had much time for anything, much less going out. Concentrated on my career. My social life, you could say, ground to an enormous halt."

I feel I am treading on forbidden ground. Something inaccessible. Some line I cannot or should not cross. I should leave it alone. We eat for a while without saying anything.

Frank and I, as close as we were in other ways, could never go to a restaurant without quarrelling. Once when we went to Toronto with Douglas and Margaret, we argued about which wine to order. It ruined the whole evening. Frank wanted a bottle of white for us all. He kept saying you have to order white with fish, but Douglas clearly wanted red. I told Frank it was ridiculous to order a whole bottle of their most expensive white if no one else wanted it but him. I don't know what came over me that night. When the waiter came, I didn't even give Frank a chance. I told the waiter to bring a glass of white for Frank, and a bottle of the house red for the rest of us. Frank was furious.

I remember he stood up then and took off for the washroom, still wearing his dinner napkin tucked into the belt of his pants. When he came back he wouldn't say a word to me. Normally he treats Margaret like she doesn't exist, but this time he turned his full attention on her, asking her all about her niece's new house and listening attentively throughout the whole meal. When we got up to leave, he ignored me, took Margaret's arm and escorted her to the door, helped her on with her coat even. And I, nervous as a foal, ran guiltily after them, sick at heart, trying to make it up with Frank and forgetting my purse under the table.

"You're probably still wondering why I showed up at your house on the weekend," Richard is saying. He puts his fork down carefully and looks at me. There is a deep black rim around the outside of those pale gray eyes. And dark shadows around the nose and under the eyes.

When he examines me like this, quite literally dissecting, I admit it's difficult to look away. I feel strange inside. For one brief insane instant, I wish that I could suddenly pull off all his clothes, one by one, watching all the while those intense, gray eyes with the deep black rings.

I look away. Squirm in my chair, taking another deep swallow of water. The back of my neck and forehead feel damp. *He knows.*

"Not really," I say, wiping at my forehead with the back of my hand and resisting the urge to glance back up at his face. "I was really glad you stopped in. And thank you again for the magazine. It's great."

The waiter brings Richard's soup along with our entrees and for a few minutes we busy ourselves with cutting meat and chewing and swallowing. Richard begins to eat his soup.

I watch him, stealing surreptitious little looks every now and again. I bet this isn't the first time he's sat here this way in this same restaurant sipping his soup and drinking wine with some woman. He has forgotten me; he is lost in the past remembering someone else, someone familiar. Maybe it's the lack of sleep for so long, but for one chilling moment I am overcome with this terrifying and absurd thought that I am *Her*, that I've somehow forgotten and I've just always been *Her* and we've always come here like this.

She is sitting here across from him, eating her swordfish and discussing the wine and a concert they will see tonight after dinner. They will debate an article they've read together in a magazine, a complex political issue. Her long hair is curling around bare shoulders and she is smiling as in the photograph, certain in the knowledge that her companion loves her. The perfect, happy couple. I can see it all very clearly. Pick up my water glass and spin it around idly, for a few moments drowsy and only half-aware that he is across from me.

"It was something you said the other night, at the bar," Richard is saying, drawing me back. "That's why I wanted to talk to you again, why I showed up at your house, believe it or not. It was something you said about what you liked to read, about Dostoyevsky and the firing squad. About if you faced a firing squad and came so close to death you could never be the same person again. I kept thinking about that. I even dreamed about it every night since then. I realized I've been drifting this past while in sort of a haze, too busy and too involved in my work to think about anything else. But then after our conversation the other night it was like I finally woke up again. I know it sounds ridiculous, like some stupid line, but I went home and started to think about what you said and realized I wanted to talk to you again. You see, Clarice, you're so different from anyone I've ever met."

He pushes away the soup bowl and reaches for his plate

of fish. I look down at my shrimp, shoving it from side to side with my fork. Lift my wineglass to my lips, realize it's empty and set it back down on the table. I have misjudged him. He was listening. I thought he was just being polite, just nodding and watching those people behind us and not thinking at all. Even Dostoyevsky.

"I'm glad I saw you there," I say. I can't think of anything else. Fortunately two people have come into the restaurant and he isn't listening. He's inspecting them. A man and a woman. I recognize the man right away. The one from the bar, the one who was sitting with Richard at Sunny's on Friday night. The other is perhaps the nagging girlfriend?

Please don't look this way; don't notice us. Please, please, please just go away.

But Richard gets up instantly, motions vigorously to them with one hand so they see us right off and come over quickly, followed by a waiter who walks directly behind them twisting a napkin in his hands.

Was this prearranged?

"Well hello. I can't believe you're here," the girl says, addressing Richard. She is short and bosomy, with beautiful olive skin and curly dark hair. "This is just amazing." She glances my way and I stand up quickly.

Amazed to find him here with me? Maybe she knows the other woman in his life. Maybe she has even met *Her.* I picture them together, life-long best friends who go out for pedicures together, tennis every week and lunch out on Fridays. What will she tell her the next time she sees her, or will she call tonight? *You won't believe who we saw Richard with tonight. I mean don't worry or anything. She was probably just some girl he works with. And she wasn't much to look at, believe you me. Kind of old too. Still, I thought you'd want to know. . .better have a talk with that guy of yours. . .*

"I know, small world," Richard is saying. "I can't believe we'd meet up with you two here of all places."

He sounds genuinely surprised, but not at all unhappy to see them. And he does not look guilty or shamefaced in any way.

Richard's friend laughs and glances at me, a strange look on his face, as though thrust into an awkward situation and not knowing what to say next.

"So, aren't you going to introduce us?" He reaches over and holds out his hand for me to shake. I take it, pump once and let go as quickly as possible. He is very interested. He wants a name.

"This is Clarice Forrest. Clarice, this is my friend Bob and this is Lisa. Here, have a seat." Richard motions to an empty table next to us.

The waiter, still hovering in the background, pulls out a chair for Lisa, begins bustling about replacing plates and cutlery. Bob and Lisa sit down, but turn their chairs toward us when we sit down again ourselves. Evidently they are planning to join us for the rest of the night. So much for well-laid plans.

"So this is the girl you've been hiding from us all this time, you old devil," Bob says, leaning over to give Richard's arm a shove with his elbow. He is clearly kidding around, but Richard looks away unsmiling. This comment, innocent enough, appears to have annoyed him a great deal.

"You could hardly say I've been hiding her," he says, folding his napkin neatly. "We've only just met."

"Oh that's sweet," says Lisa moving a little closer to me, "Bob and I've been going out for years and years, decades. We were high school sweethearts." She looks over at him and they exchange a meaningful glance. I feel guilty that I've seen this look between them and am suddenly irrationally jealous. Their evident ease with one another. They sit together, knees touching, his one hand lightly pressed over hers. They look as though they've belonged together forever, like a cup and saucer that fit neatly together, incomplete when apart. They even look alike, more like siblings than lovers: both olive-skinned, brown-eyed with perfect, regular features. He is perhaps older though, with almost completely gray hair.

"So how do you and Richard know each other?" I say to Bob.

Bob grimaces. "Oh we've been friends for ages, from way back. Played football together. Also family friends you could say."

Richard has flagged down our waiter and is ordering more wine. He looks at no one, an inscrutable expression on his face. "Do you two want some wine or do you want something else first?" This to Bob.

"You know Lisa and I, we'd rather drink beer." Bob grins at me. He and Richard begin to talk about football, a game they saw somewhere together. Lisa is wearing an enormous gold locket around her neck. Picture? Lock of hair? My eyes are drawn to it again and again.

"Nice place, isn't it? I love it here, not that we've come very often. It's so expensive." She looks around and smiles, raising her eyebrows. She has a beautiful nose: long and narrow and perfectly shaped. "So how did you two meet?" This very quietly, to me alone. She is very, very interested.

"Oh a bar in Hope." How awful that must sound. I'm that kind of a woman. I wish, suddenly, that Lisa and I were good friends already, that we'd known each other for many years, that this whole business of getting to know each other was long since over. "We were both just there for a drink and we just sort of started talking."

She smiles again and pats Bob's hand. "That's wonderful. Richard is a very nice guy, you know. So is Bob, I have to say. He and I met in church a long, long time ago. He was in the church choir and I used to sit there in the pew with my parents and stare at him during the sermon. He looked so cute and angelic in that white choir robe, and so incredibly handsome, I had trouble concentrating on the priest. Of course he was only a teenager then and I was quite a few years younger, but I was definitely in love from that moment on. So we've been living together for aeons now, and we're finally getting married, I think." She laughs and glances over at him. "Neither one of us has been all too keen to get settled down and all that, but we're finally going to do it next summer. Maybe."

"Wow," I say. "Imagine that. You met in church."

She reaches into a tiny black purse, pulls out a wallet, flipping it open neatly, as though she does this often. "There. There's a picture of us when we were first dating."

It's hard to see. The paper is quite old and creased and both of them look like mere children, but when I peer at it closely I can see that, yes, it is them after all. The two of them, together in miniature, his hair a little longer and of course without the gray, and her dark curls cropped short.

Our drinks arrive and Bob and Lisa order dinner. I stir the remaining food around on my plate, take a few tentative bites, but taste nothing. Somehow the arrival of Bob and Lisa has depressed me. I should be happy to meet his friends. But they are a part of Richard's life. I am an intruder, simply watching from the sidelines. My thoughts have become confused and I'm not sure what I'm feeling anymore. They turn their chairs a little more so they can see us better, and the three of them begin to talk about mutual acquaintances.

I take a bite of shrimp, stare moodily across the room at an old couple at a table by the window drinking their cups of tea together. The old lady's thin, white hair is combed into a youthful ponytail, although she'd be eighty if she's a day. They must have brought their own cups, which are tiny and very colourful. Surely they didn't get those here. What would a waiter say if someone came in the door bearing his own teacups? Sorry sir. No personal teacups permitted.

Glance at my watch. Already half-past eight.

"Why don't you two come over to our place for a drink after dinner?" Bob is saying. "It isn't that far from here at all."

"Oh yes, we'd love that," Lisa says, turning again to me. "Although it's a bit of a mess. You two could go for a walk or something if you're finished your dinner and then join us at our house, say about ten or ten-thirty. I'm sure we'll be done by then. Give us a minute to get home and clean up a bit."

We say our good byes and get up and leave. Richard slips his arm through mine and we walk quite companionably together. Evidently he's done this before, seems to know the way around this part of the city very well. He strides along rapidly as though not even thinking about the direction at all. I try to think of a way to steer the conversation back to our discussion before Bob and Lisa arrived, but somehow I can't find the right words and the mood has been lost.

"So tell me something. Does it bother you much that I was married before, that I'm divorced?"

"Of course not." But he has let go of my arm and pushed both hands down deep into his pockets. He is not thinking about me at all.

"Why should it bother me?" he says. "Anyone can make a mistake in life. God knows I've made a few hundred thousand myself. Every day I think about how much I have to regret. Besides which, I think I like you better that way. I don't think

I want to go out with a woman who thinks she's perfect, who hasn't made a few errors in judgement along the way."

I don't know how to answer him so we both walk on in silence. I try to match my steps to his, but this is very awkward. His are so much longer than mine, and he is walking very fast. Every now and then I must take a silly little hopping step just to keep up.

"Are you as tired as I am?" he says suddenly.

"Yes, some."

Those dark circles around my eyes. He must have noticed them. Permanent now, I would think.

"How about I call Bob and Lisa then, leave a message that we're not coming? There's a phone booth just up ahead at that variety store on the corner. I'll tell them we're beat and we've changed our minds. We could stop by their place some other time, and I could take you home."

He really does look exhausted, but I'm a little disappointed that he wants this date to end already. I have to admit some part of me has enjoyed it, or at least I was enjoying it until his friends arrived. Just being out again and talking to him like that, our dinner together. At times I almost forgot why it was I was sitting with him, almost lost sight of my plans.

At any rate, we will go out again. I know it. This will not end here. And although I don't know exactly how I will go about settling the score, I will find a way. That much is certain. I will make him remember.

-24-

I follow him through town. Then wait until I see him pull into the park before stopping my car on the side of the road. He is already parked and is walking down the main trail by the time I get out, and I have to run hard to catch up.

"Richard. Is that you?" I yell this ridiculous question at him from a quite a distance and wave my arms when he turns to look. *Irritation? Displeasure? Suspicion?*

"I can't believe it's you," I say, jogging up to him and laying a perspiring hand on his arm. "I come here all the time and I've never seen you before. Ever." I am quite literally gasping for air and have trouble talking clearly. It's been a long time since I've run this hard and evidently it's no longer so effortless for someone as old as I am.

"Do you, Clarice?" he says slowly. "Maybe you just didn't notice me before. I'm not a very noticeable person."

"On the contrary," I say very loudly, "I'd have noticed you right away, trust me. You are very noticeable to me."

"You going for a walk?" he says.

"Yes, sure."

"Well good then. I'll join you if you like. Here, this way. I always walk down this path. It goes right out of town and through the fields along the bush. I like it because no one seems to know about it and you hardly meet a soul. It's not that rough for jogging either. I've tried it a number of times."

"Great," I say. "Fine. I'd love that."

We walk together for a while in silence. It is a beautiful day. One of those summer days where it is truly hot and the sky is filled with that soft, moist hazy kind of light. The leaves on the trees appear to move a little as we pass by although there doesn't seem to be even the smallest breath of wind. I sense, almost feel in my bones, the growth of the trees around me and the grass under my feet. Everything is rushing toward maturity, headlong, before the nights grow sharp and cool and life is buried again in the snow. Everything still, so still.

"Tell me, what was he like, this husband of yours?" Richard says finally, after we've walked together like this for some time, close together, but not touching. "Or maybe you don't like to talk about it."

"Oh no, I don't care," I say. "It doesn't bother me at all. You can ask me whatever you like. I guess the best way to describe Frank is to say he's a really good person. Kind, considerate, smart. Pretty good-looking too."

"He sounds like some kind of a god. So what happened?"

I hesitate a moment. It isn't easy to explain. Everybody likes Frank. I'll admit he's a very likeable person. So open and willing to share his thoughts. So easy-going and cheerful and careless with life. The kind of person who is always smiling when he talks to you, regardless of the topic of conversation. One of those smiles that comes unbidden when speaking to anyone; that shows his teeth right back to the last molars. And a lighthearted sort of manner about him that attracts people. The kind of guy who'd offer a stranger a beer in a bar, just because the stranger looked a bit down on his luck. It is only Maggie who ever seemed on edge around him. Maggie and perhaps myself.

"We just couldn't live together anymore. We became strangers, he and I. That is, I became someone different, not the person he married and it wasn't fair to him. There was no going back to the way it was. Sometimes things happen between two people."

"People change."

"Yes, they do. They have to."

We come to a little clearing. Sit down in the grass, stretch out our feet. I reach down and begin to untie one shoe, slip it off and rub at my foot. The heels are still very tender. We sit quietly for a while. It doesn't matter. At this point, I am no longer ill at ease with him. I feel drowsy and relaxed and very tired. On the verge of falling asleep even. He leans back a little, resting his weight on his hands, a peculiar detached quality about him that I have noticed before. I settle back in the grass, begin picking the bark off a fallen branch and ripping it in little strips. I am glad he isn't questioning me any further about Frank. I don't want to go back there anymore. Back into the past. I want to let it go. And for some reason I don't want Richard to know any more than what I've already told him about Frank.

"You will have to excuse my friends butting in on our dinner. Their intentions were good. They just feel obligated to watch out for me."

A little odd, the way he phrases this, as though he isn't old enough to watch out for himself.

"Tell me more about yourself." he says looking over at me. "Tell me what it was like growing up. Did you grow up around here?"

Despite everything, I find myself telling him little bits and pieces, memories from long ago. About mother, how she scolded us with our toys and how rigid she was about mealtimes. Breakfast at seven, lunch at twelve, supper at six. Had to be so. My sisters, how different we were from each other. How Martha would steal my books and hide them outside. How Jennifer tried to sneak a kitten into the house and managed to keep it in her room for three whole days until mother found out. Why we went our separate ways once we were grown and how I've come to see my relationship with my sisters. How I miss them at times. And the parents I loved. The closeness between them. Mother's death. It all comes out unhurriedly, easily, spontaneously. He has a way of asking the right questions, of speaking quietly, of looking over at me with such an expression in his eyes that I feel he is truly understanding. A way of not saying anything sometimes and just looking up into my face so that I feel it is fitting to tell him things, to keep talking. Even about Frank. It just comes out, although I had just told myself I didn't want to tell him more. And me, leaning back, tearing at the grass all around me, talking and talking. Little bits of grass falling into the bushes behind me until the space around me is just bare dirt. And I begin to feel a little peace for the first time in a long, long while.

Later, when I look down at my watch and see that we've been sitting here more than two hours, I leap anxiously to my feet. The sun has gone behind a big front of clouds, the air is suddenly cold, and I have to run to keep up with Richard walking fast and silent back to his truck.

-25-

Snip, snip, snip. The long strands fall against my cheeks and down to the floor. Like the pieces of the letter that fell one by one while I, lips pressed together, watched and swept them quickly into the fire.

The hairdresser brushes up close with plentiful hips and cuts again, steps back to survey her work, taking my chin in her hands and turning my head first one way then the other.

"That short enough?"

The face looking back from the mirror is not my own. There is something comforting in this thought. I have changed these last few weeks then.

"Well, I'm not sure. But it's nice. Real nice."

"How about the sides?"

She doesn't wait for an answer but picks up the scissors again and begins snipping at the sides and around back. I'm not certain whether it's too late to object now without sounding foolish so I say nothing, stare at the back of the head reflected in the mirror, wait for her to complete the masterpiece.

"Do you think I need more conditioning?" I say.

She stops a moment, surveys my head, picks up a fistful of hair in each hand and scrunches a few times. Wrinkles up her nose.

"No. It's fine. Just needs a good cut. Looks like somebody took a hacksaw to your head. You didn't try and do it yourself, did you? And make sure you blow-dry it with a big round brush. You got a big round brush like this?" She holds up the tool for me to see, sticks a couple of hair clips in her mouth. "You need the right amount of hair gel too. Like this." She squeezes the stuff out into her palm and holds it up close. Rubs both hands together and scrunches here and there.

"Oh gosh no. It grows uneven and it's been ages since I've had it cut."

"Hmm." she says, clips still in her mouth. She begins fiddling with the scissors again, pulling hair from the side of my head down to the bottom of my jaw and comparing it to the other.

"Just wanted a change, a real change. Got tired of growing out the bangs, you know what I mean?"

I can't believe how much I'm talking. This hairdresser is new. I've never seen her here before, but then I haven't been in to have my hair done in a long time either. Normally when I'm at a hairdresser's I say nothing. Today I just can't seem to keep my mouth shut.

"Uh huh," she says, pulling the clips out of her mouth and sticking them into my hair at the back. "Just got mine cut last week. After spending the whole winter with it hanging in my eyes, I finally decide to give up on it. You know? The whole winter. And for what?"

***

When I get home there is a message on my new answering machine.

The first thing I did this morning before my hair appointment was to go out and buy one. It wasn't much to get it set up. I was surprised at myself. I thought it would take me all day: a huge manual to read in six different languages. But Maggie stopped by and showed me how to do it and it took no time at all. Apparently she and Paul have had one for years. Only goes to show how long it's been since I've telephoned her house.

The first words on my new machine are from Richard. The message is very short.

Hello Clarice. It's Richard. I'm at the office. Some problems here. Should take most of the day but I'll call you when I get home late this afternoon. Probably around four-thirty or five.

I play the recording several times listening closely to his voice, trying hard to read any nuances. His voice has become so familiar this last little while and at first I really can't hear any expression at all, but then, after listening five or six times, it seems he sounds a little downcast. I expect this news from work has annoyed him; something isn't going well. Or maybe calling me was an obligation he wished to clear away before starting his day, like taking out the garbage.

If Richard should stop by later this afternoon I'd better be ready. No garbage on the floor this time. Everything neat as a pin. I will look decent too, my hair freshly done like Maggie's, something flattering to wear. Heels, maybe and makeup. Lately I have begun to try a little harder.

Examine the chessboard. I am in check now. Must move the bishop again.

I begin cleaning, emptying out garbage cans and scrubbing floors. I even change the vacuum cleaner bag, which is splitting, and water the houseplants. Find a cloth and dust my antique dolls, straighten the picture in the living room, totally rearrange the birds in the front entrance.

One of the birds, a cedar waxwing, has lost her beak. I have not noticed this before. *Frank.* Plowing through with his over-stuffed suitcases and knocking the poor female waxwing over, recklessly jarring loose her beak. Then, utterly heartless, careless as always, picking up the piece and stuffing it into his pants pocket and from that moment on forgetting it forever.

But this is not being very nice. Frank is a nice person. Frank is a person I have loved and do still love in some small way. Like a forgotten toy that one finds again as an adult. A few warm feelings stir, leap awake again briefly in a small flame. But they are weak, insubstantial, fleeting. Memories only.

The doorbell rings and I confront on my front porch, dressed in a tailored cream suit with matching purse held stiffly under one arm, Frank's mother, Dinny.

"Well, hello," I say, pulling the door open a little wider. It's been years since I've seen my ex-mother-in-law, so surely I can be forgiven for the look of bewilderment bordering on panic that instantly glues itself to my face. "Sorry to just stand here and stare," I say. "You just totally bowled me over. Come on in. I can't believe it's you after all this time."

"Hello Clarice." She steps in and slowly surveys her surroundings. "So how are you my dear?" Long meaningful glance at my face. "Well for heaven's sake," She raises her eyebrows at my collection of wooden birds, "you really shouldn't make yourself such a stranger. I thought for sure you'd have stopped in to see us by now. We don't really live all that far away you know. We've moved again. I'm sure Frankie must have told you."

"I don't think so actually. I'd no idea. Frank never said."

"Well," she says, unbuttoning her suit jacket, "you look like you're doing okay anyway. And your hair looks very nice that way, dear. Since I was driving through town to see a friend I decided I just had to check in on my little Clarice."

Little Clarice. She's never called me such a thing before. Ever. In fact, I don't remember anyone ever calling me that. Not even Mother. Hidden agenda? It isn't long before I discover exactly what it is.

"It's really about Frank that I wanted to see you," Dinny says, leaning closer so I catch a good nose full of expensive perfume. "I'm really rather worried about him."

"Well. Come on into the kitchen. I was just busy with cleaning so things are a bit of a mess, but come in and have a coffee anyway."

I push aside bottles of cleaners and scrub brushes, and begin measuring out coffee. Silence for a full minute. If Dinny has something to say she'd better come right out with it. I set the coffee mugs on the table and sit down across from her. She's folded her hands and is looking around the room at my things. Her ash-blonde hair is shorter and lighter and she looks thinner, which suits her well. But she is definitely very pale. You can see that even through the carefully applied foundation. And there are a score of vertical lines above her upper lip and around her mouth that have added years and a hard-bitten look to her face.

"I like what you've done to the kitchen."

Stalling.

"Actually," I say, getting up for cream and sugar, "I haven't really done anything with the kitchen for years and years. I imagine it looks just the way it did when you last saw it." I am not going to make things any easier for her.

"I haven't been here for so long, I guess I've just forgotten."

"True enough." The coffeemaker begins to make loud gurgling noises and we both turn to look at it. "Yes, I imagine you have forgotten. How is Michael anyway?"

"Oh Michael's fine," she says. "A bit of a problem with blood pressure recently, a tad high, but nothing to worry about at any rate. He's supposed to watch his cholesterol too, but you can't tell him that of course. Butter on everything. Three eggs for breakfast. That sort of thing. Men are all the same."

"And Frank? What's so wrong with Frank all of a sudden that you came here after all this time to see me about him?"

"Well Frank's getting married, Clarice dear. I guess you

didn't know. Sorry to shock you like that. But it was very, very sudden as you can imagine. I hope you're not too upset."

Upset? I admit I am quite surprised and it must show on my face. After all, Frank made no mention of any other woman when he was staying here with me. And that wasn't so long ago at all. Not a word about another woman the last time I saw him either.

"Maybe I shouldn't have come," she says. "I know you haven't been married to Frank for a long time. But I know how much you still must care for him, and I'm sure you'd always wish what was best for him and try to help him whenever you could. I just thought..."

She looks up at me and I am amazed to see she is close to tears.

"You were a very good wife to our Frankie. I know we didn't always see eye to eye, but I was terribly upset when you decided to split up. When Frankie came back to stay here and you were obviously back together again, I thought...we had such high hopes..."

"You thought we were actually getting back together for good? Really, Dorinda, you must've realized that was out of the question. So tell me, who's this lucky girl Frank is going to wed? Funny, I never thought he'd get married again."

"She doesn't live here in town. The fact is, she's not someone Douglas and I are very happy about."

"Douglas? You're still in touch with him then?" I glance at her over my mug. Dinny and Douglas had not parted on the best of terms and as far as I knew, rarely spoke to one another.

"Oh yes. Douglas and I have talked ourselves hoarse on the telephone a number of times lately. He's still our son after all, and Douglas is of the same opinion I am, which is that this girl, this old woman, Janet, is not in any way suitable. For one thing she's divorced, twice, and she's got four children with at least three different men. It's all come about so suddenly. They hardly know each other. In fact I think he'd only just starting going out with her just before he showed up here on your doorstep. A matter of months only. Maybe six at the most. A dreadful mistake if you ask me."

Caesar emerges from the basement stairs and saunters by, tail waving slowly. He sits down in front of his dish and begins to eat greedily, spilling food all over the floor. Dinny and I both turn and look at him.

"He's getting fat," I say. "He needs more exercise."

"And it's not just the girl. Frank's been drinking too, quite heavily. His business isn't going well at all. And Doug and Margaret, despite their heaps of money, won't lift a finger. Typical, isn't it? Michael and I, of course, have helped him out all we can, but..."

Dinny pulls out a package of cigarettes from her purse. For some reason I don't have the heart to tell her I don't permit smoking in my house. Actually I'm quite surprised to see her with cigarettes. I thought she'd given up smoking years ago. And here she was always so fussy, washing her hands three times before supper and using the most expensive hand and face creams available. Always lecturing me about how a woman must take care of her skin.

"I thought you quit." I get up and look around the kitchen for something to use as an ashtray. It seems I've tossed out the black marble ashtray Dinny herself gave me years ago. Actually I now recall having given it to the Bishops next door for Earl's pipe. I find a tinfoil pie plate in the broom closet and slide it onto the table in front of her.

"Look Clarice," Dinny says, flicking her cigarette over the pie plate, "I can't tell you what to do, but I hope you'll at least give him a call. I know he still loves you. He talks about you every time I telephone him. He just doesn't want to be alone anymore. It's understandable, you know. A man needs to have a woman in his life. How can you be so cold-hearted?"

My feelings for Frank have died. My name may still be Clarice Forrest, but the person inside is not. People do change. It happens. You wake up one day and you're not the same. *An Act of God*, they said. But no one around you seems to understand. I can't change back, that's the trouble, which Dinny will never accept, and I suppose no one else who knew me before will either.

The telephone begins to ring. For a few seconds we both turn and stare.

Richard. What could I possibly say to Richard with her listening? There will be no end to the questions, accusations, especially in light of the news she just told me. I feel an instantaneous prick of guilt, a hot flush on my forehead and down my back.

On the fourth ring I stand up quickly and lift the receiver.

"Hello, Clarice?"

"Yes."

"Hi, how are you? It's Bob. Richard's friend Bob."

"Oh hello, I'm just fine."

"Sorry to bother you. Richard told me your last name, but I must've called four wrong numbers before I hit the right one. You'd think in a town the size of Hope it wouldn't be a big deal."

"Is there something wrong? Is it Richard? Is he okay?"

"Oh no, there's nothing wrong. I just wondered if we could get together and talk. There's a few things you need to know."

"What?" I am having trouble concentrating, understanding. Glance over at Dinny who is leaning my way and evidently listening very closely. I consider changing phones, moving to the bedroom, but she would be offended, instantly suspicious. And later she would make some comment, how I could certainly trust her not to listen in, that if I felt that way to just say so and she'd go.

"Look, I've got company right now. We could maybe talk about it later. Set up a time. An appointment. Something convenient for both of us. I can't really commit to anything right now, but I might be interested at some later date."

"There's something you need to know about Richard. Don't worry. I'm not trying to scare you off. Richard's a really really nice guy, a really good person, trust me."

Her. That's it of course. He wants to tell me Richard is already taken. Take me aside somewhere and explain to me like some little child that I can't have him. That I must give up this nonsense and go home and behave myself.

Dinny is fishing around in her purse and not looking at me. The cigarette is lying on the pie plate, half-finished and still smoldering.

"I think I know what it is you want to say. I think I can figure it out for myself. It probably isn't necessary for us to meet after all, and like I said, I've got to go. I have company right now. But thank you anyway."

I don't even wait to hear him say good-bye. Replace the receiver gently. Dinny is already getting up and heading for the front door.

"I'm sorry to keep you," she says with a small laugh. "I can see you're busy. I wouldn't want you to be thinking of me as the interfering mother-in-law still."

She holds out a hand. Should I be giving her a hug or kissing her cheek? She is, after all, my former mother-in-law. Not former in her eyes apparently. Once she claims ownership of a person there's no getting away. I reach for her hand and shake it, dropping it as quickly as I dare.

"I'm sorry about Frank," I say. "Maybe I can call him sometime. But I don't think there's anything I can do for him. I'm just not the person to ask."

"Oh Clarice," she says, opening the door and looking up at me with big wounded sorrowful eyes. "Oh but you're so wrong about that. You are the one person in this whole world who can do something for him. Only you can save him."

And with that ridiculous closing comment, as though he were on the brink of some towering precipice and about to stumble to his death, she shuts the door.

It isn't until I've returned to the kitchen and begin clearing away the tinfoil ashtray, the coffee mugs and the sugar and cream, that I glance up at the calendar, which I have finally hung up beside the fridge.

It is then that I finally remember that today is, in fact, my birthday.

-26-

I clean the rest of the day finding corners long forgotten. There are places in this house where the paint has inexplicably darkened from white to a disheartening and unappealing gray. Moldy little places where dampness has been breeding. Blackened corners with peeling paint. Mildewed bathroom tiles. The house is beginning to show its age in so many ways and I hadn't really noticed at all until today.

Another birthday. At this age celebrating a birthday alone isn't really all that bad. No one to say over the hill, getting on in years, you still look good for your age. And I don't really care one way or the other anymore. I used to care. I used to hate the idea of another year passing, or getting older. But now I am indifferent. What does it matter? I can do as I please. Drink a whole bottle of a really good wine in one sitting, eat loads of ice cream, whatever. No one to scold, no one to raise a disapproving eyebrow, no one to organize things for me.

I make myself a cabbage and ground beef casserole. Not fancy, but there isn't much in the fridge or freezer to work with. Next, I bake a cranberry banana loaf. I can't remember the last time I actually baked anything. When Frank was here he did most of the cooking and we ate rather frugal, uninspired meals, neither one of us paying much attention to cookbooks or interesting ingredients. Soup from the store, grilled cheese, sausage fried in the pan.

Once, a long time ago, we cared about all those things a lot. When we were first married we took a gourmet cooking class together. *Great Italian Pastas Even You Can Make* with fancy names like *Tagliatelle with Asparagus and Gorgonzola Sauce, Rigatoni with Avocado and Italian sausage, Canneroni with Coriander.* Every weekend we'd go down to the Farmer's Market in Milan for rye bread, vegetables, fruit, fresh pasta and seafood. Saturday night was feast night, our romantic date night with candles and wine.

I head out for a walk in town to celebrate the birthday. When I was a little girl, mother made a vanilla cake with vanilla icing and one candle, the same for each of our birthdays. We were permitted one friend to come to our parties, plus the dolls. Everyone dressed in their best with new hair ribbons and polished black shoes. After supper we all went for a walk through town to the ice cream shop for soft ice cream dipped in chocolate.

***

By the time I arrive, it is almost ten and completely dark. I get out of the car and pop a Tic-Tac into my mouth. A slice of moon appears briefly from behind the clouds, but it is still very difficult to see anything at all.

Lights flicker through tree branches as I approach the farmhouse. His truck is parked by the shed. I sit down under the trees behind the house and watch, sucking hard on one Tic-Tac after the other. I'm not certain how long it is that I sit this way, leaning against a tree, dozing, half-asleep, a Tic-Tac melting in one cheek. Then a door closes and I sit up straight, pushing my hands flat against the bark behind me. An engine starts. The lights of his truck turn, slowly illuminating the shed and then the house, then move away and disappear down the lane.

Everything is suddenly very silent again, and very cold and very dark. The lights in the house are now all off.

What if *She* is still in there, sitting silently at the kitchen table in the dark? I picture them together as they were only a few moments ago, he with his arms around her and she with her head against his shoulder on that enormous couch in the living room. And then it seems I can almost see her standing there at her bedroom window, just standing and staring down at me.

But I walk towards the house anyway. It is simple enough to find the basement window again. There is nothing to stop me from opening it just as I did before. It is easier now that I've ripped the screen a little and the nails are loose. The basement is unbelievably black. So black I feel my eyes are not really open at all. When I open the hallway door there is finally some light, but only just a little. There is no one standing there behind the door; the house is quite empty.

First I search through the kitchen drawers for a flashlight, but find only a small candle instead and a box of matches. The house looks more lived in this time. Dishes on the counter, a vase with flowers on the table, a loaf of bread, jam jars. The fridge hums, and from the other room there is the steady loud tock of a grandfather clock.

Upstairs I shove open her bedroom door and set the candle down on the little night table beside the photograph. Should I take it? Just walk out of here with it under my arm? It would be a small matter really. Perhaps no one would even notice it was gone. They would think it had been misplaced somehow, moved to another room and forgotten.

***

Fling the front door open wide and rush into the kitchen to check my new answering machine. There are four messages, all from Maggie.

Hi Clarice, it's me Maggie. Happy birthday. I've been trying to get in touch with you all day. I bought a dress for the party and I'm just dying to show it to you. I'm not sure I really like it though. I'll probably take it back, but see what you think first. I need to talk to you when you get home, so call me back. It's, um, eight-thirty. Talk to you later. Bye.

Clarice, Maggie again. Where in heaven's name are you? You're quite the wild party girl these days. Out celebrating your birthday with some new mystery man huh? So call me as soon as you get home. It's urgent. Bye.

It's me again, dearest. Paul's already gone to bed, but I'm going to stay up for a while so call me if it's before twelve. Don't forget.

Re-ah-lly Clarice. You're certainly out late again. I sure hope he's worth it. Do I sound like your mother? I really, really have to talk to you so call me first thing in the morning. Don't forget. Long pause. Oh and don't call now, I'm going to bed.

I turn the machine off and sit down at the table, dish out some casserole, now stone cold, and cut myself a piece of loaf. Caesar is asleep on top of the fridge, very close to the edge on the left side. For some reason he's decided lately that this is a good place. When Frank was here, he didn't want to sleep upstairs at all. Spent all of his time in the basement, only showing up when he absolutely had to in order to visit his food dish. Otherwise, if Frank so much as walked into a room, Caesar would disappear instantly. But as soon as Frank moved out he resurfaced, started sleeping in all his old places again: the chair in the living room, the spare room bed, under the telephone table, and now on top of the fridge next to the bananas.

Should I call Frank? To be very honest, I haven't thought about him once since Dinny left. Dinny's right. I'm terribly selfish. Maybe I ought to try and help. It wasn't a very considerate thing to do to one's ex-husband: leave him a note ordering him to get out of the house. It was actually very mean.

I cut one more piece of loaf and eat it in bed, crumbs falling. I've made up my mind. I will stay awake tonight. I will not go anywhere. Wide awake. Richard could still call. Maybe I have him all wrong. Maybe he's been trying to reach me but something terrible has happened. He could be very sick.

Or maybe he's perfectly happy. In his house in his bed. Asleep and holding *Her* in his arms.

-27-

Awake. Sunday morning and there is a storm.

Every few moments a gust of wind jars windows and rain whips the house walls. I lie back listening, almost comforted by the sound, drifting willingly back into the soothing nothingness of sleep. But only for four or five minutes and then all at once everything comes back; all the horrible images and the things I must think about. And then of course I am fully awake. It seems that, despite my intentions last night, I fell asleep after all, and this time slept the rest of the night quite soundly without once waking.

Race around the bedrooms slamming shut windows. There is also a puddle of water on the bathroom floor. A pile of laundry by the window has soaked up most of it, but I run to the kitchen anyway and grab a rag from under the sink. Caesar follows me, sits in the doorway carefully washing his feet, toes spread apart and pretending not to watch. When everything is mopped up I head outside, wander through the backyard letting the rain soak through my dressing gown, and watching the puddles grow under the yellow cedar hedge. These are the kind of mindless irrational things I find myself doing these days.

Twenty minutes later I am showered and changed into a pair of new jeans and a light pink T-shirt. Maggie tells me this colour doesn't suit me. She says I should wear primary colors only, blues and greens and deep reds. I am all washed out in pastels. But I suppose I am finally beginning to know what I like and I have always liked this colour. Today I look good in pink and to hell with Maggie the Terrier. My hair looks nice this morning, in fact. I blow dry it carefully, brush it back, running fingers through and turning from side to side in front of the bathroom mirror. I look good. I'm not sure I've felt this way in a long time, and who knows why all of a sudden. Maybe because I did not stay awake last night. In fact, I slept a good long stretch for the first time in months.

I walk back into the bedroom and examine the chess game. Move my queen again. The black queen is in a very bad position now. Bad for me, that is. I must be very careful. Very cautious. Must be sure to plan each and every step. Think of every possibility. Get myself into position for the final move and then of course, *check mate.*

As I head out the front door, I touch my pocket to see whether the letter is still there. It must be returned today. I told myself I wouldn't do this anymore. No more keeping these letters. So I have to find some way to give it back. Maybe I can toss it into the bushes under his mailbox so that it looks as though the mailman dropped it. *Choices.* The worst that could happen is he tells me I can't come in, that he isn't alone. And that isn't really so bad at all, is it?

***

It feels strange standing here on this same doorstep where I have stood so often before. This time, however, I'm completely legitimate, and I am going to knock and wait like any other normal person.

I lift my hand and knock sharply, twice. Wait a full minute and knock again. It's now raining hard and starting to soak through my good clothes. Why on earth didn't I think to put on a raincoat? He will think I've done this on purpose, arrived here on his doorstep wringing wet as some kind of turn-on so that he will have to take me in like a true Good Samaritan and offer me dry clothes. He will think I've purposely stood out in the rain, drenched myself and then showed up here; a pathetic gesture to get his attention, like a child who knocks over a lamp to provoke preoccupied parents. He will think I'm that kind of person: scheming, detestable, hard as wire

It takes several more minutes before the door finally opens. Richard in pajama bottoms and no shirt. His thick hair sticking up at the back and pushed away from his face on one side. Evidently he has just woken up.

There is a sudden hot, nervous feeling in my stomach that radiates out into my body until it reaches my fingertips. I reach up as though to fold down a collar. My fingers stop at my neck. I can't help but stare at his pajama bottoms and I can think of nothing to say.

"Clarice? Is that you?" He opens the door a little further, blinks a few times. "Jeez, what time is it? Sorry, I," Turns and looks behind him, toward the clock in the living room, scratches at his hair with one hand. "I just got up. What time is it anyway?"

"I didn't mean to wake you," I say, stepping back from the doorway. "I thought you'd likely be awake already. It's, uh, almost eight, actually."

Swipe quickly at my flattened hair, wipe at my nose with the back of my hand. There is water streaming down my face. Thank heavens I didn't bother with mascara. Thank the saints above. I feel like a schoolgirl, out of breath, pounding heart, hormonal, and fascinated with this half-naked man in front of me. I study the navel: a little bit of hair quite dark and curling. Chest smooth and almost without hair. Arms surprisingly muscular on an otherwise too-thin frame. Quick little darting glances.

"Oh," he says, looking back at his wall clock again as

though he can't quite believe it. As though he doesn't quite know whether I mean eight in the morning or eight at night. "Well come in. You're getting soaked out there. Get in here. Throw your shoes off at the door and come in. I'll make some coffee. Warm you up. What're you doing out here in the pouring rain anyway? Did you walk?"

"Sure," I say, slipping my shoes off and following him through the living room and into the kitchen. Glance quickly behind me. A trail of rainwater on the flawless carpet. "And yes I walked."

The kitchen is not so tidy today. There are several glasses on the counter by the sink and some empty beer bottles on the table, along with an enormous stack of mail and newspapers. It feels as though this isn't really his house somehow. But at least he does seem to be alone. There are no telltale signs of some other guest; no item of lingerie draped across a chair, a pair of heeled shoes by the door. For a moment I imagine turning towards the stairs and seeing a sleepy woman coming down dressed in a short, lacy nightgown, one strap hanging loose, the curve of one breast exposed, long blonde hair falling messily to shoulders. I can see her face, at first startled, then a lazy smile and a look of complacency settling, a look that says *I belong here. This is my man. And just who the hell are you?*

"I was just about to go through all that," he is saying. Motions towards the table and a stack of mail. "Didn't get a chance yesterday. Here, have a seat." He pulls out a chair for me and runs his fingers through his hair, attempts to flatten the back. "I should at least get myself a shirt. Make myself decent."

"Oh no," I say, "don't bother. You look great just as you are."

He laughs, and I realize suddenly what I've said. *Idiot.* Maggie would've come up with something witty to say, something to put a person at ease and make the situation all right again, but I am not that kind of person. It is impossible for someone like me.

"Maybe I should be getting you a shirt or something. You look soaked. Are you cold? You must be cold."

I shake my head and look away.

"About yesterday..." I say.

"By the way, I apologize, Clarice. About yesterday I mean. I said I'd call and I didn't. I'm really sorry. I was going to call as soon as I got up this morning and tell you. It was one of those days. Everything went wrong. And then I was up really late. Unexpected company. But here you are. You beat me to it." He smiles.

I get the impression it has only just now occurred to him that he forgot to telephone me yesterday. A little too eager to offer excuses and make amends. Also, he doesn't really explain why at all, just gets up and starts to pour water in the coffee-maker, measures out spoonfuls as though to change the subject quickly.

"You take cream?"

"Oh, no. Just black is fine."

"Me too." He sits down across from me. "About all I can offer you is toast. Don't think there's any eggs. I've never managed to make a decent pancake either. My mom used to make these fabulous pancakes. Buttermilk. Made them all the time when I was small. The greatest pancakes you've ever tasted, but I haven't a clue about the recipe. Every time I go out to a restaurant for breakfast I order pancakes, but it's never quite the same."

"Did you get things straightened up at the office?"

I look up and finally meet those intense gray eyes straight on. I cannot possibly look away. A warm surge in the area of my stomach. I wish I could reach across the table, lean over and touch his arm. A very perverse sort of thought when you consider it.

"Oh that, yes." He picks up a letter, glances at it, tosses it back on the table. Looks over at me again. "You look really nice this morning, Clarice. How do you manage to look so awake and cheery and alive this early on a rainy Sunday morning, even sopping wet?"

"But my hair. It got soaked out there. I must look awful. And it wasn't raining at all when I left, I swear." I rub a finger under my eyes, tuck my hair back behind me ears.

Richard's cat has come into the kitchen and is now brushing up against my legs under the table. He sits down at my feet, begins washing his face, unconcerned, oblivious. Does he remember?

"It wasn't raining when I left. I had no idea." I say.

"Hmm," He stares at me again in that same intense way. Strangely, it suddenly doesn't bother me at all that he is examining me like this, so openly. If any other man had done so in the past, I would've been mortified, aware at once of a thousand imperfections. Even Frank. I hated it when Frank looked at me. I mean really *looked*. It made me feel he was measuring, adding things up, calculating. And that I always fell short somehow. I stare back at Richard and say nothing.

"Cripes, I'm sorry Clarice. You really could use some dry clothes and I'm just sitting here. I can see from here you're shivering. You must be freezing. I'll find you something of mine that might fit, sort of. Something dry and warm at least."

He gets up, walks past slowly and, unbelievably, actually touches the top of my shoulder, just a light touch, and his fingers brush down a little towards my arm. Then he goes, soundlessly, from the kitchen and up the stairs.

I imagine him turning into his room at the top of the stairs, going to the closet and opening it, examining those rows of neatly ironed shirts, forehead creased, trying to determine which one might work best. I shift in my chair breathing deeply, still feeling the warm spot on my arm where he touched it. Glance back at the kitchen table. On top there are three letters from *Her.* I can tell instantly by the handwriting. Slanted and sloppy, the letters huge and uneven.

I don't move for one full minute, hardly dare to breathe. How is it she's still writing to him? Three, all from her, all unopened. They lie there, partly obscured by some other mail, bills and such like. I push the others away, just a little, so that I can be sure. Yes, they are definitely all from *Her.* That same sloppy, scribbled handwriting. As though the writer were in some inordinate hurry, scribbling the words frantically while the envelope was propped on the steering wheel of a car.

Suddenly I remember the letter in my pocket. I have forgotten it again. I should've just dropped it under the mailbox. Now I must deposit it here in the midst of this huge pile of letters. He'll never know. He will think it quite natural there is another letter from her, expect it even. He will think it got lost in the mail for a while and that's why it's arrived so late. The post office loses things all the time.

For a moment, but just for a moment, I am tempted to take one of the other ones instead. Just one. Why would he ever suspect me anyway? If I could just see what she is writing about now, maybe I could understand the situation a lot better.

I reach into my pocket for the letter and toss it onto the table with the others. I wish I could drink a glass of wine, a shot of scotch even, to give me nerve. I could ask him. I could say I'm cold, that I need a drink to warm me up.

Suddenly I am aware that he is back in the room. He has

changed into a pair of new Levi's and a green and white flannel shirt. His hair is combed and a little wet. In his hands he holds a blue shirt and sweatpants.

"Is that for me?" I say. "I'm not really all that wet. You needn't have bothered."

"They're really old," he says, handing me the clothing, "but they're the smallest ones I've got. The pants are really short on me so they might kind of fit you although you're so skinny I hope they don't just fall off. And you can roll up the sleeves on the shirt." He glances down, at my legs and feet. "I brought socks too. Thought your feet must be frozen."

"Thank you so much. I didn't mean to stop in like this, all wet, so you'd have to find me something."

He smiles again, that charming, amused smile I've already come to know.

"You can change in the bathroom. Upstairs at the end of the hall, straight ahead."

I get up and go to the stairway, pretend to hesitate.

"Oh and don't look too close at the bathroom. I haven't had time to clean this morning. Just up there, straight ahead. You can't miss it."

But it is spotless, just as before. The towels, navy and burgundy stripes, hang neatly folded on the towel bar. The sink shines. There is a full roll of toilet paper on the dispenser and the toilet looks freshly scrubbed. There is a new bottle of shampoo standing on the edge of the bathtub along with a large bar of soap, still wrapped. As though waiting for a guest.

Slip out of my jeans, pink shirt, bra and underpants, and drop them to the floor. They really are very wet, saturated. I pick up his sweatshirt and pants, pull on the shirt, doing the buttons up quickly and rolling up the sleeves. Push the hair away from my eyes and open the bathroom door. Glance towards Richard's room, but the door is closed. Move closer, stop and listen. For a moment I can almost imagine the sound of rustling bed sheets, movement, quiet breathing.

When I return to the kitchen, I find Richard has cleaned up his mail and wiped the table. He is putting bread in the toaster and there is an encouraging aroma of coffee. I feel warm and dry and strangely happy inside.

"Thought I could at least offer you something. Serves me right being unprepared. Now I know how you felt when I showed up at your door unannounced a while back."

"I was out walking this morning and I just kind of ended up here in your neighbourhood. Thought I'd stop by and say hello." I sit down at the table.

"That must have been quite a long walk. But I'm glad you stopped in. When I called yesterday and left that message, I wanted to-" he hesitates, reaches for two plates and sets them on the table along with the toast, butter and jam. He sits down across from me. "I wanted to tell you some things, so that you wouldn't think..."

He turns away, gets up again and gets two knives and two mugs. Sets them on the table without a word.

"Look Richard, I promise I'll be understanding if there's something you need to tell me. I want you to feel you can say anything to me, trust me implicitly."

I sit and wait for him to speak; knowing that something has changed. His eyelids are half-closed as though he is not quite awake. He looks troubled, ill-at-ease, and not at all the way he usually does with me.

"I should have told you," Richard says finally, looking down at the table. "I honestly truly didn't mean to mislead you. You have to believe me. But I should have told you right from the start, right from the very beginning."

In the intervening silence I can already hear the next words quite clearly long before they are spoken aloud. I can almost see them in the air between us. Written in large black letters.

"I should have told you right from the beginning, when we first met, that there was someone else."

I know I was prepared for this. Having seen the letters and having followed him to *Her* house, I knew all along of course that at some point he would say these words. But somehow I don't feel very good. I must refocus on the plan. It is time to ruin it all for him, break them apart and make them both suffer, finally settle the score. But for some reason I feel ill, nauseous even, and suddenly very, very tired.

Richard's cat is licking up the crumbs from our toast under the table. A restful sound, this licking. Somewhere outside a siren. And then a dog barks, sharply, insistent.

"I knew that, I suppose." I say, picking up the coffee mug and twisting it in my hands.

"Did you? His voice sounds anxious. "You knew? It was that obvious then?" He stops, waits. "Is it wrong, Clarice, to continue loving someone even though you know you shouldn't? My friends have said all kinds of things. They try to convince me. But it's not something you can just tell yourself to stop doing: stop loving someone, turn off your feelings like the switch of a light and be left alone. Just because you know it's somehow wrong. Just because other people think it should be like that."

He is mocking me, deliberately cruelly hurting me.

"That depends," I say. "that depends."

Richard's cat comes closer to my feet, lies down on top of them, instantly warm. I move my one foot a little, wiggling my toes.

"But don't get me wrong," Richard says, opening his eyes wider again, "I know this sounds like some kind of a cheap line, but I'd like for us to be friends, really good friends. I've been so immersed in my work this last while, I've hardly talked to anyone. You have been wonderful. I can't tell you how much I looked forward to the time we've spent together. We need to keep seeing each other of course."

"But what about her? This other person in your life? If I were her, I wouldn't be very happy if you had this special friend all of a sudden that you confided in so much."

Richard begins buttering his toast. I sip at my coffee and watch him over the rim of the cup. There is a line between his eyes. His eyebrows gather and the expression on his face changes entirely. He is thinking about *Her.*

"It's just very different," he says finally. "She... I just can't explain it all right now. She wouldn't mind. She's that kind of a person. She doesn't get jealous or anything. She wouldn't mind at all. And she has lots of male friends too. We trust one another. We've been together since we were little kids, forever really. I don't think I can remember us not being together."

I would like to ask him what her name is. To hear him say it. I begin to fiddle with the buttons on the shirt he gave me. I've done them up wrong so the buttons don't match up with the buttonholes and the hem on one side is lower.

I am just a friend. A buddy to hang around with. Someone who listens rather well.

"What's she like?"

"Incredibly smart. A lawyer, actually, although she's given up her practice for the time being because of her health. She's been ill. She was in the hospital for a bit, but she's getting much better now thank goodness. She may not go back; may pursue other things. She's from a very talented family, very musical. Her father's this famous organist and she plays the piano like you wouldn't believe. She's played at all kinds of places. Everyone says she has a real gift."

"A musician."

"Yes, quite talented, you'd love her. She's the kind of person that gets along with anyone. Everyone just adores her from the moment they meet her. She has a way with people, a way of making them feel good about themselves from the moment she walks in the door. She's one of those people that everyone says lights up a room. She really is. People just seem to take to her right away. Even if she's only met them once, people always ask about her. They never seem to forget if they've talked to her even once. She'd just love you, I know it. You'd get along really well."

"Well," I say, getting up from the table and walking toward the front door quickly. "It's stopped raining so I better go while it's dry. Thanks for the clothes and the coffee and toast. Maybe we could go out sometime for a drink or something. Like you said. We can stay friends. I'd like that."

He has come to the door and is looking down at me in a way that I can't understand. I feel awkward and embarrassed. She is this shadow standing between us.

And then, as I look into his face, I see he is now smiling a little. He reaches out and touches my hair with one hand. I look away and begin fiddling with the buttons on my shirt again, horrified. As though he were caressing some pet dog or a small child.

"I would really like that, Clarice. Believe me. Thanks for understanding. I know I should've told you before. I'm not trying to push you away by saying, let's be friends. It sounds so stupid, such a ridiculous old line. But I really mean it. Honestly. I will call you and we'll make plans for dinner. And you should stop in sometime again for breakfast when it isn't raining. Anytime. I'll show you the garden."

Yes, it is certain he will call sometime, idly, a few weeks from now, because he is finished work and *She* is busy at her office until late, or playing at some concert somewhere far away and he isn't able to go along. And so, out of boredom, and because his friend Bob is going out with his girlfriend that night, and because Richard too would like to go out to dinner, but not alone, he will call me. And I will say yes. I will always say yes. I will join him for a drink. I will meet him for dinner. I will tour his garden. I will be his friend. And I will make him remember.

I turn and close the door firmly behind me and walk away.

***

The white squirrels again. I see them as soon as I arrive. Now that the rain is over, they are out and about, chasing one another happily, a pair of children stopping now and again to dig in the wet ground. Tails twitching, moving erratically from tree to tree, they pay me no attention at all. No one else is here to see them. No one else to witness my two furry white ghosts.

I sit down on the ground despite the wet grass and watch. They climb so quickly it's difficult to see their little legs move. As though they were flying from branch to branch on tiny transparent wings.

Father died at this time of the year. Heart attack. Happened quite suddenly right after a simple hernia operation. A relatively minor procedure. He'd never had heart troubles before. No one in our family had. He'd seemed so healthy too. So slim and in great shape. Always out walking. He'd taken up golfing too ever since Frank and I got married. Frank had taken him out a few times, and from then on Dad started leaving the house more, going out for golf on a regular basis with his buddies from down the street.

The squirrels have come up quite close to me now. One fellow is actually a little bigger than the other. I had not noticed this before. His fur is also not as white: a little grubbier and yellowed in spots. They are no more than fifteen feet away, just sitting there on hind legs, motionless, watching me. Silent as always.

I sit and stare back. Wish I had something with me. Peanuts or a crust of bread. Something to entice them closer. Watch and listen. Somewhere in the distance I think I can hear music. Faint and unearthly. And then, without my seeing, the squirrels melt into the long grass and up into the trees. Gone so rapidly and completely it's as though they were never here at all.

When I get to the cemetery, there are branches down everywhere. There is even a large limb down on her grave, crushing some of the flowers. I drag it off and try to fix the flowers as best I can, but some are so broken they will likely never come back. For some reason this hits me really hard, the idea of something like that falling so suddenly and smashing everything. Yes, they can be replanted, but this seems the final straw. I just stand and cry, cry as though I will never stop, although I tell myself over and over that it's far too late for all of that. Stand and weep and weep over the cold black earth as I've never wept before.

-28-

Maggie is in my kitchen again. She's made coffee. Banana muffins sit atop the dishwasher on a deep green ceramic plate that does not belong to me. The room smells of pine sol and something that reminds me of a mixture of oil-based paint and perfume.

This time she is sitting at the kitchen table reading a newspaper, a stack of completed crossword puzzles on the table next to her. Evidently she has been holed up here for a while.

"It says here," she says without looking up as I come through the door, "someone you love is going to question your abilities today. Don't let them put you down. Stand your ground. Don't let friends take advantage of your inclination to say yes when you have too many other responsibilities. Be cautious about committing too much too soon and address relationship issues right away. There will be plenty of romantic opportunities, so keep your eyes open. Well..." Maggie lets out a big breath and rolls her eyes. "I've got quite a day ahead, don't I?"

"Apparently yes." I slip off my shoes and move the pile of crosswords to the other side of the table.

"You look beat, dearest. I tried to reach you all day yesterday. To say happy birthday of course. Don't think I'd forgotten because I hadn't. How was it?"

"How was what?"

"Your birthday." She says this very loud, flipping through the pages of the newspaper rapidly, folding it shut and smacking it onto the table. She has even brought along her own special gourmet coffee beans and ground them in my coffee grinder. Evidently my beans were not good enough.

"I was going to make you a cake but they're all so fattening and I've lost four pounds already on my new diet, so I made muffins instead with this new recipe I was dying to try. No white sugar, only bananas, and no butter or oil either, just applesauce. They didn't rise though. Turned out kind of hard again. But they're not bad, anyway all things considered. See what you think."

Poor little Clarice. I'll pop in like some kindly fairy godmother with my home baked goodies and try to fatten her up. What a mess she's made of her life.

Maggie is examining my shirt and pants. She thinks I'm hiding something.

A flash: my clothes in a small, soggy pile, panties and brassiere and all, on the spotless floor of Richard's upstairs bathroom. How could I have forgotten?

"I was thinking you and I should go out for lunch or something. Brunch somewhere to celebrate your birthday. Paul won't mind. There's leftovers to finish. The kids have plans with friends anyway."

"I don't think so, Maggie, I'm really tired, but thanks all the same. Is that why you called?"

"So you did get my messages."

"All four." Force a smile. She is clearly annoyed about something. Sits back and studies her fingernails, eyebrows tilted. The fingernails are the exact shade of her sky-blue shirt, and no chips either. She is hoping I will fill her in, tell her exactly what it was I was doing last night when I was out so late.

"So Caesar was here a minute ago. I found some cat food in the cupboard and he tore into it like he hasn't seen food in two weeks. Did you forget to feed him again?"

"He always does that. I left him a whole huge dish full. He must have a tapeworm or something and, no, I never forget to feed him. I don't know where you got that idea from."

"Anyhow, don't let me spoil your plans," Maggie says. "Heaven only knows I don't want to make a nuisance of myself. If you've got plans, a date or something, don't let me stop you. I called yesterday because of Frank actually. He showed up at my house totally drunk and acting like a madman. Lucky Paul wasn't home or he'd have thrown him out, maybe called the cops. From what I could understand Frank's pretty upset at you though, dearest."

"Me? What have I done?"

"Who knows, but he's just wild about something or other and wants to see you. Kept saying he's been looking for you. I thought you should know. Got me kind of worried actually."

"Don't concern yourself about Frank. He can take care of himself."

"It wasn't him I was worried about."

"Look," I say, "Frank isn't about to come here with a gun or something like that and start shooting people for heaven's sake. I know Frank isn't your favourite person, but he's totally harmless, a big baby. And he knows I'm not going to take him back into this house."

I consider telling Maggie about Dinny's visit, but it will take too long. She'll want to know all the unessential details: what Dinny was wearing, the exact shade of her hair. And I am in no mood to go over Dorinda's whole little speech about poor Frankie and that woman he supposedly wants to marry, let alone all the finer points, precisely itemized.

I stare moodily out the window. It hasn't been the best morning so far at all, has it? I have to admit this last while I had almost begun to lose sight of my original plans. *Richard*. Those strange pale gray eyes with the black rims. That inscrutable expression. And at the end, when I was about to leave, that peculiar look in his eyes as if he was asking me to stay, willing me, taunting, daring. Which doesn't make sense at all. I need to refocus. It is just a matter of time before I finally get even.

"What are you thinking about?" Maggie says.

She knows it's a man I'm thinking about. How sly she is, assessing me, dissecting the whole time while paging through that crossword puzzle book of hers so benignly. But she knows. She knows there is someone and she is trying to figure out a way to make me tell her. To make me slip up. That is why she is so cross today.

"Nothing important."

"Well," says Maggie, poking at the foliage of my potted fern, pulling off a few dry leaves and crumpling them in her fingers, "never mind. Anyhow, I've got to show you my new dress for the big party. Lavender, with a fringe and these little spaghetti straps. Very classy. Ankle length. I got it at Sullivan's. Two hundred and ninety bucks. But I might return it. The colour doesn't really suit me. If Paul finds out how much he'll kill me. Did you get something for the big bash yet?"

"No," I say, "Not yet. Haven't had the chance. I will this week, of course. I mean it's next weekend already, isn't it? And Margaret will never forgive me if I cancel out now."

"Cancel out?" says Maggie, brushing the crumbled leaves from her hands. "Surely not. You can't do that."

Thoroughly appalled, as though she can't imagine why anyone not lingering on his deathbed and soon to perish of flesh-eating disease would even consider canceling out on Margaret Forrest and the big Princess Theatre party. The social event of the year. I can't tell her I'd hoped to be able to take Richard, that I'd imagined us arriving at Margaret's big new house together.

Me, composed and self-assured at his side. All at once a new Clarice who smiled and chatted and was perhaps a little more at ease with people again. How they would all stare.

"Anyhow, got to run," she says. "If you don't feel like brunch today, maybe we can go out sometime this week then. Thursday, maybe. I'm free Thursday. Just lunch somewhere. You choose. And we'll go out shopping too. We can do that Monday or Tuesday if you like. That is if you're not too busy."

There is a hint of complaint in her voice, festering resentment, as though by turning down her offer to go to lunch today I have offended her deeply and she is not about to forget. She sniffs, picks up her purse from under the table and opens. "You haven't even tried the muffins. And here," she says, suddenly turning to me, as though only just remembering. "You haven't opened your birthday present either."

She points to a package on the counter; brightly wrapped in shiny blue and purple paper, with a fancy bow on top. I pick it up and tear at the paper. I am like a child when it comes to presents. No patience with fancy paper and bows. Never one to pick at tape and open carefully like my sister Martha, who made me crazy with impatience, who folded the paper gently, tucking it away to reuse on a rainy day. Life is not like that for me. I must tear and rip and scatter about the floor.

It is a blouse, white and frilly and I examine it in silence. It is so like Maggie to choose something like this: beautiful and costly, but fussy, something I will never think to buy myself, or ever wear for that matter. Once a long time ago she gave me a bright red wool skirt cut long to mid-calf. Every Christmas she asked whether I'd been wearing that skirt, and every December for years I pulled it from my closet and wore it to her Christmas open house. The other neighbours must've thought I had nothing else to wear. That skirt is likely hanging in my closet still and I will never be able to throw it out.

"Thank you so much, Maggie. It's gorgeous. I can't think when I'll have the occasion to wear something so nice, but I'm sure I'll get the opportunity sometime. A really special occasion."

I smile brightly and put the blouse down on the counter, hoping she won't suggest I wear it to the party paired with the old red wool skirt.

"Nonsense," she says, snapping shut her purse. "You can wear it to work at the bookstore every day if you like. It's very functional. And the quality, absolutely tops. You could pull the whole thing through your ring and it would come out without so much as a single crease."

"Okay," I say, "Fine then. Thank you. You're quite right and I'm sure I'll wear it a lot."

"Well, dearest," She jumps up looking much brighter, "must be off. Thursday then? For lunch? I'll call and we'll figure out where we should go. Oh yes and Monday or Tuesday we'll shop for your dress too. I'll help you choose. I know exactly what you should wear."

She is gone. I listen for her footsteps at the door and then the door closes behind her, so softly it is no more than a little breath and I have to strain to hear it close.

-29-

Shadows stir behind windows. A sharp cracking from somewhere within the house. A slamming of a door. Which one? A small voice wails piteously in the distance.

Ghosts? Let them come. I welcome them with open arms, embraces even. Certainly better than this empty house. I have learned there are things far worse in this life than mere ghosts: those who don't belong anywhere or to anyone and who are left with nothing. Disaster, betrayal, heartache that drones on and on and on. A mind and spirit that is weary beyond words.

Slamming down meat and cheese I make myself a sandwich with as much noise and activity as possible. I am not hungry but this gives me something to do and I am hoping it will give me energy to face the evening. Turn the radio on then off again. A harsh sound of cheerful voices, discordant music thrumming. Move restless from kitchen to living room and back, with Caesar trailing soundlessly behind me. When I look back, he turns his face away, stops to wash a paw, pretends to be occupied with something else.

The big party is tonight, but I have more than an hour to wait and this is tearing little bits off my nerves. I feel unsettled and uncomfortable in my own skin. Uncharacteristically I am already dressed, hair arranged in an elaborate coiffure, shoes and an elegant new purse waiting by the door. The purse matches my dress exactly and is covered in tiny glass beads. I believe I must look quite chic, a pale carbon copy of Maggie herself. Fearing creases, I smooth my dress a dozen times before sitting down on the couch, but I am too restless to sit for long and must get up again.

It was Maggie, of course, who took charge, who found the dress, who suggested the hairstyle, who drove me to her very own personal hairdresser, where she carefully supervised every lock to its proper position, every daub of scented pomade. Maggie came by my house on the appointed day, her own pale lavender dress draped carefully over one arm, and asked me to go with her to have the garment exchanged. But as soon as we walked in the boutique she dropped everything and selected a gown for me in less than the time it took me to close the front door.

"This one," she said, going instantly to a certain rack and pulling out one particular dress from a hundred others.

It is green, cut just above the ankle, sleeveless, backless. Not one I would have picked off a clothing rack myself in a hundred years. There is nothing striking about it, but I see at once that she is of course right as always. The dress is simple, but it fits my bony frame as though it were poured on, as though it were made exclusively for me. The shade of green is indefinable. Quite frankly, it suits.

"It's you Clarice, dearest," Maggie said at once, surveying me with a wrinkled forehead, eyes narrowed. "You're an absolute knockout in that one. That green is your colour, I told you so before. You look ten years younger at least. Stunning. I'd wear it myself," she sighed heavily, face tragic, "only you know I look positively *ghastly* in green."

And then Maggie decided after all on her original choice, the lavender with the fringe, and I purchased the green without one single backward glance. Even the saleslady must have been impressed with my lack of concern over the price, my nonchalant attitude as I calmly handed her all those fifties and twenties. Composed, dispassionate, unflappable, self-possessed. I saundered around after Maggie like some spoiled queen. Oh no, nothing was going to ruffle me.

At work this week I spoke to Reese and Sally as though to strangers, as though I were an imposter in my own life. No one else knew. And I myself was only watching, from a distance, from behind the scenes, sleepily, having just awoken from a most peculiar dream. A dream that stayed with me, lingered on and on like a hazy fog on a still summer morning.

Sally pulled me into her office yesterday, quite literally yanked me by the arm and shoved me in, then told me the news: the call from the adoption agency has finally come. They are getting a son, a baby boy. This time really and truly. The papers are already signed. Apparently they decided to try for adoption a number of years ago even though at that point they hadn't really given up on getting pregnant themselves. They haven't told a soul about this baby but her parents and his.

I was overwhelmed. Sally's eyes filled with tears as she whispered those three little words. *A baby boy.* Tears of joy. It is possible. Joyful tears full of hope. How long has it been since I've cried those kind of tears?

She told me she was going to change the baby's room, that she doesn't like the giraffe decorations anymore, especially for a boy, and wants to paint over the giant giraffe on the wall too. Would I come over and help her decide what she should choose instead? I nodded my head and mouthed the word *yes.* She is a very nice person. She deserves this, she and John. They have waited so long, have gone through so much for so many years. With a new baby in their arms they can now finally give up on their dream of conceiving a baby themselves. I am glad that the adoption came through. I will go over there and help her paint the room again, maybe even knit something for the baby if I can remember how.

Reese was in much better spirits yesterday as well, prancing around after customers and chatting non-stop to everyone, arms loaded down with stacks of books. The reason for his good spirits is now quite clear. He told me he has a new riding instructor, a woman who lately has been spending most evenings with him teaching him how to handle his new horse. Apparently he's learned a lot already and is much more confident in the saddle. Also, the new riding instructor is unattached, available and, according to Reese anyway, really quite attractive. He says she's taken quite a shine to him, and is making sure he gets lots of special attention; as many private lessons as he would like and he's been taking full advantage. The news gets even better. He hasn't told Sally yet, but he's also planning on quitting the bookstore by the end of this summer. Wants to go back to university after eleven years away and try to finish the Optometry program he started. This time, he said, he is not going to be frightened off by the prospect of fighting tooth and nail for top marks. I wanted to tell him how proud I was, but I just couldn't come out with it, couldn't manage the words. So I just nodded and smiled and tried to concentrate on what he was saying. I still felt like an imposter, like I was watching someone else act in a play. Dazed and groggy, like someone who had just awoken from a very realistic dream.

The telephone rings, piercingly, wrenching me all at once from my thoughts. Carefully smoothing my fancy green dress I walk as on glass to the kitchen and pick up on the fourth ring.

"Hello, Clarice?"

"Yes. Hello." There is silence for a moment on the other end. Static, a faint ominous humming. "Who's speaking?"

"It's Bob." Silence again, a crackling on the line. "Bob, you know, Richard's friend."

"Oh hi," I say. "Yes. How are you? We must have a bad connection."

"I'm fine. It must be my phone. Anyway listen Clarice, I was just wondering. I mean I know you said before you didn't really want to get together to talk, but I have something really important I need to discuss with you. I know it sounds weird, but I really need to get together with you and tell you this in person. I was wondering if we could meet tonight. Don't worry there's nothing wrong or anything. I'm not going to tell you Richard is wanted by the police or a convicted felon or something like that, so don't panic." A strained little laugh.

"Well, I'd love to, but tonight just isn't going to work out. I've plans to go out already," I say. "But not with Richard. I'm not seeing him tonight if that's what you thought. Don't worry."

"Oh no. I didn't think that. I didn't think that at all and I certainly wasn't worried about that. I was just hoping we could meet tonight. I really think we need to talk. There isn't any way you can get out of it, is there?"

"How about tomorrow morning," I say. "I can't get out of tonight for sure."

"We could meet for breakfast at the same restaurant in Milan where I met you."

"Alright, tomorrow then," I say. "Eight o'clock. I'll meet you there at the same restaurant."

I'm just about to hang up when Bob suddenly says, "You'll be there, won't you Clarice? You'll come for sure? I mean you're not going to cancel out on me or something?"

"I'll come," I say. "Don't worry. Eight o'clock for breakfast. I promise."

I replace the receiver and slide a thick gold bracelet up and down my left arm. This bracelet lay forgotten in my dresser for five whole years. Imagine. Tonight when I opened the top drawer I finally found it there, crammed beneath a box of single earrings whose mates have been lost long ago. I'd forgotten it even existed. A shining gold circle. An anniversary present from my father to my mother. It seemed a sign too blatant to miss. A reassuring gift from the other side.

There's a piece of paper stuck between the front doors. Someone has quietly thrust it there while I was talking on the phone. Someone who didn't want to knock or to speak to me directly, I suppose. It is folded in half and my name is written in large letters across the front. *Richard.*

Inside there are a few hastily scratched lines, almost illegible.

Clarice, I knocked on the door but there was no answer. I'm very sorry about Sunday. Can we meet later at my house and talk? There's so much I want to tell you, to explain or at least try to. If you don't come by eight, I'll know you've decided to give up on me and I wouldn't blame you at all. My apologies again. R.

Stuffing the note into the new purse I get into my car and head for the cemetery. This is not something I normally do in daylight, but since I am going to this party tonight, I know I must or it will hang over me all evening. Guilt, reproach, an ache somewhere inside that will linger.

One of the oldest headstones at the back has finally fallen over. I'm not sure when this happened. Maybe it took place a while ago already and somehow I hadn't noticed. The grass is already crawling all over it, strangling, unstoppable. How many years was that stone leaning over? How many centimeters did it shift each year? One? Two? Just one millimeter every decade perhaps? How many years did it resist before at last giving in, relenting finally to time and the unyielding grass?

Despite my beautiful dress, I kneel down and tear away, clearing a space all around the stone. I push my fingers under one edge and lean in hard. But no, far too heavy, a dead weight if you will, and there is no way anyone could move it alone. I try to make out the name on the front and a date, but the letters are so scoured by weather it's difficult to decipher anything at all. Edith Johansson, maybe? But it could be anyone. Amelia. Josephine, Matthew, Roger. Likely no one knows and no one will ever know whose rotting bones lie here forgotten under this fallen stone in the cold wet earth.

***

I arrive at the party at exactly seven-thirty. There's already a crowd and I have to park my car at the far end of the street and walk. The house is all lit up and the double front doors are standing wide open. People mill about on the stone sidewalk, shimmering cocktail glasses in hand. One woman is wearing a long crimson dress with a train and a tiara. Actress perhaps? She is speaking to a short, bald man who looks vaguely familiar, maybe a local politician. I should know but don't. Most men are wearing tuxedos with tails. One sports a top hat and cane.

As I wander in and turn to look behind me, a large woman in a sky-blue dress topped with an unnecessary fur coat trails in, negotiates her way past the others and approaches. She removes the coat, flings it in my direction. I lurch forward and grab for it, but it has already fallen down and I must pick it up off the floor.

"Oh you idiot!" the woman says, snatching it from my arms and moving away rapidly.

Margaret and Douglas's new house turns out to be even more wonderful than expected. The entrance is huge with cathedral ceilings and a gorgeous spiral staircase. To the left an immense room where a large number of people are moving about in a purposeless rotating mass. At one end, a bar emerges. There are flowers in enormous crystal vases and gold candles on little wrought iron tables.

"Care for some hors d'oeuvres, madam?" a girl in a short black dress says, holding out a large tray with a variety of unidentifiable delicacies.

"Oh, no thank you." But when she turns I reach out and grab two, quickly shoving them into my mouth. No sign of host and hostess. Begin to push my way through the crowd. It is all very noisy. Laughter and loud high-pitched conversation. Coughing, scraping of shoes. I am suddenly enormously hungry and a little light-headed.

Maggie said she and Paul would be here right at seven. She had a babysitter for six-fifteen and assured me she wouldn't be a minute late. I suddenly wish I had taken her up on the offer to drive with them.

"Hello, sweetheart," says a voice.

I turn around quickly and look behind me.

But the man is not speaking to me. He is looking past me over my shoulder to a dark-haired woman on my left. She smiles lazily in his direction and waves a careless hand, turns away.

"Don't you believe what they say about her," the man says quickly to another younger, shorter man with a goatee. "He only got the house. She's not with Gerald anymore either. That was over ages ago. All rumours anyway."

He turns his face away and I don't catch the rest. I wander over to another girl dressed in black holding a serving platter, and pick out three more hors d'oeuvres and a tiny gold napkin, snare a glass of wine from a tray.

"Clarice, for pity's sake. I didn't think you were here already. I've been looking for you everywhere. Everyone's been asking. What a crowd already. Someone stepped on my foot and nearly tore my dress, just look. There'll be a bruise as big as a plum by tomorrow."

Margaret pushes her way through. Solid in a long black gown cut low to display a superfluous and no longer youthful brown-speckled bosom. Heavy gold glitter on the eyelids up to the pencilled-in black brows. Absolutely perfect semi-circles. Lipstick thick and wet as though at any moment it might drip down her chin and onto those brown breasts. From her fingers she swings a pair of glasses on a thick gold chain.

"I haven't any idea whose they are. And mighty expensive too by the look of them. I was just telling Norma I found them next to the big palm tree in the music room, the one Evelyn gave us last year as a housewarming, and I've been just absolutely racing around trying to find the owner. Oh my isn't that a lovely little dress Susan McDougall is wearing. What do you call that colour? Dusty rose? You know we have our bridge parties twice a week now, but Susan insists she must quit for the summer. She plays golf you know. Every morning. She and Anna get up at God only knows what time. Eighteen holes before breakfast. Which is terrific exercise of course, if you're into that kind of thing. My hips couldn't stand it though. It's so wonderful you came, Clarice. I was just telling Douglas that I didn't think you'd show."

"I wouldn't miss it for the world, you know that Margaret. And your new house is just beautiful." I try not to look down at the bulging breasts, beads of perspiration beginning to show along the collarbone and in the crease. Margaret was always one to sweat generously. I take a large swallow of wine, then a second, scan the crowd discreetly but try to pay careful attention at the same time.

"We just thought. Well, you know. We haven't seen you in years, really. But you look wonderful, Clarice. Just wonderful. So much better, you know. You were so pale. For a while there we were quite afraid to look at you." Wipes a thick-fingered hand across her bosom. There is some gold glitter there, on the crease between her breasts.

I examine the crowd and finish my wine in a few more big swallows. Seize another glass from a waiter walking by. "Have you seen Maggie yet? Maggie Ducharme?"

"Oh yes, that beautiful actress friend of yours. Yes, I'm quite certain I saw her. Over there, in the great room, by the window. Yes, I believe she was talking with David Burroughs. Quite a well-known personage you know. I almost fell over, absolutely fell over, when I saw him arrive. I had no idea when I invited him that he'd actually come to our trifling little crush. Douglas almost had a stroke." She lifts a hand to her head, touches the elaborate updo gently. There are red orchids woven through her hair, but they are quite flaccid in this heat.

"Have you seen Frank? I don't believe he's here yet, but he did tell Michael he'd try to make an appearance. Oh now isn't that something, Edward's come after all. Well I must go and say hello and congratulate him. I certainly hope you enjoy the party, dear. Eat lots, there's tons of food. And you must meet Edward. I'll be sure to introduce you. He's very well-to-do nowadays, if somewhat a parvenu, a pig in clover, or so they say. But still a very eligible bachelor you know..."

Margaret elbows past a skeletal lady in gray and makes her way towards the front entrance, orchids bobbing as she weaves through. But I make her sound too affected. She is not really like that at all. She is actually quite nice under most circumstances. I am just being harsh tonight. She is wrong about Maggie though, who comes in a few minutes later with Paul dragging behind. Stunning as always in the pale lavender gown. Heads turn her way as she walks through. People step aside. Maggie moves as though she's rehearsed every step, every nod. Before I can talk to her though I am snared by Dinny, Michael and another woman. Trapped, just as I'm walking by the grand piano.

"Clarice," Dinny says, grabbing at my arm and pulling me close. She leans forward to press her powdered cheek lightly against mine. She feels dry and chalky and smells of flour. "So how are you darling?" she says. "You must meet my good friend Dorothy. Dorothy, my daughter-in-law, Clarice. Frank's wife. I've told Dorothy all about you a thousand times."

Dorothy nods and smiles, takes my hand in two damp ones, shaking emphatically. She says something I don't quite catch, laughs noisily displaying a mouthful of large gold-crowned teeth, hurries away. I tip my wineglass and take a few big swallows. Dinny and Michael are leaning on the piano. Has she noticed she introduced me as Frank's wife? As though I am *current*. Is this the way she speaks of me to everyone, as though our divorce never happened?

"Quite a carnival, isn't it?" Dinny says. "Who would've thought Margaret would ever pull it off? And the house. Revolting. After all that crap about our old house being too big for them, how they needed something to suit just the two of them. I mean look at this place. Disgusting if you ask me, parading your money like that and just typical of the pair of them. Real nouveau riche."

I swallow another big mouthful of wine and try to look agreeable. It always takes me a while to adjust to the sharp edges around Dinny, the hard corners. I need to ease into it, and then brace myself.

"I think it's quite beautiful," I say, "I've never even been close to a place this gorgeous, let alone inside one."

"Well," Dinny says, wiping at something on the front of her white silk dress. "Guess Margaret's family had more money behind them then she let on. Someone must've died."

"I've always thought if I ever had the money to buy a big house I'd love to have a library and a real music room." I set my purse down under the polished black piano bench. Dinny has placed her drink on top of the piano and is making a ring on the black finish. I lean over and pick it up, wipe vigorously at the spot with the back of my hand and hand her the glass.

"I'd love to have a grand piano like this or maybe even a harpsichord. Just imagine being able to play Handel or Telemann on a real harpsichord. Not that I can remember how anymore," I say.

"Well I guess it'd be nice for someone with small children to have a piano so the kid could take lessons and so on," Michael says. He's had has back to us and was staring at a group of young women over by the window, and is only now taking part in our conversation. Dinny throws him a sharp look and puts her glass back down on the piano.

"Yes," I say very quickly. "Exactly."

"Have you seen Frank yet?" Dinny says, a line forming between her brows. "He told us he was coming tonight."

At that moment Maggie trails into the music room, sees me, comes quickly to the piano, the lavender fringe rippling around her legs like fins on some gorgeous exotic fish. Several men turn and watch her walk past.

"There you are, Clarice. I've been looking all over for you. And there's been a telephone call for you Mrs. Browne. Margaret was marching about looking for you and I said I'd give you the message if I saw you first. Nothing terribly urgent, I hope."

"Telephone, for me?" A cagey look settles on Dinny's face. The lines above her upper lip stand out against the pale cheeks. She takes hold of Michael's arm. I get the feeling she knows what this call is all about, that she's been expecting it.

"Well let's go then. We'll talk with you again later, Clarice. You'll be here of course? And thank you Maggie."

Maggie and I both watch them go. I finish my wine and glance behind me to see whether there's more available.

"What's the call about, do you know?"

"I rather gathered it was about Frank, actually," Maggie says, smiling. "But nothing too startling, I suppose."

I take hold of Maggie's arm and guide her to the table with the wine and champagne. We both pick up a glass and drink deeply, move back to the piano. Now that she's standing right next to me, I notice a subtle change in Maggie. She is clearly anxious about something and it shows, which is so unlike her. Fusses with the thin straps of her dress, looks over her shoulder several times, spills her champagne a little.

"Where's Paul?" I say. "What room did you leave him in? A person could get lost for days in this place never to be found again."

She nods at a man who pushes past us. "Oh Paul." Says his name as though she's only just thought of him now. "Home by now, I expect. He just came to drop me off and give his regards to Doug and Margaret. I sent him back."

"You sent him home? Why? Is he sick? Are the kids sick?" I push the gold bracelet up and down my arm.

"Paul hasn't been sick for a day in his life. He's the healthiest person I know." She fusses again with the straps of the lavender dress, forehead creased.

"Well what then? Is it the babysitter? Couldn't she stay?"

"I'm actually celebrating tonight," Maggie says carefully, pronouncing *tonight* as though it were three syllables, *to-nigh-it*. She takes another big swallow of champagne and then holds the glass up high. "Cheers. Wish me well. Paul and I are going our separate ways, as of today. As of this very moment I'm officially a free woman and my new life begins."

I move over and sit down with a thump on the piano bench.

Paul and Maggie? Always smiling at one another, touching

and hugging. A flash: Paul and Maggie together at the hospital the day Chad is born, Paul holding his son proudly and Maggie smiling up at him as though he were some kind of a god.

"Oh don't look so shocked, dearest," Maggie says, examining her bare left hand. "So prudish. Don't you see how much happier we'll both be on our own? Can't you see how wrong we were for one another? You must've noticed, especially this last while."

"Why Maggie? I can't believe it. What happened? And you said nothing to me. Not a word."

"It's been coming for years now. We talked about it a lot. It wasn't like we had a big fight or anything. We made the decision a long time ago to call it quits."

"But why didn't you say anything? Not a word. You could've told me. I don't believe this."

Maggie tugs at a diamond earring, twisting it around in her fingers, sips delicately again from the champagne glass.

"*Ree-ah-lly*, Clarice. As if you needed me dumping my troubles into your lap with all you have going on in your own life. And it's not so bad. I'm happier already."

"Maggie," I say this so loud that a few people in the room stop talking and look over. "For heaven's sake, Maggie, you're my best friend. Didn't you think I could put aside my own troubles for a while and help you out a little?"

"Well I tried to tell you," she says. Turns away and sits down, folds her legs under her, smoothing the fringe of her dress carefully around her feet. "I did try. I told you about some of our little fights, and I'm sure I mentioned stuff that's happened lately. There just wasn't much to say. He doesn't love me anymore. I don't love him. I haven't for years. I want my old life back. As simple as that."

"But the children. Melissa. Chad. What about them? You've only one shot at all of this."

"Oh we've worked it out. We're not going to fight over the kids or make it hard on ourselves. Paul is getting an apartment close to where I'm moving to in Milan. He's moving in to the apartment tonight, actually. It seemed a good time to do it, with me out of the house for a few hours. The kids can spend time with both of us and I'm going back to acting of course. I'll put the house up for sale and I'll move into Milan close to the theatre as soon as it sells. A nice semi-detached with a backyard. Kids are old enough now they don't need me so much anyway. They took the news quite well, all things considered. I expect they knew."

"I'd think the kids would need you even more now," I say quietly, getting up from the bench. "Especially Melissa, being a girl and getting to that sensitive age."

"Oh, I suppose so," Maggie says, sighing. Surveys the room. "It'll work out. It's got to. Anything's better than how things stand now. I would've thought that you of all people would understand best. With you and Frank, I mean. You've been through this. You know how it can be."

"That was different," I say quickly. "There were things that went wrong outside of our relationship. You know that. Frank and I could have been quite content together. You can't compare your life to mine."

There is a commotion at the door. I get up quickly. Dinny is pushing through the crowd and bearing down on me in her white dress like a ship in full sail.

"Clarice, you have to come with me right now, right this minute." Her voice so loud and abrasive I feel goose bumps start on my arm. A sick feeling rolls through my stomach. Dinny's lipstick has rubbed off and her lips resemble two thin lines of wax. She clasps my arm and pulls me away from the piano.

"It's Frank. I promised I'd get you and we'd be there in fifteen minutes, no more."

"Be where? What's wrong with Frank? I'm not going any-where." I glance at Michael who is standing behind Dinny look-ing put out and tired.

"Of course you're coming," says Dinny, squeezing my arm even tighter. "It was you he asked for. I promised him you'd come. *Promised.*"

Maggie has gotten up from her chair and is studying Din-ny, twisting her diamond earring, a small smile on her face.

"Is he in jail or something?" Maggie says laughing. "Some-thing else to celebrate tonight then."

Dinny and Michael exchange a meaningful glance but say nothing.

"Well, is he?" I say. They are not refuting this ridiculous suggestion after all.

"As a matter of fact," says Dinny, reaching for her gold purse, "as a matter of fact, he is. It's all a big mix-up, I can assure you. A huge mistake. Douglas and Michael and I are going over right away to get things sorted out and get him out of there. I told him you'd come. I promised. It was you he asked for, spe-cifically."

"Jail?" I say slowly. If they'd told me Frank climbed the Acropolis tonight and was at this very moment inside the Par-thenon drinking tea with the Pope, I'd have been more likely to believe. "What in heaven's name is he in jail for?"

"I told you. A mix-up. You know the police. They're forever arresting the wrong person. It's his girlfriend's fault, of course. She's gotten him mixed up in this. She and that delinquent son."

"Assault," Michael says by way of explanation, and shrugs his shoulders. "The girlfriend's son. Frank said on the phone he didn't do it; that it was all an accident, that the kid hauled off and bashed him across the head and he just slapped him back, but who knows? Anyway, the kid's in the hospital. Broken jaw and God knows what else, or so they tell me."

"Who knows," Dinny says, sharply. "I'll tell you who knows. That stupid girl with her idiot son, that's who knows. Of course Frankie wasn't involved. He isn't like that. He's never been the fighting type, even as a boy. Always backed down from the other boys that made trouble. Never so much as raised a fist. I told you this girlfriend was no good, Clarice. I told you to call him and talk to him, help him out, get him out of there. I suppose you never did?"

What is there to say? She's right. I never did phone him. I turned a blind eye. It is decidedly all my fault and I can only look at her in guilty silence, appalled at my own selfishness.

"He's an adult," I say very quietly. "He's entitled to make his own decisions. We'll talk later Maggie. I'll be back."

I turn again to look at Maggie once we have pushed our way through the crowded room. She is leaning against a chair talking to an extraordinarily handsome black man in a silver suit. Smiling indolently, head thrown back, one bare hand flung carelessly across his glittering arm. I didn't notice it before, but I can see now, even from clear across the room, that her wedding band, that thick shining gold circle, is missing from her left hand.

We are already through the front door and Dinny is hastening away, Michael running ahead to fetch the car and Douglas pulling up in his, when I remember my purse. The music room. The piano bench.

"Go ahead," I say. "Go without me. I'll take my car in a minute and follow. I know the way. I just need to run back for my purse."

Dinny throws me a look, stiffens both arms and lifts her chin. Turning away I walk slowly through the double doors feel-

ing all at once, as one sometimes does in life, a real moment of
déjà vu. I have done all this before. There is the woman with the
crimson dress and the tiara and the bald politician. And there
are the men in tails and the man in the top hat and cane. They
are all still here, standing and talking and looking just the same
as before. I almost expect the big woman in the fur coat to shove
past and toss her fur in my direction.

You idiot.

It still rings in my ears. Again and again. I walk past them
and into the room with the bar. Laughter a little wilder now.
Conversation harsher, more jarring. The music room is almost
empty and the champagne table is littered with empty glasses
and bottles. Maggie and the handsome black man have vanished. I move towards the piano, certain I've left my purse under
the bench. Dinny's glass still stands, half-empty, on top of the
piano.

It is at this moment, while bending down slightly to peer
under the bench, that I finally become aware of someone, actually *feel* him standing not far off, just to the left and just out of
my peripheral vision. Another finely-pitched moment of déjà vu.
I turn my head, just a little.

Richard, of course. Who else?

-30-

I do not freeze or fall or drop something or crash into the piano.

I simply stop, lean down to retrieve my purse, and then turn to him, as naturally as though I were a normal person and he just an ordinary man.

He is standing quite close now, dressed in a plain dark suit, hair damp and uncombed. Pale gray eyes watch me with some curiosity. And he is smiling that same amused smile I have seen before, as though enjoying some private little joke completely at my expense. I get the impression he knew all along this would be where we'd meet tonight, that he'd planned it all, had simply been waiting here by the piano knowing I'd forgotten my purse and would return alone to find him here.

"Imagine meeting you at this party of all places, Clarice," he says, moving a little closer and placing one hand on the piano. On top of it stands an enormous bouquet of deep red roses in a beautiful ceramic vase, very dramatic against the shining black wood. Strange how I hadn't noticed them when I was talking to Maggie here earlier. I reach up and touch one rose very gently. So soft, barely open, so exquisitely perfect they don't even appear to be real.

"Richard. I had no idea you were coming here tonight. I didn't even know you knew Margaret and Douglas at all. What a coincidence us meeting like this again."

"Oh I don't know them really," he says, still smiling. "A friend of a friend you could say. Margaret and Douglas's next-door-neighbour happens to be the publisher of the *Urban Gardener.* I actually got the invite last minute. And you?"

"Douglas is my ex-husband's father. I guess they felt obligated to invite me," I say.

"Amazing isn't it? Meeting up with you here like this. Did you find my note? I knocked twice at your place but there was no answer," He moves closer, watching me, appraising. "You look absolutely beautiful tonight, Clarice, you know that?"

"Oh the note," I say, clutching my purse as though he might see what's inside. "Yes I found it, but I didn't have time to call. There was no way I could miss this party. They would have killed me."

"I can certainly see why. You wouldn't want to miss all this. Quite a celebration."

"Margaret would've been terribly upset if I didn't show up. And I didn't know you would be here, of course. When I got the note, it was too late. There was no time to call, to explain..."

I can't stop looking at the piano, at that beautiful vase with the roses, glowing as though it has life of its own. That vase must be worth a fortune. I have never seen anything like it. What would it feel like to lean over and grab it now and launch it into the air, watch it come crashing to the floor. Ten thousand little pieces. I move closer to the piano and reach up, touch it gently with one finger.

"Have you read Dostoyevsky's *The Idiot*?" I say, turning to him. "There's a part in the story where Prince Myshkin goes to a party and sits as far away as possible from an expensive Chinese vase belonging to his host, one that a friend has warned him not to knock over. But the Prince is obsessed by a sort of unshaken conviction, an absurd presentiment that he will most certainly break that vase, however much he keeps away from it and however hard he tries to avoid the disaster. And sure enough, as the evening wears on, he forgets his premonition and sits down in the armchair next to the vase. As he suddenly gets up from his seat, unthinkingly he waves his arm and somehow bumps into the vase, which crashes to the floor."

I stop and catch my breath a moment, lean towards him a little.

"Don't you see?" I say softly. "Don't you see it? Sometimes when you try so hard not to do something, to avoid some horrible catastrophe, and you warn yourself to be extremely careful, you become so obsessed by the idea that you become convinced it will happen anyway. And that is precisely the moment when disaster will strike. In a sense, you make it happen yourself."

"Clarice." He takes another step closer and grabs hold of both my arms. The roses in the vase on the piano, crimson spots against the black polished wood. I pull away. He is no longer smiling. There is something there in those eyes, incomprehensible, secretive. I want to ask him why he's doing this. I want to scream, What about *Her*? But I know that things are going as I have planned them and I should just be quiet and let it all happen. This is what I'd hoped for after all, a way to get even. To destroy something of value in his life. To make him remember.

"I have to go," I say finally. "It's Frank, my ex-husband. He's gotten himself into some kind of trouble and needs my help. I promised my mother-in-law I'd go. I'll try to come back to the party after if it's not too late."

Richard reaches into his pocket, pulls out a small notepad and pen and writes something down.

"Promise me," he says, ripping out a sheet of paper and taking hold of my arm again. "Promise me before I let you go that you'll meet me tomorrow. I have a house, an old farmhouse I just bought out in the country, just about a half-hour outside Hope. It's just beautiful. I've wanted to show it to you before, because I know you'll love it too, but I just couldn't. I'm going to move there as soon as possible. Sell my house in town. Promise me you'll come. I've written out the directions for you. It's really easy to find. Promise me. I won't let you go until you promise."

He hands me the paper and I take it, fold it without a word, push it into my purse.

"Promise?" he says again. "Late morning maybe. I'll make us something for lunch and we can sit outside on the patio and talk and I can show you everything. We need to talk."

"Okay," I say, "All right then. Yes. I'll come. I promise."

He lets go, and as I flee from him, holding my purse so tight across my breasts that it leaves a mark, it occurs to me that I've made a lot of promises to a lot of people today. And when tomorrow comes I suppose I will have to find a way to keep them.

-31-

As it turns out though, I don't end up going back to see Richard at the party at all, and I don't meet up with Maggie again until many weeks later.

It takes much longer than I thought to bail Frank out of jail, owing to the fact perhaps that Dinny is so argumentative with the police, creating a huge and unnecessary disturbance at the station. For a while I am convinced they will lock Frank in there for good and Dinny with him to boot. When we finally get him bailed out, we drive back to Dinny's and Michael's with Frank sullen and silent in the seat next to me, unwilling to say much at all about the whole thing.

"The kid just comes up to me and hauls off and hits me," he says when we arrive at the house. "What am I supposed to do? Stand there and take it? Of course I nailed him back. He's bloody well three inches bigger than I am, and I bet he's got fifty pounds on me."

He adds nothing more other than that he and Janet are through for good and he's already moved out of her house. There will be no wedding. It was all a mistake right from the beginning.

After Frank makes this little announcement, Dinny becomes downright cheery, serving drinks, making up cheese and cracker trays, and smiling brightly at everyone as though this were meant to be a party all along. Frank knocks back four gin and gingers in short order while the others stand around the kitchen sipping wine and admiring Dinny's new maple cupboards.

"Thank God you came, Clarice, and got me out of there. I'm sure mother could never have managed it on her own the way she acts," Frank says moistly in my ear, just as I am contemplating my escape plan. "You were all I could think about while I was in there locked up. And us getting back together. I figured you didn't really mean for us to break up for good, that you were hoping we could work it out somehow now that so much time has passed."

I bite into a cracker and move as far away as I dare. His breath reeks of cigarette smoke and gin, and his clothes are filthy.

"If it weren't for you I think I'd be ready to throw myself off some bridge somewhere," he says smiling his usual big smile. Moves closer again and rests a warm hand on my wrist.

"Frank," I say, rubbing a hand across my cheek. "Stop this. Don't be ridiculous."

"I told myself in jail tonight if you came to get me it would be like a sign that you still cared about me, that you wanted us back together. I really had no intention of marrying Janet at all. You know that. It was all just talk. Mother blew the whole thing out of proportion as always."

"Frank," I say, "Don't be a idiot. I didn't...don't say things like that. For heaven's sake Frank, lay off."

He takes my hand in his and grips it so tight I feel his wedding ring bite hard into my fingers. He still insists on wearing his ring. I've never seen him without it.

"Promise me you'll give us some kind of a chance. Promise me we'll try it again."

"Frank, it's over. Forever. We will never, ever get back together. We are divorced. It's final. You can't come and live with me anymore, not even for a week, not for one night. You and I, it could never happen for us again. Maybe I haven't made that clear enough before. I know I haven't made it clear enough, even in that letter I left you. I should have told you in person. I should have explained myself. Maybe I didn't write down the things I should have. But tonight you are going to hear it. It's really *over*."

I pull my hand away from his and get up quickly. Has my face started to sweat? Are my eyes red and are the tears now coming? The others would notice. Dinny will tell me I look sick and need to lie down. Michael will pour me a big glass of whisky and thrust it in my hands.

But no one appears to notice anything at all. Not even when I pick up my things and walk quickly to the front door. I announce I am going back to the party, that I promised I would go back and that Margaret is expecting me. No one says anything in response, not even Frank, and I am able to slip away quite easily.

But of course I don't dare go back to the party.

***

In the morning I rouse to the sensation of little feet pattering down my back. Jumping onto my bed is something Caesar knows is forbidden, but for once I lay still and leave him alone. *Let sleeping cats lie*, Maggie would say. She is not a dog person.

Ten minutes to seven. I get up and walk to the bathroom slowly, toes cracking. I have slept badly again. My head aches and my stomach feels hot and unsettled, and I wonder how I'll face a big breakfast with Bob at the restaurant in Milan.

I shower and dress and attempt to blow-dry my hair. Caesar sits outside the shower door and reaches for the water drops, claws outstretched. I move slowly to the chess game. My next move is very, very clear. Slide the white queen across the board. *Check mate*.

***

When I arrive at the restaurant, Bob is already standing at the door waiting. He holds the door open, grabs my hand and shakes it hard, pumping it up and down several times. I pull it away and wiggle my fingers a little, look around. There is hardly anyone here this morning; it is actually quite deserted. We stand impatiently for a minute or two saying nothing, throwing little glances at one another and pretending to examine our surroundings with interest. Eventually a male waiter in a very short brush-cut arrives, shows us to a table at the back, hands us menus and rearranges cutlery with much noise. Bob and I both watch as he pours the coffee, then turn and look as he strides away rapidly.

"So," says Bob, "I'm glad you made it, Clarice. I was worried you wouldn't show."

"I said I would. I promised you." He is watching me, calculating. He is thinking this girl is pretty dumb, the unintelligent sort of person who doesn't know when it's time to leave well enough alone, the kind who needs things spelled out clearly in black and white. *Back off. The man is taken.*

"Sure is quiet here this time of day, isn't it?" I reach for a napkin and unfold it in my lap.

"Oh just wait. Wait for about another half-hour or so. It'll be standing room only." He gestures widely with his hand. "The place is usually packed for brunch. Ordinarily there's only a few tables left by the time we get here."

"So where is Lisa this morning anyway? I thought she'd be joining us."

He has not taken the time to shave this morning. The stubble of a two-day beard makes his olive skin look even darker. There is hardly a hair on his head that isn't gray.

"Oh, she couldn't make it. Working today. Starts at eight."

I flip open the menu and close it again. Coffee and toast is all I can manage this morning. Wine, champagne. How many glasses? And all those rich hors d'oeuvres.

"So what was it you wanted? What were you so anxious to talk to me about?"

The waiter with the short brush-cut returns and takes our order. His left eyebrow is pierced with a small gold ring. Several toe rings peek out from under brown leather sandals. Do they allow that sort of thing in a restaurant like this? Is there no dress code?

Bob unfolds his napkin, glances over.

"How long have you known Richard?"

I take a moment to consider this. How long? What would be the truthful answer?

"It's alright," he says when I don't say anything. "It doesn't matter how long anyway. It couldn't have been very long or you'd know some of the story. You'd understand what this was all about."

"Understand what? What is all this? What are you trying to tell me?"

After all it was Richard who left the note at my door and Richard who gave me the directions to the farmhouse last night. I am suddenly angry. I am about to shove back my chair and get up, tell Bob that I'm not interested in hearing any of this, that I'm perfectly prepared to drop Richard like a rock, that I know all about his woman. But then I notice there are tears in his eyes. There really are.

The waiter has returned with our order. Toast, juice and coffee for me. Bacon and eggs over easy and pancakes for Bob. We wait until the waiter walks away, flip-flopping in his sandals. Bob looks down at his plate but doesn't pick up his fork.

"What is it?" I say quietly. "What's wrong?"

"Did Richard tell you about Jenny?"

There it is. The *Name*. It drops from the air as though weighted with lead, crashes to the floor in front of me, echoes again and again through the room. *Jenny. Jenny.* I look around me half expecting that others have heard it too, that people are looking.

"No." I say. "Yes. That is he told me about a woman he was going out with, someone he'd been together with for a long, long time."

"What did he tell you?"

"Oh not much. She's very talented, isn't she? A lawyer and a musician too, I gather. Very popular and everyone likes her a lot. Everyone that meets her likes her right away. Yes, I think that's what he said."

Bob says nothing, picks up a fork and pushes the eggs around his plate.

"And quite a personality too." I say this easily, as though it doesn't matter at all. I can be generous. Who cares whether she's talented and smart and beautiful? Twist the juice glass in my hands, around and around.

"Jenny was a wonderful person," he says slowly. "She was actually a cousin of mine, second cousin I believe. Our grandmothers were related somehow as I recall. That's how Richard got to know her actually, through me. They hit it off right away, even when they were little kids. Always together. She was perfect for him. When Jenny was in the room it was like Richard was a different person. I don't think he ever saw it himself, how much he lived through her. I guess that's why without her he just seemed to waste away."

"Without her?" I say, clinging to these last two words and losing the rest. "But where is she? Where did she go?"

Bob doesn't answer. He still hasn't eaten anything and looks down at his plateful of eggs and pancakes without seeing.

"I don't want you to get the wrong impression," he says finally. "That's why I don't quite know how to say this. He's going to be okay. I know it. He just needs some time to work it all through. He needs to talk to someone. He's really a great guy, believe me. Anybody would be shaken up over something like this. It takes a whole lot of time and you need other people around you to get over something like that. Heaven only knows it would take me forever to get over it myself. It's only natural. You see," he says, picking up a fork and spearing an egg yolk, "Jenny got very sick and she passed away. She's been gone for almost two years now"

I don't think even in my wildest, most irresponsible, self-indulgent fantasies did I ever once imagine her dead. Passed away. Gone.

"She can't be," I say, feeling my hands get ice-cold. "There were letters. I saw them myself. He told me. He told me there was someone else in his life. He told me all about her. You have to be wrong. A mix-up. It's someone else you're thinking of."

Bob does not look at me. He's put the fork down again. The yolk from the egg is running all over the plate and mixing with the pancake syrup. In the background there is suddenly noise. More people have come into the room and have begun to sit down at tables around us.

"Believe me she's gone. But they were together all the time since they were little children. They were always together, always best friends, always in love with one another. I don't think he remembers a time when he didn't have her. So he goes to her house every day still. He's bought the place now, and I think he goes there to remember, to feel like he's close to her still."

"Her house?" I say. "He goes to her house?"

"A place out in the country, not far from Hope. An old farmhouse that used to belong to her family. My mom's cousins' family from way back. Beautiful old place. They were going to get married, live there. It was all set. The wedding date and everything."

"And then?" I say. "And then?"

"She was really beautiful, you know. Really a good person. Everyone loved her. She never said a bad thing about anyone. Everyone said they would get married eventually. It seemed so natural. They were inseparable. Two of a kind."

"But what happened? What?"

"She got sick. Headaches at first really bad. And she blacked out once when she was driving and had some kind of a minor accident. At first they didn't know what it was. They did all kinds of tests and then they found out. She was in the hospital for ages. But it was too late. She wanted to come home for a while. She didn't want to stay in the hospital. She liked to play the piano. It was something she could still do for a while even when she was so sick, until it got close to the end. And then she couldn't even sit up anymore and eventually she went back to the hospital. She wasn't there two weeks before she was gone."

"Died," I say. "Dead." I should feel relief. But I can't. I feel pain, a knife in my chest. As though it were happening to me, as though I were lying there in that hospital bed unable to move with something horrible growing in my head. I have felt this way before. Suffocating. I want to get up and go outside, breathe in fresh air loaded with oxygen. Beside me a woman in a purple dress is scrubbing the grubby hands of a little girl. Evidently the little girl has been playing with the maple syrup pitcher.

"But the letters," I say, clasping my cold hands together. "I saw letters at his house. They were from her, I swear it. I saw them myself, with my own eyes. She sent them. There must be a mistake."

"It's not a mistake," he says. "He went to see her every day while she was sick, staying with her at the house when he could. Even took a leave of absence from work. But since then, since she's been gone, I think he's been going to that house every day anyway, every day since she died. He's driven all the way out there after work, and God only knows what he does there, just sits and thinks and looks at her things, I guess. And I know about the letters. I know about them all. He sent them himself."

I take a big swallow of juice. Set the glass down again carefully and twist it in my hands.

The child beside us is crying now. In her excitement she's jumped up and spilled the entire maple syrup pitcher all over the table. Her mother is yelling, yanking her by the arm and making her sit down. Yelling and scolding, voice rising. The waiter with the brush-cut hurries over with a cloth and a new pitcher of syrup, a plateful of pancakes.

"I don't believe you. You're making this up," I say.

"It's true. He sent them himself. He didn't write them of course. She must've written a whole bunch of letters to him after she got sick. Never sent them off though. Just tied them all up with string in a big bundle and put them away for him to find when she was gone. A sort of diary, I guess. I think he found them later, afterwards, and then he started sending them, one or two a week, maybe. I know. I saw them arrive at his house too. I was there once and I saw his mail on the table and one of the letters was open. I know I shouldn't have done it, but I read it. Just a few lines. Then I knew. Then I knew what he was really about."

"What is it? What was he thinking? Why did he send those letters when he knew she was dead?"

"That's just it. Don't you see? Don't you see it now? She's not really gone. Not to him, anyway. He doesn't believe it. He hasn't accepted it. I truly think he goes there every day believing in some way that she's still there. He goes to see her, to visit her in that old grave of a house. Maybe talk to her. Maybe he thinks he sees her there, I don't know. I followed him in my car once. I never even told Lisa. It would give her the creeps if she knew. She'd want to tell someone. She's got a friend that's a doctor at the psyche hospital in Milan. She'd probably tell her all about it and before you know it they'd have Richard locked up in there or something. Who knows? And he isn't crazy. Believe me, he's as sane as you and me. He just needs some help getting over this, getting through it. Some professional counseling maybe. All I know is he doesn't believe she's dead. I'm sure of it. I've tried to talk to him, but he's touchy about it. Denies everything and changes the subject right away. I guess if he keeps getting her letters in the mail it makes him feel she's still alive."

The little girl is eating her pancakes now, but her nose is still running and she flashes quick, angry looks at her mother through untidy bangs.

He goes to see her. He visits her. Keeps her alive. Like a wake before a funeral. A vigil over a corpse that goes on and on.

"He won't say where he goes? He won't talk to you about her? Has he seen any kind of a professional at all then? Has anyone tried to help him?"

"Oh no, I don't think so. I've tried to get him to, but he's furious if I even mention it. And no, he won't say where he goes. Just says he's going out. When I first saw you here in the restaurant with him, I thought for a second it was you he was going to see all along, that I was wrong about everything. That he'd met you and you were dating one another for a long time and that for some reason he hadn't told me, hadn't wanted me to know. I thought maybe he figured I'd blame him for forgetting about Jenny too quickly. Even though she's been dead for years and anyone would think he should move on. But then I realized you two had just met. It wasn't you he was going to see every night at all. My suspicions were correct. It was Jenny. Jenny all along. I wouldn't believe it, even now, but like I said, I followed him. I saw the letters. I have the proof."

I want to tell him that I've followed Richard too. I want to tell him about seeing the farmhouse, going inside, about the letters, the photograph. But I can't. There is no way I can explain. I can just imagine Bob's face if I said something now: the eyebrows gathering together, the anger in his eyes. He is Richard's friend. Naturally he will want to protect him. The plan. It's dissolving, falling to pieces, even as we speak. I feel panic rising, flooding in my chest, and my throat is suddenly tremendously dry.

"At first, right after she'd died, I thought Richard was just going to the house to be in a place where he could remember her," Bob says, "where he could sit quietly and grieve. It was the place where they spent so much time together. They were going to get married and he was going to move in there with her after all. But later, when I watched him go there night after night and spend hours and even days there, I knew there was more to it than that. And then he bought the house from the family and he started going there more and more. That's when I began to suspect things were not right. He has himself convinced she still lives there. I know it. He goes to see her and he talks to her. He's told me so himself. Not in so many words, but he did."

We both sit and look down at our plates. Neither one of us has eaten. My toast is cold. His eggs congealed. The waiter has come by now twice and looked at our uneaten plates, eyebrow ring twinkling in the morning sun. Poured more juice, asked if the food was okay or if there was a problem.

I pick up my coffee, which is now cold, and swallow deeply. Bob picks up his and drinks as well, watching me intently over his cup. He is wondering what I am thinking, wondering what I make of all this, wondering if I will now bolt like a shy horse. I can tell by the way he keeps glancing so searchingly at my face, by that speculative look. He rubs an index finger across his lips, looks down. He is expecting me to say something. He is ready to challenge me.

"So now what?" I say at last. "Why did you ask me to come here? What do you want from me?"

"Nothing. Nothing at all. Of course I don't expect you to want to continue seeing someone who's an emotional wreck, who's unstable and ..." He stops there and looks back up at me. "I just thought I had better tell you before you started noticing things, before you got all the wrong ideas about him. Before you got scared off. You seem like the right kind of person for him, the kind of person he needs right now. Down-to-earth and dependable and rational and sane. Jenny, despite all her accomplishments, was so flighty, given to fits and a wild temper like you wouldn't believe. Flaky. On cloud nine, Lisa always said, Volatile. You, on the other hand, seem so solid and steady, the kind of person one could rely on. So perfectly normal."

"Oh no," I say quickly, feeling my hands get colder. "You've got it all wrong. I'm not like that at all. I'm not any of those things you said. You don't know anything about me at all."

He smiles. "On the contrary. I think you are exactly what he needs right now."

I bend over my coffee cup, rub my hands together in my lap. My neck and forehead are beginning to get damp, but I still feel cold and my stomach feels a little sick. "Do you think that it's possible to love someone the way he loved her, even if you knew them only a short time? Is it possible?"

"I don't know," he says.

He doesn't understand me, doesn't know what I'm asking. To him, love is simple. Black or white. It's either there or it isn't. And there is only one kind of love. He and Lisa have been together for ages. They were high school sweethearts after all. There are no different levels of love in his world. You love someone, they die, you go on and find someone else and love them the same way. He cannot understand someone like Richard or like me. He has no idea that there can be different kinds of love, in every shade and intensity. That there can be countless reasons for it too. Not everyone loves for the same reasons.

"Not everyone loves for the same reasons," I say unnecessarily.

"No," he says. "I suppose not. But there's no reason why he can't get over this. It just takes some people a while. I have an aunt whose husband died when she was only twenty-five. She didn't marry again for fifteen years, but then she did and had two children in thirteen months and as far as I know is as happy as the next person. Richard just has to let the past be the past. You can't live life tied down to a dead person. That's just not what life's meant to be. He's my friend. My best friend. I want him to be happy again. And he will be. He just needs time. And he needs someone like you. Someone normal and rational and really nice."

"But you can't force a person to forget. You can't force someone to let go. They have to want to. And some people don't. Ever. Some people are just as happy continuing their lives with their memories to keep them company. Letting go can be a very bad thing for some people. They can wither and die if they are forced. Clearly Richard is one of those people. That's why I know there's nothing I can do for him. You can't possibly understand."

"No, you're wrong," Bob says, his voice suddenly very loud. He is angry. I am not listening, not complying. "You're dead wrong there. There's a hell of a lot you can do. I've seen big changes in him in the last while already, ever since you came into the picture I imagine. Big changes. Just going out on a few dates is drawing him back into some kind of a normal life already. He's willing to drop the past if he finds someone new, I'm sure of it. Don't let go now. Don't give up. I can guarantee you he will change and settle down into a normal life again. It's just a matter of time."

Should I tell him about Richard at the party last night, about the note in my purse with the directions to the farmhouse? But I'm not sure yet whether I'll go. And he will try to convince me. The truth is, I'm afraid to go there now, afraid to face whatever it is that still exists in that house. Maybe in a way she is still there, lingering, watching over Richard and whispering to him in his sleep. Maybe I'm just afraid to speak to him again. Now that I know my little plan has failed, maybe I should just abandon him too and forget about it all. It is all too complicated for someone like me. I should just stay out of it.

"I don't know," I say. "I just don't know."

"Look," Bob says, "just promise me you'll at least give him a chance. You're the first woman he's even spoken to that I'm aware of, or shown any interest in whatsoever since the day she died. He's gone to work and done his job and as far as I know he's perfectly okay when he's writing for the magazine, but that's been it. He's buried himself in his work totally. I made him go out for drinks at *Sunny's* on Friday nights with me, absolutely forced him, but other than that he's spent every night in the past two years out there in that house with her. I'm convinced of that."

With *Her.*

"I need to think about this," I say. "I need to think it all over. I can't make any more promises."

He leans back in his chair and looks at me, waiting.

"Lisa and I, we're having a few friends over next Friday night. Just a few people that Richard knows too. We're going to ask him and I want you to come too. Please. At least tell me you'll come to that. It'll only be a few hours and there'll be other people around. You can just relax and enjoy yourself and meet a few people. You hardly have to talk to him if you don't want to. No pressure. Just say you'll come. Say you'll help us out. I have this feeling if I tell Richard you're coming too, he'll decide to show up. But he'd never come alone."

"Okay," I say. "Alright. I'll maybe come to that. But I need to think about it all for a while. About everything you told me. I need some time to sort it all out. So I'm not making any promises. Just remember that. No more promises. I came here and I heard what you had to say, but I'm not making any more promises. I have my own life to think about. I'm not at all like you think. I'm not the person to help you in this, believe me."

Getting up from the table I slip some money under the plate and push it away, turn towards the door.

"Thank you for breakfast."

"No don't thank me. I'm just grateful you were willing to come and listen to what I had to say."

And then, as I walk towards the door, I hear him come up close behind me, touch my arm.

"I'm so glad you came Clarice, really. At least now you understand. Finally I've been able to tell someone else all of this, get it off my chest. And you're wrong. You're very wrong. You are definitely the person to help us in this. I knew it from the moment I laid eyes on you the first time. Believe me. I promise you that. You alone are the one person Richard so desperately needs."

-32-

It is already past noon when I arrive at the farmhouse. The sun shines dully from behind a film of clouds, thin as onionskin. Not even a suggestion of wind. Trees motionless as in a painted landscape. As still as death, if you will.

It seems a little odd not to drive right up to the house like a normal person this time. The lane way gives the impression of being narrower than I remember, trees crowding in close and branches reaching suggestively for the car windows. I am driving too fast again and the end of the driveway takes me by surprise so that I have to brake sharply. I have not been paying attention, lulled to complacency by the unnatural stillness, the flatness of the light, the watercolor trees. I am a little dull myself too, apathetic. It seems I hardly care that I am here, that I have finally arrived at my destination. I have to keep shaking myself, telling myself, *this is it. Pay attention.*

In my hands I clutch the directions he gave me last night. I'd just about persuaded myself I wouldn't come at all following breakfast with Bob this morning. How could I carry on with my plan knowing what I do? Nothing can destroy him now. Like aiming your gun at an enemy and just as you are about to pull the trigger you discover the target has already dissolved, melted into mirage.

After breakfast I went home and took a look at the map Richard had given me, along with the note he'd left at my house yesterday. And it was then, idiot that I am, that I finally realized this was the same backwards, slanted handwriting I'd come to know so well from the letters: scribbled, extraordinarily sloppy, as though the writer were in some huge hurry. Bob was telling the truth. The letters from *Her* had been sent by Richard. He himself had written the addresses on the envelopes. She did not exist anymore. It was Richard all along. And this made the decision for me. He is not the person I thought, and all of a sudden things are not so simple, not so black and white. There are so many choices before me. Alternatives to my little plan. It seems I must figure out some other way to go on with things, find some other end I can live with.

And then I permitted myself to think about my little girl again at last.

Her face: the beautiful eyes, the long dark hair, that sweet extraordinary smile that made people, perfect strangers, always look her way. The amazing way she would throw her arms around my neck and hug me tight. *I love you as big as this*, she would say, stretching out her arms. *As big as all the pieces of sand in the whole wide world and all the stars in the whole big sky.* People said it was unbelievable how she spoke in such long, complicated sentences when she was barely two. And the most wonderful imagination. Always finding little things outside, pine cones and acorns and little stones, and making up long, elaborate stories about them. She adored music. There always had to be music at our house, day and night. *Play the piano, Mommy. Play for me!* She'd pull me into the living room and then she'd dance while I played, faster and faster and faster, spinning around the room like a tiny storm. I'll tell you what kind of mother I was. I turned down everything to be with her, stopped working at the newspaper, stopped going out with friends, stopped going to parties and seeing people. No one else. I focused on her alone. I took her to the zoo and the parks and the museums and taught her as many words as I could. How to read and write her name and then my name and Daddy's too. She learned to read and write much earlier than most kids, and her printing was that of a much older child. Everyone remarked on it. When I was still a reporter and I was supposed to go out to cover a big story I called in and said I was sick, just like that. *I'm too sick to come in. You'll have to send someone else.* Just because she asked me to take her to the city that evening so she could see the Christmas lights in the park. I drove her there and we looked at them together for hours. Hours. I will never forget the wonder on her face, the fascination, joy. That's the kind of mother I was.

Today I permit myself to remember, and this time I will not allow it to break me into little pieces. I must hold it together now. I am not Richard. I do not believe my little girl is alive and living in some old house. I am not sending myself letters. He is much worse off than I am. There is no point in trying to settle the score. He is already broken.

Slowing my car to a crawl, I head for the back of the house. His truck is there, parked over by the small shed. I stop my car next to it and get out. Try to shake myself awake, to shed the indifference that has settled around me this morning. I must caution myself that I need to concentrate, that everything matters now, that *this is it.*

I approach the house very slowly. He has asked me here after all. I am an invited guest. There is no reason why I should be afraid. But somehow I feel I am the unwanted intruder again, peeping in windows, breaking screens, meddling with someone else's things. To give myself courage I march around the front of the house and walk right up to those massive front doors. No hidden away backdoor for me today. No broken window screens and rotten basement stairs. Finally I rid myself of the apathy that has dogged me all the way here. I feel it recede the moment I step onto the front porch. I am quite suddenly very wide awake.

Lifting my fist, I knock sharply, twice. Any moment now the doors will swing open wide. But I must knock again and again, six or seven times at least, and many minutes pass before there is finally a noise: faint at first, then louder, and at last the scraping of a lock and the slow movement of the door, inwards.

He stands motionless, a sheet of paper in his hands. For a moment we both just stare at one another. His face appears so different that I believe I really am mistaken, that it is not him after all but someone else, a long-forgotten ancestor resurrected from the grave. But I am wrong. Waiting here these long minutes I have worked myself up into a state of nerves. In the back of my mind I had almost expected, almost convinced myself, that these doors would be opened by Jenny herself. A grisly specter in a long gown.

Of course it isn't like that at all. Just Richard, perfectly ordinary, calmly holding open the door, and now, presumably now that he has recognized me, a faint smile on his lips.

"Hello Richard," I say, moving toward him. "I followed your directions. It wasn't hard to find."

"Yes," he says. "I thought you might come back to the party last night, but you didn't. So I wondered whether you'd even show up here today at all."

He takes my arm and leads me quickly down the long corridor, turning into a room I know I should recognize. But for some reason it is all bewilderingly different. I stumble back a little, pulling away from him.

"This," he says, motioning with his arm, "is the living room. Great, isn't it?"

No longer is there an air of neglect, a smell of disuse. The windows are all open and the room is spotless. There is no dust, no dirt. The heaps of dead flies on the windowsills have disappeared. The black mildew on the wooden window frames has vanished. Mouse droppings have been swept away. Everything clean and bright as though used every day by a large and bustling family.

And then I notice something in the room I hadn't noticed at all the first time I was here. A black grand piano. Maybe it was covered over with a dustsheet before or perhaps it was just too dark in here that day. It stands in one corner to the left of the big stone fireplace, immutable, as though it has always belonged here to this house and to this room. It waits, poised, polished, silent, a book of music already open, anticipating the long, elegant fingers that will press down the keys and bring it to life. There is even a crystal vase with yellow lilies resting on top looking very fresh and alive.

"It's a beautiful room," I say. "As though someone lived here all along. You've really done a nice job fixing it up. Was the furniture already here?"

"I just bought the house," he says, very quietly. "I haven't actually moved in yet. But as you can see, I've spent quite a bit of time getting things ready."

He is watching me, eyes half-closed, arms crossed. He looks very relaxed, sleepy even, as though at any moment he will drop down into one of those enormous armchairs, raise his feet onto a footstool and close his eyes, fall asleep.

"It's a beautiful house," I say again. "I can't wait to see the rest. It's just gorgeous from outside too. What a lovely property. I can see why you'd want to move here."

"Yes," he says, crumpling the piece of paper in his hands. "It's always been like home. I can't imagine living anywhere else."

"You knew them then?" I say. "You knew the owners well? The people who sold you the house? You've been here often before?"

"Oh yes, I still know them," he says and turns away, shifting the ball of paper from one hand to the other. "And I've certainly been here many times before. I'll go get us something to drink. You're probably thirsty. And I told you I'd make you lunch. I haven't had time until just now to get it in the oven and I didn't know for sure whether you were coming anyway. So lunch should be done in about an hour or so."

After he is gone I turn around again and move over to the piano, pick up the music. Beethoven's *Moonlight Sonata in C Sharp Minor*, open to the *Presto Agitato* movement, a very difficult passage for even the most accomplished pianist. Looking down at the spotless ivory keys, I can see *Her* sitting on the gleaming bench, blonde hair falling over her shoulders, hands floating above the keys, long, elegant fingers reaching for the difficult notes.

Shivering a little I turn away, will myself to look elsewhere but at those cold, ivory keys and those long-fingered hands.

"Clarice."

I replace the piano book as fast as I can, quickly turning the pages back to the where they were before I touched them. Holding a hand to my neck and clearing my throat noisily, I turn, hoping he can't see I am actually shaking a little. My heart is even pounding.

"Your drink. House special." He hands me a glass, unsmiling. "Do you play?" he says, motioning to the piano.

"Oh no. Only a little. I used to, but certainly not this," I reach for the music, almost touch it again with the tips of my fingers, let my hand fall back to my side. "It's really a difficult piece technically. Very fast. It sounds as though there's more than one person playing. I always wanted to be able to play something like that. I just couldn't and certainly not now. I don't even have a piano anymore."

"I wouldn't know," he says. "I don't play myself."

I look away and take a large swallow. I'm not sure what it is. It tastes very good. There's lime juice in it and something else that I can't quite identify. Cranberry maybe.

"Well, let's sit down," Richard says. "Have our drink. Then I'll show you the rest of the house."

We sit down in the two big armchairs placed close together in front of the fireplace. Even without a fire burning it is a very comfortable room, bright and cozy. I cross and uncross my legs, twist the glass in my hands. He is seated so close to me our knees are almost touching. I can feel the heat from his body radiating to my skin. I wish I could reach out and touch his leg, rest my hand lightly on his thigh, caress him slowly. And he would lean back and close his eyes and smile, and we would sit here together, comfortable, belonging as much together and to this house as the grandfather clock in the corner.

He has finished his drink already and is gazing into the fireplace, as though watching real flames, bouncing one knee up and down slightly.

"You said you knew the people that had this house before," I say softly.

But he only nods. For a few minutes we sit like this and I wonder why suddenly we are like two strangers when any time we've been together before we talked more freely than I've talked with anyone. As we sit here so close together, the minutes slipping away, I can't help remembering how warm his fingers felt when his hand touched my shoulder at his house. And last night at the party, taking hold of both my arms and pulling me closer. Now I'm not sure any more why I felt so unnerved by it, why I was almost repulsed by his touch.

So we continue to sit and I sip at my drink, and slowly, as the minutes tick away, I find myself lost in some kind of a peaceful state between wakefulness and sleep, forgetting, almost, that I am here in this room and he is seated only inches away.

"I've changed my mind," he says so suddenly that I pull away from him a little. "I'll show you the rest of the house some other day. After we eat we can go outside, go for a walk. You could walk for miles here and not see another soul."

"I'd like that," I say.

But I wanted him to show me the house. I wanted to see what he would say when he opened the door to that bedroom upstairs. Is the bed still made up and are the clothes still in the closet? Is the photograph still there? Or will it all be changed now, altered completely just like this room? I shift uneasily in my chair. I have to see that room.

"Well I'd better go and check and see I'm not burning our lunch," he says. "Tarragon chicken potpie. Recipe I learned a long time ago. Tremendous with a good white wine. That is, if I don't burn it first."

"Can I help?" I say, but he is already gone, sweeping up both glasses in one hand and striding rapidly from the room. I get the impression he couldn't wait to get up and go, to leave me sitting here alone, that he is not in the mood for company of any kind today. The truth is, he regrets his rash invitation of last night; I'm quite sure of it.

Rub at my arms. I am cold. It may be a beautiful hot day outside, but in this old stone house it is really quite chilly and my shirt is quite thin. Get up slowly, look behind me. No, he is still in the kitchen. A clatter of pans and the sound of a tap being turned on. Moving as silently as possible, I head for the doorway and make my way to the stairs. There is nothing to stop me. I am at the top in a matter of seconds and find my way to the room quite easily.

And here is the little night table with the slim curved legs, and the antique hoop bed with the gorgeous quilt. It is spotless, this room, just like the living room downstairs, but here nothing much has changed from my most recent visit. There is a strong scent. I recognize it instantly. Lilies, fresia. The window is open a few inches but there is still no wind. Nothing moves at all.

Open the closet door. Dozens of dresses, blouses, skirts, shoes. Everything as though just worn yesterday, freshly washed and pressed. Searching through I find the pale pink dress I saw the first time. Pull it out and hold it briefly in outstretched arms.

How beautiful it is. My green dress from last night seems quite ordinary and dull in comparison. And surely this one is real silk. I hold it up against me, feeling the softness and warmth against my cold skin.

And then I catch sight of my own reflection in the big standing mirror at the foot of the bed. A thin woman with dark hair pulled into a hasty ponytail, deep shadows beneath the eyes, indistinct, pale, skeletal, ghost-like, clutching before her someone else's elegant pink dress.

Turn to the photograph, conscious it is still there on the little night table next to a vase of fresh lilies and fresia. I am being watched. I hang the dress back carefully in its place in the closet and move towards the little night table.

Jenny.

She is smiling and her eyes are very blue, hair illuminated as though the sun were really shining on it. Her eyes look straight and unflinchingly into mine. The picture looks so real, the colors so vibrant; surely she is really standing there looking at me and I am the one who is the shadow.

A noise behind me and I know that those eyes in the picture are not looking at me.

"Why are you here in this room?" he says. *Accusation?*

"I just thought I'd look around while you were busy in the kitchen," I say quickly. "I knew you wouldn't mind if I wandered a bit, toured the place. It's such a beautiful house I wanted to see the upstairs."

"Yes, it is beautiful," he says. He doesn't move, just stands there in the doorway arms crossed in front, a bottle of wine still clutched in one hand.

I turn back, unwillingly, to the photograph.

"Who is this? Who is this here in this picture? Did you know her? Why did they leave everything furnished like this when they moved out, with clothes still in the closet and pictures on the table? Or are they yours?"

"Come back downstairs," he says, turning away as if he hasn't heard. "Come back downstairs and I'll open a bottle of wine. We can have a glass before lunch. It's going to take a while for our lunch. It needs to cool a little after it comes out of the oven. I can light a fire in the fireplace. It's quite a warm day outside, but it stays so cool in here in this old place. And I wouldn't want my guest to be cold now would I."

I turn and follow him from the room. *Come down at once you unruly child who can't be left alone for a moment without wandering off and causing trouble.*

Richard busies himself lighting the fire and I sit down again, this time on the couch. There is a pile of kindling next to the hearth in a copper container, some paper and a small pile of wood. Everything has been laid out as though prepared in advance for some important event.

He pours us each a glass of wine and sits close to me on the couch. We sip our wine for a few moments and he leans back and rests his head against a pillow, eyes half-closed. Picks up a ball of paper and tosses it carelessly into the fire. We both watch the paper catch and begin to burn, flaring briefly to an enormous flame and then crumbling just as swiftly to ash. I stare enthralled, unable to tear my eyes away. She is in the room with us, watching, waiting. I am almost afraid to look away from the fire and towards the piano.

The time has come. I have to tell him. To make him remember. It is enormously difficult to say the words but nevertheless they must be said if I ever want to see him again. I can't continue on with this deception now that I know what has happened to him. Now that I've made my decision.

"Do you remember," I say slowly, concentrating on speaking clearly, "something that happened to you a few years ago?" I stop, push the hair back from my face and wipe at my eyes. Shift a little away from him. "I saw you. I saw your face in the newspaper and I read a story about you, about something you did."

No emotion, no sign that he remembers anything at all, no indication that he is even listening. He is looking into the fire again, eyes half-closed, sleepily, one knee bouncing rapidly up and down.

"I read that story. And I remembered your face. I remember it all. You were at a store one day, a corner store in Milan, and something happened. You were inside buying something and when you came out you saw there was a car in the parking lot and it was driving around, crazily, in circles, around and around in one big, crazy circle, totally out-of-control. The newspaper said the car was left running while the owner, the mother, went into the store. And that person, that mother, left a small child alone inside with the vehicle's engine still running. The mother was only going to be gone for a moment, you see. She had to go in because she needed milk and some cereal, and she couldn't trust her husband to go and buy the right kind, the more expensive kind, the kind the child would eat. And somehow the child, who was asleep when the mother left, woke up and managed to get out of her booster seat, although the parents hadn't ever thought in a million years that she knew how. But one way or another she had, and she'd crawled to the front of the vehicle and pushed the gear shift into drive. And then it began to lurch around the parking lot in circles, around and around, and the mother didn't even know. She just kept on waiting in the store in line, waiting to pay for her things, not even hearing the commotion outside, not guessing the tragedy unfolding behind the doors. But you had seen it. No one else was out there. No one else was close by. You stopped and waited and watched it, trying to decide what to do, whether to do anything at all, whether to involve yourself. Then, finally, after a very long time, you ran over and tried to stop it. You tried to get into the driver's side door to stop it from going in circles because you saw there was a child, and you saw that she was crying and very frightened and you saw that one door was open a little. But it was too late. You didn't get there in time. You waited too long. You waited and you didn't save her. You were afraid if you moved too quickly the car would run over you too."

"Yes, it was me. Of course I remember. It was awful, a terrible tragedy," he says finally, "Of course I tried to stop it. I tried to get to it in time, to get it stopped because I saw that the door was open just a little and I saw the child could easily fall out. But it was too late. I was too late. She'd fallen out by the time I got to it and got it stopped. It was too late. There was nothing anyone could do. I knew there was nothing more that could be done. If only I'd come out a few seconds earlier. I asked myself that so many times afterwards. Why couldn't I have come out of that store just a few moments earlier? But you're wrong. I didn't wait. There was no time. I didn't hesitate at all. I didn't. I just ran as soon as I came out of the store, I swear."

I look away. I can see that little face. Until today I haven't seen it so clearly even in dreams in many years. I haven't allowed myself that little luxury, you see. But finally today I see that face again quite clearly, that little face just as it was the day it happened, the little dark curls, and the beautiful eyes. So beautiful. People always asked who she resembled most. But she didn't look at all like me or like Frank either. She was so perfect. A perfect little angel. Resembled no one in either family. Like she dropped from heaven into our lives for such a short, short time. The day it happened we had been to the park and then to the zoo in Milan. She said *isn't that a spider monkey, Mommy? Isn't it?* Imagine, she actually remembered that exact name from the last time. And she knew the panda bears too, and many of the birds names. She was so tired and was finally drifting off to sleep when I pulled into the variety store parking lot. I didn't want to turn the engine off and wake her up. I didn't want to lift her out of the booster seat and disturb her when she needed so badly to rest. You see I didn't want to wake her up. That was the kind of mother I was.

It wasn't his fault. It wasn't his fault. He tried to save her. He did all he could.

I know there are tears streaming down my cheeks but I don't try to stop them. I know he is looking at me and waiting for me to say something, but I can't say anything at all. I can see him moving towards the car, the car spinning around wildly, the door partly open. I can see him reaching out desperately to grab at the door, reaching for her. Too late.

"I'm so sorry, Clarice," he says, comprehension at last dawning on him, the expression in his eyes changing as he raises one hand to his lips. "Good God, Clarice, it was you, wasn't it? It was your child. I didn't know. I didn't get it until just now. But I saw the mother there. I saw her standing at the doorway of the store when I finally got the car stopped. Now I can remember it quite clearly although I'd forgotten that part. She'd just come out at that moment when it was all over already. I saw her face and I realized she could see it was too late. Then the ambulance came and all the people crowded around, and someone said she was gone, that the little girl was gone, and there was nothing more anyone could do. I'm so sorry, Clarice. Now I know. Your little girl."

"And so you see," I say. "I had to tell you the truth. I've seen you before. Before that night we met in the bar. Only I couldn't tell you then. I couldn't very well tell you about it and try to remember it all again that night in the bar. Not until now." I look down at my hands, at the nails. They are ragged, splitting. I must've chewed them to pieces last night. "You see I've lost someone too. I've lost the one, the only person in this world that mattered to me, the only one I really loved. And so I thought when I saw you that day when she was taken away from me, that you could've saved her, that you could've done something. There was time for someone to save her, surely. I thought I knew that for certain. I wanted to ask you. But you disappeared so quickly afterward I didn't even get a chance to say anything to you. And then I saw you again years later walking down a street in town. I didn't even know you lived in Hope."

"You saw me before that night in the bar? You knew who I was all along?"

"Yes, I saw you." I stop, uncertain how to continue, how to explain it all, seeing suddenly before me the stolen letters as though they are still in my hands. If only I'd known about Jenny from the beginning. "I saw you a number of times before I tried to talk to you in the bar. I knew who you were. And I blamed you. You could have saved her and you chose not to."

He is looking at me now, looking intently at my face and into my eyes.

"Richard, I know all about her. About Jenny. Your friend Bob told me just this morning. And I understand. I know how hard it is to live with. It's just like Frank and I. There was always this shadow between us, her little shadow. We could have been satisfied living together, Frank and I. We were content enough before it happened. Happy with the life we'd built, and we loved each other. I loved Frank in my own way. He's a good person. Her death changed him for the better, while for me it made me worse, worse in every way. There was no way. There was no way we could continue on together and that it could work for us again."

I pick up the glass, take a long drink swallowing hard. The fire is burning well now, consuming the larger pieces of wood, and I am beginning to feel its warmth on my face.

"When she came along," I say slowly, "she became the love that drew us together. Before she arrived, Frank and I were something like two strangers living together. When she came, she changed everything, made us both better people. We loved each other because of her. And then, when she was gone, it was like it crushed me. I no longer existed; the other person that remained was just a shell. I couldn't see anything the same after that: not people, not work, not anything. I stumbled around looking for a way to live with myself, to keep from falling to pieces. There was no way Frank and I could go on together. Not that I blamed him. There was no room for him in all of this. Then the guilt took over. The terrible, terrifying guilt. It didn't get better with time. They lied about that; it got worse. Much worse. Each day, each week, each year. Time doesn't heal all things. It's a lie. A horrible, hideous, awful lie that people make up."

Twisting the glass in my hands I glance up at him. His eyebrows gather and his face begins to change, subtly, all at once inscrutable, guarded. He has begun, again, to think about her.

"You're right. It doesn't heal all things. Time just begins to rob our memories of little details." He begins to speak very quietly, so quietly and rapidly I almost don't catch it all and have to lean towards him. "At least she will always be here in this house, and I will always be here with her. I don't mind, really. I don't. I'm at peace here. I talk to her, tell her everything. I'm moving here you know. I've put the other house up for sale and I'm moving here for good. She wanted me to move here for so long and for some reason I fought it tooth and nail, God only knows why. Now she'll finally be satisfied. I'm happy when I'm here. It's all I need."

I pick up my wineglass, take a deep swallow. I feel calm now. The tears are gone and the words have been spoken.

"Richard, tell me about her. About Jenny."

I feel a sense of relief having said her name aloud at last. It sounds so ordinary, commonplace. And after having said it, it is almost as though her presence in the room begins to fade, recede, just a little. I try not to glance over at the piano.

"It's funny my closest friends don't understand her," he says. "For some reason they never liked her either. They are the only ones. They have never admitted it, but I always knew. Even though everyone else just loves her. Anyone that meets her likes her immediately. You can't help it. She just has a way with people. They love her on the spot from the moment they lay eyes on her. But Bob and Lisa, for some reason, they have never liked her."

A sharp crack from the fire. I find myself listening to the clock, listening for sounds in the house. It is difficult to pay close attention, to think clearly and concentrate on each word.

"Richard, why did you ask me to come here? Why did you ask me to go to dinner with you? Why did you come to my house? You just said yourself you have all you need here. You have her. You say she is here in this house. Richard, Richard, look at me."

I don't know how long we sit and watch the fire. We say nothing and the minutes slip away. The clock chimes the hour but I am not really listening, and then I'm not certain whether it's two o'clock or three. Did he ever go and turn off the oven? I struggle to remember. It seems to me that maybe he did go to the kitchen, but I can't be sure. I see a little face everywhere I look. A sweet little face. I see it in the fire. I see it in the window and there, behind the door.

The minutes slip away. He has forgotten I am in the room and I'm afraid to move, afraid I'm going to get up and walk away and that somehow life is going to return to the way it was and nothing will be different. Minutes tick by. Sometimes silence can be as shrill as shouted words.

"Clarice." He finally turns to me. I lean over and very slowly reach out and take his hand in mine. His hands are very cold and still.

"I was wrong, Clarice. I shouldn't have said it like that. I shouldn't have said the things I said to you. Sometimes I have trouble believing it. Other times I know I'm wrong, that I'm just fooling myself, but sometimes, especially here, it isn't so clear anymore."

The expression in his eyes has changed again and his hand begins to grip mine very tightly. He does not try to pull away.

"I know it's difficult for you to understand, but I realized that first night in the bar that I was drawn to you, really drawn to you, although you were a perfect stranger. I knew that night when I went home that I needed to call you and talk to you again. I feel like I'm alive again when I'm with you, like waking up after a long deep sleep. Maybe buying this house and coming here was a mistake. Maybe I should just stay in town where I'm closer to people like you."

"You said you didn't need anyone. That you had everything you need here. That you don't mind."

"No," he says quickly, grips my hand even tighter, pulls me closer so that his face is just inches from mine. "It's so hard for me to explain it all. I don't want to just let you walk away. You have to understand that."

"Tell me what happened here," I say, trying to pull my hand away from his. "Try to explain it to me." But he doesn't loosen the grip he has on my hand. He holds it even tighter, pulls me even closer. For a few moments I am afraid, really afraid. But then, in spite of myself, I feel my heart begin to race, feel the heat from his body next to mine. I swallow hard and set down the glass.

Ironically, this whole scenario was something like my original plan. How stupid is that? This is what was supposed to happen in my little revenge plot; him pulling me closer and closer.

"That day in the hospital when Jenny got so sick she didn't recognize me anymore, I told them I wanted to bring her home. I told them this was where she belonged. And so I did. I'd been awake for days sitting by her side, watching her, and I think I was beginning to get feverish myself. I was so tired and they, her family, all told me I needed to go home and sleep and rest and that they'd call me, that I didn't have to try to stay awake and stay with her anymore, that they would look after her. But I didn't want to listen. So I took her home, like I said I would, and dressed her properly and laid her down on her bed where she'd be more comfortable. And I closed the curtains in the bedroom and put some flowers on the night table. There were lots of flowers in every room that people had sent. She liked to have flowers on the night table so she could see and smell them the moment she opened her eyes in the morning. Lilies, fresia. Her favourites. She said they gave her strength, made her think about being alive. And then I took a chair and set it down at the end of her bed and another at the foot end, and I lit a candle and I stayed with her. I don't know how long I watched over her like that. It must've been the rest of that day and all that night, but I think I must've fallen asleep too, in the end, because suddenly I thought I saw the arch-covered gate of a cemetery in amongst some enormous trees and her lying underneath waiting for someone to take her away, and in the distance there was the hooting of an owl like some strange and ridiculous nightmare. Of course when I woke up it was long since past sunrise, and there was no gate and no owl, and the candle had burned down and gone out, and she was gone too. I suppose they'd come and taken her away or maybe she hadn't been there at all. But I stayed, stayed awake with her in this house after that and I never went away."

I can see it all very clearly now, everything that happened. He held a wake for her, a real wake like they used to have; a vigil over a corpse before burial, sitting up with someone all night to keep away evil spirits and safeguard the soul's passage to heaven. A *lykewake*, they used to call it. And somehow this wake continued for days, weeks, years. He never allowed it to end, even after her body had long since been buried. Simply continued on here in this house and watched over her, and because he persisted in doing this, it was as though she was not really dead and gone at all. It was easy to believe she still carried on. It was easy to come here and bring flowers and talk to her and read her letters. A wake. Richard sitting on a chair beside her with a candle in his hand watching over her all day and all night. It would be simple thing to sit here in this old house day after day and pretend she is still here, just in the next room, around the corner, just out of sight for a moment but never far away. And pretending would gradually become believing. The two realities would melt together and it would be difficult to tell which one was really true. One can trick one's mind so easily. Under the circumstances, wanting it so much, and being alone day after day in an old house that lends itself to ghosts and that kind of thing, anyone could become confused.

We sit still together for a few minutes listening to the sound of the clock and the fire. I listen for her too. I can feel his hand gripping mine, the warmth of his leg next to me. He is pulling me closer so that I am leaning fully on him now and he has taken my hand into both of his. His hands are no longer cold. Warmth radiates from him and when I look into his face, I am startled by the intensity of the expression. He lets go of my hands and reaches up and touches my face, and then he begins to kiss me, not gently, but forcefully so that at first I'm not sure how I should respond. I should just turn away, get up and leave. He is only thinking of her and I am simply a warm body close by. If he closes his eyes he can forget, and she can take my place.

But then I feel my heart beating and my own desire becomes so intense that it replaces everything else, any thoughts, any plans, everything. And even for a moment wipes out any thoughts of her. Feeling the hard muscles under my fingers, I draw my hand up from his side to his chest and touch his face. Originally the plan was that he say my name, say it out loud. But he continues to kiss me, my mouth, my face, my neck, and then his hands reach for the buttons on my shirt and begin to open. I feel the shirt slide from my shoulders and his hands on my breasts, and I reach down and begin to open the belt of his jeans, slide the pants down, feel his hardness.

As he lowers himself down on me I open my eyes and for an instant I see behind him, on the other side of the fireplace, the piano, standing there waiting, poised and silent and black.

The plan was that she suddenly walk in on us like this. Somehow I was to trap him into deceiving her, and somehow I was to time it in such a way that she would walk in at this crucial moment. I don't know exactly how I thought I would manage to arrange all this so perfectly. But I held him accountable for my little girl's death. He should have saved her. He let her die. It was his fault. And this was how I was going to get even: I was going to destroy them both. She would walk in and see us and cry out, and I would get up and laugh at them both. It was this that I looked forward to: standing there and watching their pain as I destroyed them.

I glance over to the piano again and it is almost as if I can see *Her* standing there, watching, waiting. But then I forget even that image and for a few moments everything is darkness. They say the climax of making love is sometimes called the little death, and so it was with me.

I look up at him afterwards, after a long time when I finally feel that I am awake and alive again. He is smiling at me in the curious way that is his alone. As though amused by some private little joke he isn't sharing with anyone else and least of all me.

"Promise me you won't leave, ever." He strokes my cheek gently. He is not pretending. He is not thinking that I am Jenny. He knows it is me. And he wants me to stay.

"Do you believe me now?" he says. "That I need you. That I need you to bring me back to life again."

I want to say something, to answer back, to reassure him, restore confidence. But then, while I get up and carefully button up my shirt, I can suddenly see it all very clearly: the whole future that lies before us. He will ask me to come here again and again, and we will talk about everything, and we will understand each other in a way that we didn't think was possible with anyone. And we will make love to each other. I will want him, desperately. I won't be able to stay away even though I know all of this has not turned out the way it was supposed to and that I have so many things to hide from him forever.

But I will love him, fiercely, despite the past, in a way that he will never love me. We will go out together, go to dinners, dances, parties. I can see us standing at Bob and Lisa's house, at their party later this week, holding glasses of wine in our hands, Richard's arm around my shoulders, and me leaning casually against him, feeling his warmth. I can see already the years ticking away, our intimacy and need for one another growing. His friends and mine will believe we have finally found happiness together, that we've been able to put the past behind us now that we've found one another. Everyone will speak of happy endings, of how lucky we are to have made a new beginning, what a nice couple we make, how perfect we are together. And we will smile and nod and agree, and he will kiss me and we will be together, in our own way.

Maybe he will even put some of her things away, or some day in the far distant future even sell some of them, pretend to himself that he doesn't think about her at all. I can see him taking boxes and gathering together some of her things, her clothing, folding it away neatly and carrying it away. I can see him moving the bed out of that room, taking it apart and carrying the pieces up to the attic. And the piano? It will stay, of course, but it will be moved into a less prominent corner, out of the light and in a place where it does not draw my attention.

We will get married, very soon, because that will be what he will want. He will ask me to marry him suddenly, just a few short months from now, and we will have a quiet, beautiful wedding with all our friends around us.

And on the surface we will be a normal, happy couple together. Quite ordinary. Even he won't be able to tell the difference. In the end, he will even begin to depend on me very much.

I can see us together in this house, with cats on the windowsills, and him working at a desk in a corner of the room writing an article for the magazine, and me sitting before the fire holding a book in my lap, watching him, waiting. Empty.

Even he won't be able to tell the difference.

But I, for one, will know that something is different, that something is wrong, that there are no happy endings for us, for people like us.

Some of us can never be restored to what we were. It isn't possible. Some of us can never recover from the events we've lived through. Life is filled with hardship, sorrow, misfortune. Time does not heal all wounds. Time does not fade our memories. Time has nothing to do with it. If anything, it makes them sharper, makes them bite more.

And this would've been the year she would've learned to ride without training wheels, would've learned her times tables, would've lost her first tooth, her first love, graduated from school. This is the year she would've gone to university, married, turned thirty, given birth to her first child, taken the trip to Spain she always dreamed about.

He will not love me the way he is supposed to, although he himself will believe that he does, and I will never be the person he thinks I am. Maybe he won't ever know it. Maybe he won't see the difference. But I will know.

There will be shadows that will live with us for always in this house. Two shadows. And they will never, ever go away.

This isn't, of course, the way it was supposed to end for us. I didn't know, after all, about Jenny. It wasn't the plan. I was supposed to come here and destroy everything in their perfect little lives the way in one moment, in one second years ago, I thought he'd destroyed everything for me. How was I to know I was wrong about it all? How was I to know he was not to blame? And how was I to know Jenny was already a ghost? How was I to know that someone had done my work for me and left behind a pitiful, broken man and only the ashes of my revenge?

Why did I feel I needed to avenge myself anyway? It doesn't seem believable now, that I could shift the blame that easily. It seems the plan of a lunatic. An idiot. You would think it wouldn't be possible for a sane and rational person to come up with a plan like this. But I did. For such a long time it was the only thing that kept me going, the only thing that kept me alive. My little secret. This feeling that I was at least doing something, *anything*, to make things right again, anything but just simply existing and forgetting about her as though she never happened. Time wasn't healing anything. It was pulling me to pieces. No one knew. Everyone thought I was so strong. I needed to find some way to stop myself from falling apart. To stop my own guilt. I was so torn to pieces that I couldn't even permit myself to think about her, to remember. And then I found him and could shift the blame and it made it all easier somehow.

I get up from the couch slowly, walk through the room towards the door.

There are footsteps. He is following me. A hand tightens on my arm, pulls me around. "Clarice. Where are you going? You're not going already?"

I say nothing. This was the plan originally. This moment, at least, is unfolding as it was supposed to.

"What is it? Why are you looking at me that way?"

I continue to stare, to look into his pale gray, black-rimmed eyes. He can see how I feel. Surely it is clear from my expression. He looks astonished, puzzled, hurt. The feelings ripple across his face one after another like the movement of water in a lake.

"Please stay. Tell me what's wrong. God, say something. What have I done? I'm sorry if I...I shouldn't have..."

But I can't do it. I can't go. I can't carry out the ending and walk out the door forever. I know I will come back. I will stay here with him and when he asks me to marry him, I will not flinch when I say *yes*.

"I wasn't leaving," I say very slowly, shivering because I am suddenly very cold again and can hardly feel the ends of my fingers. There is a feeling that comes over me too, something unearthly, as though I'm not really sure I am actually standing here, like I'm looking down on myself and watching. "It was just I thought I heard someone in the house. I'm sure there was someone standing right there, a moment ago, right over there by the piano."

Then I turn and go to him very slowly, unwillingly. Just like earlier today, a feeling of indifference, apathy, settles over me again, as though in a sense I am not altogether awake.